THE MACKINAC *Incident*

THE MACKINAC *Incident*

A Thriller

Len McDougall

Skyhorse Publishing

First Skyhorse Publishing paperback edition 2016

Skyhorse Publishing books may be purchased in bulk at special discounts for sales promotion, corporate gifts, fund-raising, or educational purposes. Special editions can also be created to specifications. For details, contact the Special Sales Department, Skyhorse Publishing, 307 West 36th Street, 11th Floor, New York, NY 10018 or info@skyhorsepublishing.com.

Visit our website at www.skyhorsepublishing.com.

10 9 8 7 6 5 4 3 2 1

Library of Congress Cataloging-in-Publication Data is available on file.

Cover design by Brian Peterson

Print ISBN: 978-1-5107-0417-6
Ebook ISBN: 978-1-62636-515-5

Printed in the United States of America

This, my first novel, is dedicated to Michelle Elliott and Bert Notestine, whose generosity during hard times made it possible. And to my lovely soul mate Cheanne, whose expertise and advice are evident on every page.

Table of Contents

Chapter One

The Insertion

The North Atlantic rippled gently under a moonless sky, fifteen miles east off the coast of New Brunswick, Canada. A frothy ripple preceded the rising of a black periscope. The periscope swiveled about tentatively for less than a minute before it began to rise swiftly. The conning tower beneath it emerged above the ocean like a mythical kraken, followed by the black steel hull of a Soviet-vintage diesel submarine. The vessel had been repainted flat black, and it bore no markings of any kind.

Water still streamed from the decks when a hatch amidships opened to emit a muted red glow that would be invisible from a hundred yards away. As soon as the hatch cover was fully open, four black-clad figures exited with trained precision. Each pushed a large black duffel bag onto the deck before leaping nimbly after it. It was obvious that the duffels were heavy.

When the four men had clambered onto the deck, they shouldered their bags, and ran a few steps to where a sixteen-foot Zodiac Bombard Commando assault boat waited, lashed to the sub's deck. Each man laid his bag in the center of the boat, securing it with straps and quick-release buckles before taking his place at each quadrant.

The small crew were barely seated when the submarine beneath them began to sink. With practiced smoothness, they pulled free the quick-release mooring knots at each corner, and the coxswain started the silenced 150 horsepower Mercury outboard. As soon as the submarine had descended below propeller depth, he gunned the throttle, swinging the Zodiac around with a muffled whine until the bow pointed west toward the Canadian shore. The pilot referenced a handheld Magellan GPS, adjusted their heading a few degrees, and then opened the throttle to full.

As they skimmed westward at more than thirty miles per hour, each man pulled his balaclava up over his mouth and nose to help ward off the North Atlantic chill. Based on previous dry runs, they had precisely thirty-four minutes before reaching their landing point. Time enough for each man in the boat to reflect on his own reasons for being there.

♦ ♦ ♦

Twenty-eight-year-old Philippe Aziz was piloting the Zodiac. He was the driving force behind the whole operation—and the money that was making it happen. Born in Saudi Arabia to wealthy parents with oil-rich relatives in Syria, Jordan, and Kuwait, young Aziz had wanted for nothing throughout his youth. Being fantastically wealthy in an Islamic land gave him license to do virtually anything he desired; since puberty, girls and boys of all ages had been his for the choosing. Once he had strangled to death a thirteen-year-old blonde American girl who he had purchased off the white slave market—while he raped her. The memory of that experience gave him an erection even now. Aziz had known the power of a god, and he liked it.

But those pig-eating American bastards, with sins far greater than any that had ever been committed under the mantle of Islam, would ban his way of life. Under the pretenses of equality and fairness, America and its puppets would outlaw his noble culture that had existed for a thousand years, and turn his proud Muslim brothers into just more fat, lazy scabs on the ass of humankind. Already the United States had begun to entice some Muslim women into shirking their most fundamental and holy duty, to serve the needs of men, who, in fact, had always controlled the world, and—Allah willing—always would.

Aziz saw himself as a holy warrior. Allah had seen fit to test his faithful by bestowing superior weapons onto the Great Satan, so he and his brothers did not meet their enemy in open battles that they couldn't win. Instead, they fought the juggernaut United States as the Hebrew

King David had battled mighty Goliath. With every airliner that they brought down, with every skyscraper they crushed, with every bomb in every crowded place, Aziz and his brothers-at-arms took a toll on the great evil that was America. The Prophet Muhammad had promised his faithful rewards and glory, even after death, but Philippe Aziz intended to have both while he still lived. He meant to return to the Middle East a hero of Islam.

Canadian-born, thirty-year-old Paul Richarde was an al-Qaeda–trained explosives expert and the team's guide through the wilderness forests of southern Canada and northern Michigan. Born to an unmarried sixteen-year-old Canadian girl in southern Ontario, Richarde, too, had grown up hating America. His birth father, whom he had never met, had been an American Coast Guard sailor. His mother, a young farm girl alone and unable to support herself and her baby, who was castigated by the people of her ultra-Christian home community, emigrated with her bastard son to Sault Sainte Marie, Ontario, just across the border from an American town of the same name.

Growing up in the "Twin Soos" had been a nightmare for Richarde as a boy. With no street savvy and little sense to boot, his adolescent mother had been easy prey for petty criminals on both sides of the border. In almost no time, she had been lured into drug addiction. Crystal methamphetamines were plentiful from the Michigan side, where impromptu manufacturing took place in ramshackle mobile homes, and even in the rented motel rooms that dotted its sparsely populated, heavily forested Upper Peninsula. The Canadian government, for all its rhetoric about law and order, enabled its citizens to have access to virtually unlimited quantities of high-potency marijuana. Ironically, the alcohol that had killed his mother before she'd reached thirty-five years old had always been available and legal on both sides of the border. His mother was the reason her son wouldn't touch alcohol to this day.

Young Paul hadn't had much of a chance at life. At barely thirteen years of age, he'd come home from school one day to find four American sailors in the small apartment provided by his mother's pimp. Hard drug use had robbed his once pretty mother of her good looks, and she found herself having to perform ever more degrading sex acts just to make grocery money. The filthy American vermin he walked in on that day were using her like an animal, making her perform any sex act they desired. In shock, young Paul had tried to escape the naked free-for-all, but one of the sailors, a fat, hairy gorilla of a man with yellow-stained teeth had grabbed the boy's hand on the doorknob.

"Where ya goin' kid?" the sweat-beaded man slurred, with breath that stank of cigarettes and whiskey. "Don'tcha wanna join the party?"

Richarde was horribly sodomized and his screams for help went unanswered by his mother, as she pretended not to see the agony that was being inflicted on her only child. The fat sailor had scarred him emotionally and physically; he'd bled from his rectum for weeks afterward. The nightmares had gone on for years after that. Even now, he was suffering with painfully inflamed hemorrhoids that only made him hate Americans all the more.

Peter Grigovich was a thirty-three-year-old, Bosnian-born Canadian citizen whose parents had fled his homeland in 1993, when the once peaceful socialist republic of Yugoslavia had fragmented into ethnic and religious violence. His father had been a quality engineer for the Yugo car plant when the Soviet Union had collapsed under pressure from the United States, and with it fell the only stabilizing force in that part of the world. With no job and no prospects for the future in his homeland, the elder Grigovich had applied for a work visa to the United States, believing that he was a shoe-in for an engineering position at Ford or General Motors.

But that wasn't the case. The American automakers had refused to recognize his father's engineering degree from the University of Belgrade, and after six months, the State Department had refused to renew his work visa. For him, the land of the free had become a trap. Unable to return home to a country that no longer existed, his father had been imprisoned indefinitely in a windowless jail "pod" in the American Sault Sainte Marie with drug addicts and thugs, even though he'd never committed a crime in his life. His equally blameless mother had been imprisoned in another federal holding facility—Peter never found out where—while her ten-year-old son was sent to a foster home.

His foster parents were devout Baptists, strict to the point of being slightly abusive, and downright pious in their claim to a Christian life of self-denial, although it soon became clear to Peter that they applied their religious philosophies more often to him than to themselves. To them, he wasn't a little boy who needed love and guidance in a frightening new world; rather, he was a means of placating their own guilty consciences. When they ordered a pizza, he was allowed to eat only their discarded crusts. There was a padlock on the refrigerator; but his caseworker from the Department of Social Services seemed not to notice. He ran away once when he was fourteen years old, but there was nowhere to escape, and the American police who caught him had handcuffed his wrists so tightly that his thumbs still ached from nerve damage. Then they had held him in a filthy jail cell until his foster parents retrieved him two days later. He was punished physically and mentally by them for several months for that transgression. His foster parents actually told him that someday he'd thank them for the way they abused him. He never did.

When he turned sixteen years old, the State Department had deigned to award him US citizenship, but he was never allowed to forget that he was a second-class citizen. In school, his classmates dubbed him "Polack," even though he was almost entirely of Armenian descent. He was arbitrarily accused of every infraction by his teachers, and punished for the actions of other classmates, even when they were the culprits and he was innocent. At the only home he'd ever known, he was treated like an unwanted burden and severely punished for the most minor trespass. When he was eighteen years old, his pent-up anger found some release when he called his foster parents motherfuckers as he strode away from their door forever. With a deep hatred for them, and for Americans in general, he'd successfully applied for Canadian citizenship, and had been recruited soon after by al-Qaeda.

Timmons McBraden was a thirty-two-year-old American and the son of a retired sheriff in Michigan's Upper Peninsula. He had grown up on Whitefish Point, fifteen miles from the shoreline of Ontario, across Lake Superior's Whitefish Bay. He hated his own countrymen for reasons that were different than those of his companions, but with a passion that was equally deep.

McBraden was the son of a single, alcoholic father who had used the law and the authority of his office like it was his own personal bludgeon. Even while he claimed to be enforcing it, the elder McBraden had always considered himself above the very law that he used to eliminate citizens that he didn't like. Lack of attention by the state government situated in Michigan's vastly more populated

Lower Peninsula had allowed local Upper Peninsula governments to become kingdoms unto themselves, where the ruling elite pretty much had things their own way for generations.

In school, Timmons had been highly regarded among both classmates and faculty. He sooned learned, however, that the respect he received from others wasn't for himself, but out of fear of his father. His grades were good, even when he didn't deserve them, and he came to expect preferential treatment in everything he did. He was made captain of the varsity football team in high school, even though his athletic prowess was mediocre. When he and his classmates had been busted for drinking beer and smoking pot after a game one night, he was driven home in a squad car, while his friends were booked and charged. When the father of one of his classmates protested the injustice, he served a year in the county jail for a felony that everyone knew he hadn't committed. He had since moved away.

After Timmons graduated at the top of his class, he attended law-enforcement training at Lake Superior State University—his father's idea, not his. Ironically, it was there that he'd tried mainlining heroin for the first time. After less than a year of college, he was inevitably arrested for drug possession, along with a dozen other students at a boisterous party. By that time, he was thoroughly addicted to heroin.

His father intervened again, and the matter was swept under the rug while he worked through his withdrawal at a private clinic in Indiana. The incident never made the local news, and even residents of his hometown were mostly unaware that he was a felon. But he was aware, and his father's perversion of the laws he had taken an oath to uphold was just another form of terrorism to him. His father had never been physically abusive to him, and he loved him as a parent, but he despised him for being a self-serving hypocrite.

♦ ♦ ♦

The fast-moving Zodiac made the Canadian shore in less time than Aziz had anticipated. A dim red light flashed seaward from a covered boathouse when they were a mile offshore, telling Aziz precisely where to land the craft. Shining from inside a boathouse, the light would be invisible to anyone watching from land, and all but invisible to anyone at sea.

Aziz piloted their vessel expertly into the boathouse's opening, and then cut the motor. A low-intensity red light came on inside the enclosure, and a lithe young girl emerged from the shadows to grab the boat's bowline. The boat crew could see that the windows of the boathouse were blacked out with squares of cardboard as the girl deftly tied off the stern and bowlines.

Nineteen-year-old Brenda Waukonigon had become an expert at marine skills while fishing with her father on Lake Superior. A member of the Sault Ojibwa tribe, she'd learned the fine points of navigation and all-around seamanship while dragnetting for whitefish with her father on that huge freshwater sea. She was as skilled a commercial fisherman as any man she'd ever met, thanks to him.

Brenda had also learned to hate the white man—and Americans in particular. Her father, a callous-handed fisherman all his life, had been her greatest hero while she was growing up. Her mother had disappeared from their lives while Brenda was too young to remember her, and Brenda's father had never quite gotten over the broken heart she'd left him with. Amos Waukonigon drank a bit more than he should have, often crying to the shadows late at night in a drunken stupor. But he was up at the first light of dawn every morning, spreading and mending his nets. It was clear to anyone who saw them together that Brenda was his pride and joy.

One day, when she was fifteen years old, they'd come over to the Michigan side of Sault Sainte Marie to do some shopping, to take advantage of the lower prices offered in American stores. It was common for Canadians to still do that; in fact, the economy of the American Sault depended in large part on Canadian shoppers. While they were shopping that fateful day, Brenda and her father visited some old friends on the Ojibwa reservation near the village of Brimley.

It was on the reservation that they ran into trouble. A rusted old Chevy pickup truck filled with Cheemookamon rednecks had run their car into a ditch near Naokoming Creek. When her father jumped from their hopelessly mired vehicle to confront the three white men who smelled of whiskey and beer, they'd descended on him in a gang, beating him with their fists, cursing, and kicking him when he fell to the ground. Brenda tried to help her father, but one of the drunks felled her with a hard fist to the side of her head. When she regained consciousness, they were gone, and her father was dead. He was killed by asphyxiation and internal bleeding when a fractured rib punctured his lung. He died from choking on his own blood. Brenda still cried herself to sleep at night, thinking of how he must have suffered before he died.

But Amos Waukonigon was just a drunken Indian, and a Canadian citizen to boot. The Yankee police hadn't looked very hard for his murderers, and whoever they were, they probably still walked the streets of America. Meanwhile, the orphaned Brenda was forced to return to Ontario, where she lived with an aunt ever since. When Brenda met Philippe Aziz at an anti-American rally a year ago, she was willing, even eager, to join a cause against the Yanks she hated.

♦ ♦ ♦

When she secured their craft to the dock pilings, bow and stern, the four men threw their heavy satchels onto the dock and jumped out after them. Aziz grabbed her and pulled her to him, kissing her hard on the mouth. She felt a stirring in her loins from the embrace of this dark and exotic man, just as she always had since their first meeting. For his part, there was no love, only sexual passion. She didn't mind; it was enough. Their shared passion was a mutual hatred of Americans.

"I couldn't get us a car," she said in Canadian-accented English. "But I got an extended-cab pickup truck with four-wheel drive. It'll haul your gear, and it should be comfortable enough for the four of you to ride in. Besides, I think you might need the four-wheel drive. I drove it here myself." She jerked her head toward the back wall of the boathouse, where she'd parked the truck.

Aziz took her by the shoulders and held her at arm's length, as if admiring her. "I'm sure that you did well," he said. "Did you get all of the other items?"

"Yes, I got you a Garmin GPS loaded with the most current highway maps, and the iPad that Timmons asked for. There are four, fully loaded backpacks, each of them packed with dried food enough for three days, and each of them weighing fifteen kilos."

"Did you get the guns?"

"Yes," she answered, with obvious pride at the accomplishment. "A Desert Eagle 50 caliber for Peter,"—she looked appreciatively at the well-muscled Bosnian—"two 9-millimeter Glocks for Tim and Paul, and for you, my love, the Ruger Security 6 you requested, in 357 magnum. One box of fifty cartridges for each gun, two extra magazines for each of the automatics, and two speed loaders for your revolver." She handed him a briefcase with the guns inside. She intentionally brought no holsters for any of them; having a holster only defeated the purpose if one of them got searched by a policeman and had to throw his gun away.

Aziz nodded his head. "Good. Is everything untraceable?"

"Yes, the guns are orphans. I bought them all from the wife of a private collector who died recently. The truck was purchased from a farmer in British Columbia. It's registered to a man who passed away last month. It's a solid beige Ford F-150, the most common pickup truck in North America, in the most hard-to-remember color. There's a nylon jet bag with two changes of clothes in it—civilian and BDUs—for each one of you."

"You've done well, Brenda," Aziz said. He pulled her to him again with his left arm. But the embrace was hard enough to be brutal this time. In Aziz's right hand was an ESEE Knives RAT-6 survival knife. He drove the razor-sharp blade, edge upward, forcefully into the girl's soft solar plexus, pulling her forward onto the blade while he twisted the handle, making sure he made a wide hole in her heart. She gasped, struggling against him in an effort to pull herself back from the blade. But it was too late, blood was pouring into her abdominal cavity from the hole Aziz had rent in her heart's ventricle. She stared over Aziz's shoulder, directly into Peter Grigovich's eyes, and whispered in a failing voice, "Help me . . . Please."

Aziz felt blood spurt from the knife wound, hot against his hand. He smiled cruelly; he liked it. Aziz pressed harder, keeping the pulsing blood mostly inside her convulsing body as his hand helped to seal the outside of the wound. He held her until she went limp, less than a minute later, then he released her lifeless corpse to fall into the water. The tide was going out, and her body immediately began to drift out to sea through the boathouse door.

Grigovich stared at the girl's receding body while Aziz knelt on the dock and washed her blood from his hands. Grigovich fancied himself a tough man, but Brenda Waukonigon's wide, frightened eyes locked onto his own as they glazed over with the veil of death disturbed him deeply. He knew that he'd never forget that awful sight. He also knew that if he showed what he was feeling to the others, he would join her. They'd simply carry on with three members, instead of four. It was one of the contingencies they'd trained to meet.

Chapter Two

The Survival Instructor

Well, wouldn't that just frost your ass? Only he, Rodney frigging Elliot, could lay some damned thing down for one second, and then turn to find it gone. The blood rose in his neck until it started to throb. Every time he tried to accomplish even the most minor chore, there was some goddamned, mother . . .

"What's the matter, Rod? Lose somethin'?"

He looked up from where he knelt on the concrete barn floor amid scattered gear and backpacks. He was only half worked up into a fine rage when the fires of his frustration were quenched by the approach of a pretty blonde woman with mischievous blue eyes and a smile that had always made his chest feel a little tight. In her hands was a cup of steaming, hot coffee.

After a whirlwind romance that led to a decade of living with the most incredibly beautiful woman he had ever seen, Rod still found the mere presence of his wife, Shannon, to be like a soothing balm whenever he was pissed off about something. And he was often pissed about something. Shannon liked to joke that he was a triple-A personality.

He took the steaming mug she held out to him, and answered in a gruff, slightly embarrassed voice, sweeping his other hand across the array of equipment spread before them.

"Aaahhh . . . I'm just bitchin' because I can't find that stupid MSR water filter that was right in front of me a minute ago . . ." His sentence trailed off, because there in his outstretched fist was the item he'd gotten so worked up over losing.

Rod looked sidewise at Shannon, who was grinning with that look of hers that said, "You're a dumbass, but I love you anyway."

He grinned sheepishly and said, "Y'know, I'm getting too old for this stupid survival instructor stuff."

She pulled him to her by his collar, and kissed him on the cheek. "No you're not. Fifty-five is not old today—besides, I'm older than you."

"Yeah, two months." He appraised her muscular, athletic form with an eye that remained appreciative of it even after a decade. She still possessed the womanly attributes that got him excited; maybe more than ever. Even now he felt a stirring of lust.

It must have shown in his eyes, because Shannon grinned even more widely in feigned surprise, then pushed him away. She said, "You're a dirty old man," and walked away.

"Wait," he called after her, "you said I wasn't that old." He pointed to his distended trousers, "And what am I supposed to do with this tent pole?"

She called back over her shoulder, "You erected it. You take it down."

His anger dissipated, Rod turned back to assembling the backpacks he was issuing his clients for their weeklong survival class with him along the wild Betsy River in Lake Superior State Forest. They were three thirty-something professionals from Chicago, a husband and wife, and her brother. He had interviewed each by phone, advising them on clothing, footwear, and personal items. As with every survival class, he had a full medical and personal dossier on each member, and he felt he knew the three students without having ever met them. When it came to wilderness survival, he didn't like surprises.

Each of the backpacks they'd be carrying was tailored as closely as possible to have a mass equal to no more than one-third of its bearer's own weight. They'd be humping them through rugged backcountry for up to seven miles a day, and excessively heavy packs resulted in injuries. When medical assistance might be more than half a day away, he really wanted to avoid the need for a paramedic.

Rod had taught wilderness survival classes for almost twenty-five years, the last eleven of them in Michigan's Upper Peninsula. Whitefish

Point, jutting northward into Lake Superior, twelve miles from the tiny village of Paradise, was a good environment in which to teach his type of real-world survival. An average twenty-three feet of snow fell during the six months of winter, with ambient temperatures occasionally falling below −35°F. During the nonsnow months, mosquitoes, several species of blackflies and midges, deerflies, stable flies, and the UP's infamous horseflies—said to require killing with a knife or a gun—were more voracious than those in the Amazon rain forest, due to their short breeding period and life span.

Rod's no-nonsense approach to wilderness survival training was popular with some law enforcement and most military personnel, but especially with sport hunters who had enough real-world experience to know the difference between fact and fiction. Like any self-employed professional outdoorsman, Rod always needed money. But Rod had no compunction about recommending that casual survival wannabes seek training with another survival instructor. A student who thought that he already knew what he was doing usually wasted Rod's time arguing about every little thing, and those who expected some sort of magical enlightenment weren't there to learn survival at all. Rod wasn't there to debate or to elevate anyone's consciousness; he was there to teach his clients how to not die in the woods.

His own survival training was almost a cliché. Originally from Saint Clair County, in Michigan's Thumb area, Rod was born to Jane Mitchell, a twenty-year-old farm girl from Imlay City and Michael Elliot, a twenty-four-year-old army private from Port Huron. Square dancing was popular then, and that was how Jane met Michael and later became pregnant. Because it was considered the right thing to do in those days, they rushed into marriage three months later. Rodney was born first, then his sister Margie two years after.

It had been a failed union from the start. With her husband stationed in Fort Leonard Wood, Missouri, the naïve and lonely Jane had been easy prey for a nineteen-year-old bad boy named Melvin James. His ebony hair, sexy spit curl, and rebellious attitude made him irresistible. Michael abruptly divorced her as soon as he learned from his own parents that Jane was not only cheating on him, but actually living with Melvin.

For his part, Melvin came to see Jane's son and daughter from her previous marriage as a guaranteed source of income from the Social

Services Department. Every month, she received a healthy sum from the state for their welfare, and would do so until they were eighteen years old. That was all Melvin cared about, as far as Rodney and his sister Margie were concerned. The two children were merely beer money and a source of rent when Melvin was down on his luck.

Worked like a slave when he wasn't in school, with plenty of physical abuse thrown in for good measure (his mother didn't object when her second husband beat and kicked her kids), Rodney's lust for nature had sprouted at age ten. His stepfather, fearful of Rodney's birth father, had moved the entire family three hundred miles north to Charlevoix, Michigan.

Young Rodney had become entranced by the dark-skinned people who lived in nearby "Indian Town." These communities of tar-paper shacks inhabited by Native Americans descended from the Ojibwa, Odawa, and Potawatomi tribes were common to almost every northern Michigan town in those days. Generations of racial bias had kept the Indian bloodlines mostly pure, and the tribe members were generally spurned by their white neighbors. The Indian elders, some of whom remembered pulling stumps with mules, had provided a welcome and fascinating escape for Rodney from the hardships of being at home. He remembered them as poor but honest people who didn't give or rescind their friendship lightly, and who always treated children with kindness.

But while the elders held to a tradition of passing down what they had learned to their young, Indian youngsters who were being raised in the white man's schools rebelled against the traditional ways. To them, an eagle feather was worthless, but wearing Levi's blue jeans garnered respect from their peers. Where once an Indian teen had sought wisdom from the grandfathers, he now yearned for cars, music, and other trappings of white society. With few students who wanted to learn from them, the elders had grudgingly accepted a white Scots-Irish boy who seemed fascinated by their culture.

That was when Rodney had developed an obsession with wilderness survival. He learned to run a trapline and hunt raccoons for fur when he was twelve years old. He'd tube-skin the carcasses, sometimes cape them completely, leaving claws, nose pads, and even whiskers intact. When he had a dozen or more salted pelts in the freezer, his stepfather would take them to a local furrier and sell them for drinking money—Pabst Blue Ribbon beer, a brand Rod still hated to this day. Even though young Rodney never saw a dime from the sale of his furs, trapping them had meant getting away from his abusive stepfather, often for days at a time, in the solitude and serenity of nature. It had been worth it.

During those first few years, there were many times when Rodney found himself caught in a blizzard, or some other dangerous situation in the woods he was sure he wouldn't survive. His first winter outing—alone, because no one would go with him—had resulted in frostbite so severe that skin peeled from his fingers and toes for the following weeks, like he'd been badly burned. He'd suffered from hypothermia, encountered hordes of biting bugs, and been lost at night. He'd even survived being bitten by a Massasauga rattlesnake when one took shelter in his old Korean War era sleeping bag. He was convinced he was a goner that time, but after lying alone in the woods for three days—no one even reported him missing—he'd somehow found the strength to hike six miles back home.

Between having a natural talent for survival and a tribe of good instructors, he had honed his woodcraft skills to a fine edge. By the time he was fourteen years old, his abilities had begun to earn the derision of some full-grown hunters and other sportsmen, who had, in fact, begun to fear his growing skills. For Rodney, the objective wasn't to achieve some macho image, but to learn self-sufficiency in the place he loved most of all. He was reassured knowing that no matter what happened, his loved ones would never starve or freeze to death.

Rodney was the first to leave home and managed to survive in society by lying low, working hard, and fooling people into thinking that he was older than he was. When Rodney's sister Margie started to show the first signs of womanhood, their stepfather took notice. After several years of physical and sexual abuse, she ran away to their birth father, and charged their sick, son-of-a-bitch stepfather with statutory rape, which finally resulted in his imprisonment. Even after getting away from his family, it seemed that a black cloud hung over Rodney's head everywhere he went. At twenty-two years old, he'd gone to prison for his part in an ill-fated convenience store robbery. When he emerged after serving only three years, it was with a changed attitude, a trade school certification in drafting, and enough college credits to claim an associate's degree in statistical process control. He figured that his main reason for turning to crime in the first place had been stupidity caused by a lack of viable options; having lived among the human animals that society kept behind prison walls, he swore to never be without options again.

He had become a maverick—a mercenary, really—after his parole. Beginning at a United Technologies automotive plant in Traverse City, Rod had bucked his way up from dimmer switch assembler to quality technician in less than two years. Over the next twelve years, he worked his way up to quality control manager, and then further widened his areas of expertise by working a year at several different manufacturing facilities.

Never did he stray too far for too long from his beloved northwoods, though. They were his refuge when the burdens of life got too heavy, his solace when sadness was overpowering, and a place of solitude when his mind got too noisy to think straight. His weekend escapes to the forests and swamps of northern Michigan kept him sane when the world around him grew more insane.

Regardless of how much he accomplished, the state never let him forget the fact that he'd been in prison; that single transgression would haunt him for the rest of his days. He couldn't vote; it was illegal for him to own a firearm; and he was forever restricted from holding a number of job positions. He still avoided driving around Charlevoix, because every cop who saw him would find a reason to pull him over.

The final blow came when it became clear to him that no matter how hard he worked, no matter how much of an expert he was, he'd never get any farther on the career ladder unless he regressed to being a liar and a cheat. The only difference was that now he was expected to commit crimes with an ink pen. Disillusioned at finding that the pillars of society were as bad or worse than the people with whom he'd done prison time, he'd relocated to the sparsely populated Upper Peninsula as soon as he could get free of his obligations.

It was near the village of Newberry that he'd met his soul mate, Shannon. He was working as a freelance wolf tracker for biologists from a local tribe—the irony of a white guy tracking for Indians wasn't lost on him. Shannon was known locally as the "Wolf Lady" because she had a weird fascination with wild canids, and had actually obtained a legal permit to raise gray wolves.

They'd met at a seminar about wild wolves migrating from the Upper Peninsula to the Lower. It had been love at first sight; that sounded hokey to him even now, but it had been true. For the first time in his life, he'd felt truly accepted by a woman. For the first time, a relationship had been based on more than just sex. Shannon made him understand what the poets and singers were trying to convey about romance in compositions that he'd always thought were corny. For the first time, he'd understood what love really was.

♦ ♦ ♦

The trio of survival students he was scheduled to take out this time seemed to be a good-enough bunch. The two men were engineers who'd worked together at the same firm. The woman was wife to one of them, and sister to the other. Aside from necessary medical contact information, Rod didn't think their personal details were any of his business, but he was sure that he'd learn all about them during their week together. The forest had a way of bonding people, making them divulge aspects of their lives that they'd normally never tell strangers. He'd experienced that with almost every survival class he'd ever taught.

He read over each medical dossier and signed liability waiver, still thinking that he really was getting too old for this. They'd scheduled their outing to coincide with the Labor Day weekend. Survival classes never got cancelled on account of bad weather, so the timing didn't really matter to him, except that it would happen during the best part of the UP summer. Bugs would be minimal, and the nights would be the warmest they'd be all year.

Early autumn was the nicest part of the summer on Whitefish Point, for more reasons than weather. Most wild plants were in blossom, every species of animal was actively preparing for the onset of winter, and the wild blueberries and huckleberries for which Whitefish Point was known were in full abundance. It promised to be a fun outing, but he wondered if maybe a growing number of aches and pains were telling him that this might be his last time.

Chapter Three

The FBI

"Good morning, Melanie."

Melanie Grunier looked up from her desk in the anteroom of the small office to smile at Special Agent Thomas Colyer as he removed his jacket and hung it on the coat tree near the door.

"Good morning, Tom," she replied. "How was your evening out?" Last night, Colyer had celebrated his fifteenth year of marriage by taking his wife Lanie to the crab buffet at the Ojibwa casino in Brimley. There wasn't a lot of night life in the Upper Peninsula, and casinos offered most of it. At forty-nine years old, with just over five years to go before he could retire with a handsome pension, he was just as happy to be away from the bright lights and excitement of the big city.

"Very good, as always. I've never had a bad meal there yet." He noted a pile of paper in the tray of his fax machine. "How long has that been there?" he asked with the jerk of a thumb.

"Must've come in sometime during the night."

Colyer exhaled forcefully. There was quite a pile there, and the cover sheet was marked "Eyes Only." Pretty unusual for boring old Sault Sainte Marie. Like so many cops, he had specifically requested assignment here, where nothing major ever happened. The little city was a confluence of almost every type of law enforcement officer, from the

Immigration and Naturalization Service to city cops, and living here should have been an ideal situation for anyone who wore a badge.

But after spending three years here, he felt like he'd been duped; this seemingly quiet border town had converted an old Strategic Air Command base in nearby Kinross to a prison when it had been shut down by the air force. Even worse, from his perspective as a law officer, the city fathers had seen fit to entice convicts' families to relocate and take up residence in the old servicemen's quarters. For that reason alone, this place teemed with crime as much as any major population center. The university had become a target for dealers of every kind of recreational drug, and impromptu meth labs had been busted in every place, from motel rooms to national forests. Street violence was rampant, and there was more smuggling across the Canadian border than was let on. This wasn't the sedate Yooper town it was supposed to be.

Colyer flipped past the cover sheet, and read the body of the fax message. Nothing specific; it was just a blanket warning that had been issued to all border town FBI offices. A Soviet-era submarine had been intercepted by a Navy Los Angeles-class attack sub. The *USS Hardwick* had picked up the diesel off Iceland, and identified it as a fourth-generation Amur, one of the boats being sold wholesale by Russians to any third-world tyrant with enough money to buy one.

The *Hardwick* had quietly trailed the diesel until it surfaced off the east coast of Canada. The sub had let off a small, fast boat with four men in it, and the *Hardwick* had video-recorded the incident. But being an international matter, Washington, DC had to be involved. By the time Washington had contacted Canadian authorities to strategize, the small boat had almost certainly landed on Canadian soil.

While the report went through various channels, the *Hardwick*'s captain had tailed the mystery submarine halfway back to Iceland. At that point, the unidentified submarine had executed a standard Russian "Crazy Ivan" maneuver, kicking her rudder fully starboard and coming around fast to face her bow toward the American boat.

Trained to counter this well-known Soviet-era turn, the *Hardwick*'s skipper had ordered an all-stop. The sonar on the diesel sub must have been updated with the most sophisticated hardware, because the American boat had been detected immediately from nine-thousand yards. Before the *Hardwick* could coast to a stop, the other boat's outer torpedo doors had slid open and her forward tubes flooded. The *Hardwick* went to "battle stations" fast, as two torpedoes were launched toward her.

Thinking quickly, the *Hardwick*'s skipper had ordered "full ahead." Its nuclear-powered engines drove the boat forward in a surge of speed, presenting as small a target as possible as it closed with the pair of oncoming torpedoes. When the torpedoes had armed their warheads, the *Hardwick* launched "bubbler" countermeasures from either side of her hull.

Drawn to the sudden, violent disturbance of the countermeasures, the torpedoes had veered away from the American sub and detonated. The *Hardwick* had then opened her own torpedo doors even before the explosions stopped reverberating. Her captain had requested and received permission from COMSUBLANT, the command center for submarine forces in the Atlantic, to respond with lethal force as soon as the enemy had launched its torpedoes. With a firing solution computed and torpedoes ready to fire, sonar reported the Russian sub had flooded its ballast tanks and was crash-diving. The *Hardwick* gave chase, but sonar reported that it sounded as if the entire boat had been flooded. That was confirmed when the boat smashed with uncontrolled force against the sea bottom.

Colyer dropped heavily into his chair and tossed the sheaf of papers onto his desk. The file contained only a brief summary of events, but the veteran FBI agent knew that it was implied that he should advise local and state authorities to be on the lookout for at least two people most likely traveling west. A lot of planning and a whole lot of money had gone into getting a submarine to make a delivery of personnel off the coast of Canada. The apparently suicidal scuttling of the boat pointed to a fanatical refusal to be taken alive, probably religiously motivated, and probably Muslim. Nutcases came in all flavors, but most Christian extremists weren't so eager to die for their beliefs, and Muslim countries had been buying fleets of surplus Soviet submarines in recent years.

Colyer felt that something very big was about to happen. It would almost certainly be a terrorist attack, and most likely not on Canadian soil. An attack on Canada would hardly raise an eyebrow in the international community. New York? Probably not. Ever since the Trade Center fiasco, security there was tighter than a gnat's asshole. Niagara

Falls? Maybe. Lots of people there . . . but how to get enough victims in a single place to make a meaningful impact?

Colyer sat back in his chair and pressed his fingertips together. He made a long exhale. It would help to have some idea of what the intended threat might be. A bomb—in that case, the target would probably be a crowded building. Maybe a chemical attack. The boys in DC had been expecting some sort of nerve-agent pesticide fog for a long time. Or fifty-five gallon drums of cyanide salt dumped into the sewer system of a major city, which would produce cyanide gas through manholes and grates. It was routine to monitor steel-hardening corporations that bought the stuff by the pallet.

He swiveled his chair to stare out the only small window in his office. This was the tough part of the antiterrorist game; there were just so many potential threats out there. About all he could do was wait and see. But by then it was usually too late to do anything but pick up the pieces.

Chapter Four

Crossing Whitefish Bay

Waves from Lake Superior lapped like liquid sighs against the sandy beach of the Canadian side of Whitefish Bay. Fifteen miles to the south, on the American side, was the projected landing point, near the lighthouse. Except for an occasional iron-ore freighter, marine traffic was almost nonexistent on Whitefish Point. Even the American Coast Guard mostly ignored this easy entry point, complacent in their knowledge that no one would ever try to illegally enter either country from there, when all they had to do was drive across the International Bridge at Sault Sainte Marie. Even pleasure boat traffic was nil, because except for the fishing docks at Whitefish Point, there wasn't a slip within fifty miles. There was no place to get fuel, and not even a grocery store within a dozen miles.

Aziz and his crew wasted no time retrieving and loading a second Zodiac from the dense brush where the now-dead Brenda Waukonigon had hidden it on the Canadian shore. Grigovich parked the truck in a stand of hardwoods at the end of an old logging road in the low mountains of southern Ontario. Across the bay, he could see the forested sand dunes of Whitefish Point silhouetted against the night sky, and the tower of the now-defunct lighthouse at its end.

Grigovich came trotting back down the road toward where the other three men waited, already seated in the boat. With him he carried the truck's license plate and the aluminum VIN tags from its dashboard and engine manifold. He'd drop them over the side of their boat when they reached deep water. It would be several days before someone found the brush-covered pickup, and several more before it could be identified. Only Aziz knew all of what they were about to do, but he calculated that the job would be done well before anyone could figure it out. Aziz was pretty smart, Grigovich thought.

The drive here along Highway One from Canada's eastern coast had been uneventful. There had been no trouble with the pickup the Indian girl had provided, and only once had a Mountie given them more than a passing glance. That Canadian cop had followed the four men in their rusted, half-ton Ford for about ten kilometers before exiting the freeway. Lucky for the cop, because the team had prepared for that event; they'd simply kill him and drive away. By the time anyone even began to formulate a theory about that, Aziz and his team would have left the country.

It appeared that their decision to avoid back roads where a curious cop might pull them over just because they were strangers had been a sound one. By alternating their times behind the wheel and driving straight through, they'd made the approximately twelve-hundred kilometer drive in less than twenty-four hours. There had been no stops at motels where a clerk might have remembered them. There had been no bathroom stops except at filling stations, where they bought packaged food that could be eaten while driving. All the sleep that any of them had gotten had been in the truck. Each man carried a bottle of prescribed Dexedrine in case he needed to stay awake, and Ambien for forcing himself to sleep if he needed it. The prescriptions were legitimate, and would pass muster if the police checked them. But they'd never find the doctor, because he'd taken a position at a hospital in Cairo, Egypt.

Now, Aziz thought, was the time to divulge all the details of the intended operation. All of them knew that they were going to make a political statement to the Great Satan, and Grigovich and Richarde must have deduced from the fifteen kilos of C4 plastic explosive that each of them carried that it involved blowing something up. McBraden hadn't the slightest inkling of what was contained in the fifteen-kilo sealed and padlocked 50-caliber ammunition can that he was carrying. Aziz carried an identical ammunition can. Now was the time for Aziz to let each member of his team in on the nuts and bolts of what they were about to do.

Aziz squatted on his haunches on the remote beach, and motioned the other three to come close. When they were squatted next to him, he said without preamble, "Our target is the Mackinac Bridge on Labor Day." The Mackinac Bridge, a five-mile-long suspension bridge, had connected Michigan's Upper and Lower Peninsulas since Eisenhower was president. Aziz knew it was the busiest stretch of Interstate 75 in the United States—especially on Labor Day. During the annual Bridge Walk, tens of thousands of Michigan residents and visitors, led by the state's governor, filled the bridge's northbound lane. With projected casualty rates that would make the World Trade Center disaster look like a minor tragedy, the Bridge Walk would be the perfect time and place for Aziz to strike a meaningful blow for his brand of Islamism.

The other three looked quizzically at their leader, and he continued, "Paul and Peter are carrying conventional plastic explosives. Timmons and I are carrying fuel-grade plutonium. Our objective is to bundle the plutonium in plastique, and place two bombs, one mile apart, on the stanchions below the bridge's roadway under cover of darkness. When we detonate the bombs by telephone at the height of Michigan's annual Bridge Walk on Labor Day, the plutonium will become aerosol. The fallout should be carried on prevailing winds to Mackinaw City and Mackinac Island, as well as onto the Americans walking the five-mile span of the bridge. If the wind is favorable, we might even irradiate the Upper Peninsula community of Saint Ignace and Bois Blanc Island. Immediate casualties should number up to three thousand, with thirty or forty thousand more suffering the effects of radiation sickness for years afterward. The bridge should remain impassable to commerce for at least a month, with a severe, negative impact to America's economy."

He paused, waiting for the gravity of his disclosure to settle into the minds of his comrades.

McBraden was first to speak. "My mom and dad are on the Bridge Walk every year . . ." His voice trailed off under Aziz's hard gaze.

"I'll say this one time, McBraden. You're either with us or against us. At this stage of the operation, there can be no backing out."

McBraden lowered his eyes, because he knew what Aziz was implying. He'd known the kind of people he was dealing with when he'd been smuggled into Afghanistan without a passport and trained in the black arts of terrorist warfare. But while his Arab masters had been teaching him to manufacture bombs and handle various weapons, he'd been too caught up in the camaraderie he hadn't known since his high school days to let himself believe that there was a sinister end to his lessons.

Aziz paused to let his words sink in. The same applied to every one of them. He'd personally bleed the carotid artery of any man in this group, and leave him to die in the woods, if he even suspected that man wouldn't carry out his part of this mission. Aziz had murdered before he'd reached puberty, and many times after, and the act had always brought him pleasure beyond any sensation that he'd known. He wouldn't hesitate to do it again if it became necessary. Right now, he needed every member of this team, but if one of them faltered . . .

"Okay," he said, "that's the mission. Are there any questions?"

There weren't. The question was rhetorical; he'd just told them what the mission entailed. And he'd made it abundantly clear that while each member of his team was important, no one of them was considered invaluable. All that mattered was the objective, and the closer they got to accomplishing their goal, the greater the need for unconditional loyalty from each of them.

"Okay," Aziz said. "Let's go."

Just as they'd drilled a thousand times before, each man clambered to his assigned corner of the boat, and snapped his backpack into place with quick-release buckles and straps. When the bags were secured, each of them announced his readiness with a single word: "Clear."

Aziz pulled the Generation Two Nite Owl Starlight monocular headgear over his eyes. Crossing from the Canadian shore to Michigan's Whitefish Point would typically be an uneventful, forty-five-minute trip. But the American Coast Guard sometimes patrolled this narrow waterway without running lights, and they'd probably been alerted about the submarine in the North Atlantic. The invaders also needed to be watchful for American Border Patrol vehicles, whose presence had increased since 9/11. It was unlikely that anyone had yet pieced together a cogent picture from the puzzle fragments, though.

The team had no way of knowing the fate of their submarine, but Aziz had known that it would almost certainly be detected by coastal defenses; probably an American hunter-killer attack sub. They were very good. For that reason, Aziz had handpicked a captain and crew who were willing to trade their lives to holy Allah for the good of this mission. Aziz had to assume that all of them were now dead, their vessel scuttled as planned, and now on the floor of the North Atlantic. The thought of their sacrifice didn't sadden him; it only filled him with anger, and renewed his determination to see the job through.

Aziz pushed the electric starter on the Evinrude 150 horsepower outboard motor. It fired immediately, its silenced exhaust making little more than a high-pitched hum, as he backed stern-first from the shore. When the water had deepened enough, he shifted to forward gear, and the Zodiac came around smoothly. He pushed the throttle to maximum, and the four men ducked their heads against the slipstream.

Whitefish Bay was an historic refuge for ships whenever Lake Superior grew rough. Known as "The Graveyard" by merchant seamen who earned their livings transporting iron ore and other goods across it, Lake Superior had killed more sailors than any other of the Great Lakes. Fully half of the graves in the cemetery on Whitefish Point were marked by a simple aluminum placard that read "Unknown," their occupants mariners who'd washed ashore and were given a decent Christian burial without ever being identified. Some of those in caved-in plots were probably Americans from an era prior to the time when everyone was identifiable by computer, and some were doubtless Canadian.

The distant shore along Whitefish Point was dotted with only sparse lights. There were few year-round residents there, most of them Indian fishermen who netted the whitefish for which this area was known. There were numerous resort homes that sat empty most of the year—to the men in the boat, their owners were the enemy, rich Americans with lavish incomes that they used to suppress and enslave their own people, while gobbling up clearly dwindling resources. Having themselves been victims, Grigovich and Richarde hated these types of hedonistic, superior-acting Americans most of all. McBraden, who had associated with the wealthy elite through his father, as he enforced the laws they told him to—and ignored those they told him to—hated them only slightly less. He'd seen for himself how above the law people with money could be. Aziz simply hated Jews, Americans, and Christians, in that order.

The water was calm, and the trip across Whitefish Bay was relatively uneventful. To the north, in American waters, there was a westbound cargo ship. The maritime shipping chart carried by Aziz identified it as the *SS Humphries*, an American-flagged, iron ore carrier on its way to Wisconsin. They passed a mile astern of her, as anticipated, and there was no sign that the *Humphries* had detected their passing.

The only real unknown in the landing on Whitefish Point were the so-called "owl people." This group of visiting biologists and biology students gathered near the lighthouse each summer night to erect fine nets that ensnared owls. Funded by numerous universities and foundations, the eclectic group was charged with identifying and banding the various species of owls found around this haven for migratory wild fowl. There was no way for Aziz and his companions to know where the owl people would gather from one evening to the next.

The muted glow of a map on McBraden's iPad clearly showed the outline of the Point, and the few roads that traversed it. He could zoom in to magnify points of interest, but he would have liked if it were real-time, instead of just dated satellite photos. They'd already decided that the best landing place would be slightly past the point, on its north shore. There was an almost unused, township campground there, blown over with beach sand that had buried the outhouse-type public restrooms halfway up their doors. It wasn't a popular place with tourists or locals. Ironically, some of their best reconnaissance photos had come from Facebook and other Internet sources.

Even without a GPS, they could take a visual bearing from the flashing lighthouse beacon. A tourist attraction now, its continued operation was merely symbolic; even recreational boats were guided by satellite now. To the right of it, relative to their own course, was a federally protected, endangered, migratory-bird preserve. The owl researchers might be there, so Aziz stayed well offshore as he followed the coastline around the point to the township campground.

The wind was stronger on the north shore, and the water choppier. He killed the motor and scanned the beach with a night-vision binoculars, while Grigovich did the same with optical binoculars. It was difficult to survey the beach from their small boat as it bounced on the waves, but neither man saw any indication of movement.

Aziz restarted the motor and ran the Zodiac at full speed toward the beach. They made ground in less than two minutes, but he maintained full throttle until the boat was completely out of the water, and the propeller stalled from churning against wet sand. With practiced precision, the four men leaped from each corner of the boat. Grunting a little, they carried the half-ton load across the beach and into the underbrush, leaving as little sign of their passing as possible. Strong breezes along the windward-facing shore should blow over and fill in whatever drag marks and tracks they'd left within a day. Until then, they could hope that none of the few skilled trackers who still existed there would enter onto the nesting preserve and notice their activity.

Chapter Five

The Dragnet

Colyer hung up the phone and then pinched the bridge of his nose between a thumb and forefinger. You'd think that the nexus of federal, state, and local police authorities that this town represented would produce at least one cop with sufficient brainpower to comprehend the potential gravity of this situation, he reasoned to himself. Of all the police agencies represented here in Sault Sainte Marie, only Immigration and Customs Enforcement had seemed to do more than pay passing interest to his phone call informing them of possible terrorist activities. The rest seemed to blow him off as someone with paranoid delusions from an agency that they had little to do with on a daily basis.

But even as he imagined that local and state police units across the Upper Peninsula were circling their ears with their forefingers to demonstrate how crazy they thought the FBI must be, he used his authority as a federal agent to issue an All Points Bulletin. He couldn't force any of these officers to do their generally boring jobs with more enthusiasm, but he could create a paper trail that enabled him to assign blame if they let the terrorists slip through their fingers. Maybe that would help to motivate them to be on their toes.

He groaned as he looked at a map of Michigan's Upper Peninsula. There were almost three hundred miles of open border here, with just one FBI agent and a couple of hundred various police officers to cover it. It didn't help that most of the cops he'd spoken with seemed to think that he was overreacting. So few real crimes happened here that the judicial system made front-page news of minor occurrences that more urban environments would hardly note.

It was such an ironic situation; the confluence of police agencies in Sault Sainte Marie ensured that every minor infraction was punished with extreme severity. Yet, when a real and potentially grave threat arose, it was considered too remote a possibility to be taken seriously. Even his contacts at the Royal Canadian Mounted Police in Ontario seemed to think that it was a stretch to imagine that a rogue submarine in the North Atlantic had any importance to their area of interest.

To give his frustrations a rest, Colyer opened his laptop computer and punched up his personal email account. There was a message from his wife Lanie asking how his day was going, and if he felt okay. He smiled to himself. So many men and women he'd known searched their entire lives for the kind of romance he'd found with this cute little brunette. Without thinking, he ran his fingertips over the framed photo of her that graced his desk. She had short hair in the photo, kind of a pageboy that framed her elfish face perfectly.

He loved her more than he'd ever loved anyone. She'd been a small-town, local cop when he'd met her on a kidnapping case in Illinois sixteen years ago. She'd been totally enthralled by the strapping FBI agent from Saint Louis, and he'd just wanted to get laid. Somehow that mutual attraction had blossomed into a white-hot romance, and that had led to their marriage a year later. Lanie undergwent a full hysterectomy their second year of marriage, so they'd never had children. Neither one of them were saddened by it, however; based on visits with their families, they both figured their lives together had probably been better for it.

When he'd answered Lanie's email, Colyer typed in the sixteen-character password needed to access his agency account. The first file to make an appearance was the international police blotter update. He figured it was a part of his job to give it at least a cursory perusal every day. Mostly it was a glossary of mundane petty crimes that had no bearing on his job as a federal agent, but occasionally something popped up that helped to solve a bigger crime.

Like today . . . There, a one-paragraph mention of a not-inexpensive Zodiac boat being found by tourists walking along the shoreline near Whitefish Point, west of here. Attached to it was a powerful and apparently new outboard motor. Neither boat nor motor had identifiable serial numbers. When a local deputy had finally gotten around to responding several hours after it'd been reported, he'd tried the motor. It had started right away.

Curious. The boat was well off the beach and haphazardly concealed. Whoever had put it there had tried to make it difficult to find, yet they hadn't put a lot of time or effort into its concealment. He googled the boat to get a retail price: more than five thousand dollars. The fuel-injected outboard motor that was attached to its stern sold for more than twice the price of the boat. Total weight of the craft and motor was almost eight hundred pounds, so it hadn't been dragged off the beach by just one man, and probably not by two. Presuming that the boat had been carrying some sort of meaningful payload, there were probably three or four occupants, obviously stout, fit, and probably young.

Not too young, though, because a boat and motor that cost as much as a new car weren't usually kids' toys. There were some well-to-do resorters along the coastline of Whitefish Bay, but this seemed pretty cavalier for even the richest of them. No one had reported a boat stolen, and a resorter wasn't likely to leave his own boat stashed in the brush along a national lakeshore.

Colyer pinched the bridge of his nose again. He was getting a headache. He reached into a desk drawer and retrieved a bottle of ibuprofen. As he twisted the cap, he wondered at the apparent abandonment of such an expensive watercraft in a region where the annual income of the average year-round resident was well below the poverty line established for the rest of the nation.

He would've liked to have reviewed the scene when it was first reported. Local cops had found no reason to treat it as a crime scene. The boat hadn't shown up on a hot sheet, so local deputies had simply trailered it off the beach to an impound yard here in Sault Saint Marie.

It was probably nothing, but this incident irritated something in Colyer's brain; it just didn't make any sense, and he was accustomed to finding logic in everything. From his computer he accessed the police report that was written by the deputy in charge. To his credit, the young deputy, who'd probably been assigned the task of retrieving the boat because it was mundane, had overreacted by dusting it for fingerprints. Nothing had been done with those prints as yet, but they were available, part of the evidence gathered at the scene.

He punched up the digitized fingerprint images from the agency's Combined DNA Index System. There seemed to have been no attempt by their owners to conceal them, although some of the existing prints looked like they were smudged over by someone wearing gloves. Probably someone whose hands had gotten cold; probably while the boat had been on the water. Maybe at night, because this was the warmest time of year in Michigan's Upper Peninsula.

The CODIS system returned only one match. Timmons McBraden, the son of a retired sheriff, who'd quietly undergone treatment for a heroin addiction in Grand Rapids, Michigan. The wording of the official record left Colyer with an impression that the elder McBraden had exerted his influence as a sheriff to cover up the incident, but there'd been no way to stop his son's prints from being entered into the national CODIS database—he'd apparently tried, though.

Timmons McBraden had dropped off the map two years ago. No work history, no known address—not even a cell phone bill. Now that was reason for Colyer's intuitive mind to grow suspicious. No one could survive in America today without leaving some trace of his existence. Even homeless street bums had cell phones.

Whoever they were, the other occupants of the boat weren't known criminals. Although he wasn't supposed to do it without consulting one of the international agencies first, he ran the only other pair of identifiable fingerprints through the International Criminal Police Organization, or INTERPOL. He knew that his log-on would be registered and recorded, and that he'd surely be asked some pointed questions about it by his own supervisors, but he needed to satisfy his own curiosity.

Nothing. No matches. Still, his brain nagged. An abandoned boat was suspicious enough, but there was more to this, he knew it. None of the police agencies he polled seemed to be concerned, though. ICE and Border Patrol acted as if he'd been alone here for too long without a vacation. In fact, he had to wonder if that weren't true. Still, maybe he'd better check out the boat at the impound yard in Sault Sainte Marie, then maybe drive to Whitefish Point and check over the place where they'd found it.

Chapter Six

The Survival Class

"Do you think there are any bears around here?"

Rod grinned. He heard that question every time he taught a survival course.

"Sure there are," he said, "and wolves and coyotes, and even the odd cougar. But I'd be more concerned about other dangers—the most fearsome predators in these woods have six legs."

His survival students didn't believe him. They never did. He could see in their eyes that their heads were filled with television docudramas that touted the dangers of wild animal attacks. Based on his decades of real-world experiences, some of which had nearly killed him for a variety of other reasons, the danger posed by wild animals was so negligible that it could be ignored. He permitted his clients to carry their sidearms if it made them feel safer, but he himself carried no more weight than he needed, and a firearm had proved itself to be just extra pounds that he didn't need to lug.

Rod ran a critical eye over this most recent survival class. Bill Morgan was an electrical engineer who worked for Schneider Electric, the manufacturers of the Square D circuit breakers found in most homes across America. Shawn Hennesy, the man who'd asked about bears, was his brother-in-law and brother to Sue Morgan, who was the third student in this survival class. Rod didn't like taking less than a full class of five people—as many as he felt comfortable with. Smaller classes paid less. And he wasn't generally amenable to taking women, because they complicated things. For one thing, the camp "pee tree" had to be farther away from the main camp, for the sake of decorum, at least.

But Sue Morgan seemed a likable enough sort, pleasant to talk to, and not unpleasant to look at. Maybe a tad wide at the hips from having borne the three grown, successful sons and daughter she mentioned frequently during conversation, but she was a well-maintained, middle-aged woman. Her permed brown hair was colored to hide the gray, and she was carefully plucked and manicured. Sue was what many young men would call a MILF.

Her brother Shawn was production manager at a metal stamping plant that fabricated Square D circuit-breaker boxes from sheets of steel. That was how Bill and Shawn had gotten to know one another, and it was how Bill and Sue had first met at a Christmas party in Chicago twenty-seven years ago this year. When Bill Morgan had approached Shawn with this idea about getting away from the city of Southfield, Michigan, for a week of survival training in the Upper Peninsula, he'd jumped at the chance. He needed wilderness survival skills like he needed astronaut training. But it sounded like an enjoyable few days of respite from a terrible, boring life that had become a series of awful days.

♦ ♦ ♦

It was seven miles to their first campsite on the Betsy River. Rod kept an eye on his clients to make certain that it wasn't too much for any of them. He'd had a few clients who hadn't been able to make the entire leg of that trek, especially when they were on snowshoes in winter. During one or two of those times, he'd feigned exhaustion or some sort of joint injury, and made camp right on the spot. Probably a few of his more perceptive clients had caught on to his ruse to help them save face, but none of them had ever called him on it. And Rod had learned that consideration for the self-image of his clients was as important to their overall well-being as learning to navigate with a map and compass.

These three were in better than average shape, though. Like most young executives, Shawn and Bill owned a paid membership to a gym where they lived, and proudly proclaimed to him that they worked out three times a week. Sue was a full-time mother and wife who sold Mary Kay cosmetics in her spare time, and subscribed religiously to Jillian Michaels and almost every other aerobic exercise system. None of the three were work-hardened, but they seemed fit enough.

Per usual, Rod had set up a phone interview with each one of them in order to instruct them about clothing and footwear, even socks and underwear. Here in the UP, there could be snow every month except July, and every rain shower was cold enough to induce a potentially terminal case of hypothermia. It was all pretty routine: for example, no cotton, because it absorbed lots of perspiration and precipitation; it lost its "dead air" insulating qualities when it was saturated; and it dried very slowly. Cotton was wonderful material for a bath towel, but lousy for thermal long johns.

Another common problem was footwear. Most of his survival students bought a new pair of hiking boots just for his class. Most students were used to what he termed "street" shoes, slip-on types and sneakers that were fine for walking on a mostly flat concrete-covered environment, but offered little in the way of ankle or arch support, and had little traction. They'd probably never again wear the unfashionable lace-up boots he demanded that every client have in the backcountry.

The most common, most immediate problem after that was that the boots they showed up wearing were almost always new and not creased at the natural break-in points of their feet. Rod's own well-worn boots practically walked themselves, as he liked to say, but his clients caused him to include moleskin and Guard-Tex tape in his first-aid kit to treat foot abrasions and blisters on the trail. He always recommended beforehand that clients walk at least five miles in their new boots before putting themselves into the do-or-die situation of the Lake Superior State Forest. But he'd had to insist that more than a few of them walk in water to saturate and soften the leather, then wear the boots until they dried; sort of an accelerated, break-in technique.

In fact, Bill had already begun to complain about "pinch points" in his obviously unworn hikers. Sue and Shawn had apparently heeded at least some of the advice he'd given in his emails and phone conversations; both of their boots looked like they'd been walked in for a few miles. Bill's new Raichle boots were top of the line, but he clearly thought himself too well educated to take advice from a dumb hick who lived back in the woods—after all, how smart could anyone be who actually chose to live in these boondocks?

Rod noted the ill-concealed air of superiority in his client, but he didn't take it personally; he'd endured worse from the people who hired him. Most clients were never going to find themselves in a genuine wilderness survival situation anyway. In fact, most would never find themselves in the woods again. For a majority of them, his wilderness survival course was on the same level as any other exotic adventure vacation.

But Bill Morgan's egotism that he was smarter than the man he'd hired to ostensibly be his teacher would bear watching. The nuts and bolts of wilderness survival were alien to most people, urban or not, and a refusal to listen to an expert denoted the potential to do things that were self-destructive—like picking up a bale-handle pot off the campfire with bare hands, when it was hot enough to brand skin. Or just slipping and falling on dew-dampened reindeer moss. Rod had seen it happen more times than he could recall, usually to the same type of folks who were convinced of their own intelligence. But common sense depended on a person's background experience and frame of reference; he'd seen for himself that it wasn't only a hillbilly in a city who was out of his environment and apt to do stupid things.

Sue Morgan picked up on Rod's wry amusement with her spouse. "Is there any poison ivy around here?" she asked.

Rod could see that she was being more apologetic for her husband's arrogance than she was being curious. He favored her with as kindly a smile as his experience-hardened face could muster, and said, "Not much in this terrain. I'll let you know if I see some. Are you allergic to poison ivy?" He asked the last question loudly enough to be overheard by the other two and watched their reactions.

The three of them looked at one another, and the two men shrugged. "I don't know," Hennesy said, "I've never had poison ivy before." He looked at Bill Morgan, "You?"

Morgan shrugged again. "Me neither."

"Well, I have," Sue said. "When I was a teenager, I had such a bad case that I couldn't go to school for two weeks. My mom said that I'd caught it on the wind."

Rod grinned at Sue with genuine sincerity. "The reaction comes from direct epidermal contact with oil on the leaves. Don't worry," he said, "I promise to warn you if anything comes along that'll hurt you."

He himself was immune to everything in the woods. Like some of his childhood friends, he'd suffered through enough long, miserable bouts with aquatic parasites in his youth to be at least resistant to them. But he'd seen enough people, friends and clients, who'd suffered from allergies to know that they could range from uncomfortable to life-threatening, and were never to be taken lightly. Some people had become deathly ill from things they didn't even know they were allergic to. Those people were the reason he made capsules of over-the-counter diphenhydramine antihistamine a permanent part of his first-aid kit, and carried an illegal prescription-only epinephrine styrette. No one was going to die on his watch if he could prevent it. Especially not someone as genuinely nice as Sue Morgan.

"Okay," Rod said, "we're here. Let's make home for the evening. The first thing on our itinerary is to set up camp and build a fire. Then we'll learn to build a debris shelter."

They dropped their backpacks where he indicated, then walked to the bank of the river to survey their surroundings and stretch their tired limbs.

"Oh, what a gorgeous place," Sue Morgan said.

"This is awesome!" her brother exclaimed.

Even Bill Morgan was impressed; he exhaled a little sigh of contentment in spite of himself as he looked up and down the river. "This is a pretty cool place," he said.

Rod said nothing, but the slightest upturn at the corners of his mouth revealed that he knew this pretty little campsite on the Betsy River would have that effect on these first-time visitors. Only the rarest of people was immune to the charm of this forest.

Shawn Hennesy slapped his neck. "There are a few mosquitoes here, though," he said, grimacing at the squashed remains in his palm.

Rod grinned, "That there are. Thank goodness it isn't hot and sunny, or they'd be joined by horseflies and deerflies. Here," he said, reaching down to pluck a frilly leafed plant from the shoreline. "This is yarrow. Smell it. It contains natural pyrethrins, basically the same stuff found in commercial flea sprays and shampoos. Crush the plant and rub the juices onto your skin. It'll help to keep the bugs away."

All three of the survival students immediately started gathering the plants to follow his instructions. Rod smiled to himself as he dug out a shallow excavation for their campfire. Then he raked together a fistful of dried grasses in his splayed fingers and struck a shower of hot sparks onto them with his flint-and-steel fire tool. The tinder flamed instantly, drawing an impressed "ooh" from one of the men—he couldn't tell which one, because his attention was focused on the tinder. Rod added shreds of birch bark and small twigs as the fledgling fire began to flare in the prepared fire pit.

This was the first and last fire he'd start during the course. Not only was daily fire-making a part of real-world survival training that every client should know how to perform in a number of ways, but experience had taught him that there was a relaxing component to fooling with an open fire. From watching his students, he'd figured out years ago that there was considerably more than just heat within the embers of a campfire. Poking coals and rearranging wood seemed to have some sort of therapeutic effect on the most troubled soul, so he let clients maintain the camp's fire as much as possible.

When the fire had grown to a crackling blaze, he began unstrapping and laying out the shelters he'd buckled to his clients' backpacks. One of the first lessons he taught them was constructing shelter against the elements from whatever materials an environment offered. But at the end of a day, nearly everyone opted to sleep in the bug-screened, watertight, zipper-doored, folding domiciles he'd strapped onto their packs. His personal bivouac shelter was a five-pound Observer from the Canadian company Integral Designs. Shawn carried a four-pound Eureka! Zeus bivy; Bill's pack had a two-person Kelty Acadia that provided enough floor space to sleep him and Sue comfortably. They could sleep in a debris shelter that he showed them how to make, but he'd be in his bivy at night, and he was betting they would be, too.

When the tents were up and situated in places that were selected to guard against rain runoff and "widowmaker" dead trees that were infamous for dropping large pieces of deadwood onto the heads of unsuspecting lumberjacks, he led the trio into the woods to search for shelter materials. With the exception of fast-growing bracken ferns that served as the shelter's rain repellent outer covering, no living plant materials were needed. He set Sue and Bill on the task of cutting free bundles of useful ferns with a machete and leather gloves to protect their hands, while he and Shawn chose the main beam and wall supports from dead saplings and limbs. Without leather gloves, fibers in the ferns' stalks could slice unprotected fingers like a razor.

Having built hundreds of debris shelters, he was always impressed that they withstood the full brunt of a UP winter with as little damage as you'd expect in a quality stick-built home. Livable shelters from previous classes dotted the forests around here; they didn't have satellite TV or central heating, but he liked to leave them there for lost deer hunters and such, who might be happy to have a roof on a cold and stormy night. Bears and other animals frequently found moving into one preferable to building their own dens. He smiled to himself at the memory of backing out of one of them in a hurry when he came face-to-face with a striped skunk who'd taken up residence there. Lucky for him that skunks were reluctant to use their spray defense in an enclosed place where they'd victimize themselves.

Chapter Seven

The Encounter

Grigovich froze. His piss stream involuntarily stopped. He stood staring while drops of urine splattered onto his boots. Bill Morgan stared back, equally surprised. The Kershaw machete Rod had provided him for the class was gripped in his leather-gloved right hand. In his left hand was a handful of ferns, held by their stems like a bouquet of flowers.

His nerves already stretched taut by the murder of the girl, on top of the stress of their mission, Grigovich grabbed for the big Desert Eagle 50-caliber pistol that he carried tucked into his waistband. Morgan's eyes went wide at the surreal image of a large man standing before him, penis hanging down from one hand, his other hand on the butt of a huge handgun.

Morgan freaked. He turned and ran blindly in the opposite direction, not caring which way he was heading, so long as it was away from the gun.

"Stop!" Grigovich shouted, pulling the large automatic fully from his waistband. His command seemed to have the reverse effect on Morgan, who only ran faster.

Almost of its own volition, the big pistol's Tritium sights appeared before Grigovich's eyes, and the gun rocked back in his hand as the woods echoed with a booming report. The large-caliber bullet struck

Morgan between his shoulder blades; he lost control of his legs and pitched forward onto his face. His mind knew that he'd been shot, but his body felt no pain. He was helpless to stop his forward momentum as his face plowed into the thick bed of pine needles that lay on the ground. He felt the impact, knew that his nose had been injured. He registered the fact that one eye socket was filled with dirt, but he could do nothing about it. Then Bill Morgan died.

Grigovich stared dumbly, the Desert Eagle hanging loosely in his hand, a wisp of white smoke curling upward from its barrel. His ears still rang, and he could smell the odor of burnt gunpowder. He hadn't meant to pull the trigger; it was just an automatic reaction brought on by adrenalin.

Aziz was first on the scene. He could hear Richarde and McBraden close behind.

"What the fuck have you done?" Aziz shouted, his voice trembling from barely controlled anger. "Can't you even take a piss without fucking killing someone?" He put his own Ruger Security Six revolver to Grigovich's temple. "You've jeopardized our entire mission, you stupid fucker."

"I'm sorry, Philippe," Grigovich muttered, trying hard to fish in his mind for a justification that might explain what he'd just done. "He surprised me and I thought he might have a gun . . ." His voice trailed off. That excuse sounded lame in his own ears.

"Shut up," Aziz said. He thought fast. "We've still got a job to finish. Let's at least hide the body. This guy probably wasn't out here by himself. McBraden, you said you know these woods. Where do we hide this carcass?"

"If we had a shovel, I'd say dig a shallow grave, and then camouflage the hole with forest duff. But grave-digging wasn't one of the contingencies we'd planned for, was it?" McBraden shot Grigovich a dirty look. "More important, I'd say, is to put as much distance between ourselves and this body as quick as we can. Let's cover this guy with brush to make him hard to find, then haul ass away from here."

Aziz wasn't happy with that plan. It was oversimplistic. Someone was going to come looking for this guy, probably within minutes. As far as he could see, McBraden's value to the team was limited to having grown up while riding a snowmobile or four-wheeler through these woods. When it came to crunch time, he was proving to be about half the expert woodsman that he'd bragged he was.

"Enough," Aziz spat harshly. "Find out how many more there might be and then kill them."

The other three looked at him in surprise, as the very real gravity of what Grigovich had done and what Aziz was demanding sank into their brains. McBraden was wrong; they couldn't simply hide this body and then run for the Mackinac Bridge. This guy wasn't out here alone. His clothing showed no signs of discoloration or wear, and his boots weren't well-creased at the break points. They were new. The man was a tourist. And since he was back here in the deep forest around Betsy River, not only did it make sense that he wasn't alone, it followed that he'd probably been part of a group led by an expert woodsman. That expert had to be found and dispatched before he made it out and alerted authorities.

"Quickly," Aziz hissed in a low tone through tightly locked front teeth. "Spread out and find the rest of them. They can't be that far away. This guy looks like he was making something. Hurry, we need them all." There was a cruel meaning in the way he said he wanted them all together.

They left Morgan where he laid, plowed face-first into the forest floor. Richarde and McBraden drew their automatics. They didn't have to open the actions of their pistols to see if they were loaded the way American actors always seemed to do in Hollywood movies. Their Spetnatz-style Russian training in Afghanistan made it second nature to have a live round in the chamber ready to fire. Grigovich replaced the magazine in his Desert Eagle with a fresh one, bringing it once again to full cartridge capacity. With a hand signal that showed spread fingers, Aziz silently told them to split up and search between here and the river for this man's companions.

Chapter Eight

The Escape

A gunshot. Its loudness and short, sharp boom indicated that it had come from a short-barreled pistol. The survival instructor's brain went into self-preservation mode instantly, because years of experience had impressed upon him the value of immediate reaction. Whether it was the overhead crack of a widowmaker limb, or getting his kayak off Lake Superior at the first sign of a blow, swift response had saved his life more than once over the years.

His alert mind worked at furious speed. A pistol shot back here spelled trouble. This region was closed to hunting this time of year, and almost nobody hereabouts hunted with a handgun. Besides, voices usually didn't echo through the woods until *after* a kill had been made. The voices he'd just heard had preceded the shot, and there were sounds of feet moving fast through the bush.

Rod screamed to Sue and Shawn, "Move! Get your asses to the road, like I showed you, and don't stop till you reach town!"

They both just stared at him. He didn't have time to wait until they regained enough of their mental faculties to comply before Grigovich and Richarde burst from the underbrush. Shawn Hennesy turned to face them, his mouth open wide with fear and surprise at the sight of two armed men charging toward him. Before Hennesy could utter a syllable, both gunmen had fired bullets into his chest. His mouth still open in astonishment, he gasped once and fell backward onto the ground, dead before his body had fully collapsed.

Sue was frozen, stunned at seeing her younger brother shot lifeless before her eyes. But Rod's survival instinct caused him to react like a deer, sprinting immediately for safety behind the concealing brush. Grigovich fired two rapid shots at his disappearing figure. Aziz fired once, the reports of their pistols sounding loud but flat in the sound-absorbing forest.

They both missed. As Rod knew from having grown up as a meat hunter with no extra money and a limited ammunition supply, shooting at a fast-moving animal in the woods amounted to a waste of rounds. It generally meant that you were desperate, too, because you'd blown any chance you might have had for getting a clean second shot. A serious hunter who was out to put dinner on the table for a hungry family concentrated primarily on tracking and stalking skills, and then on putting a well-placed bullet into a stationary victim that had as little chance of dodging it as a hunter could manage.

"Son of a bitch," muttered Aziz. Compared to the sand and rock terrain that he was accustomed to, to him this area was a thick, green nightmare where large man-eating animals lurked behind every tree and bush, especially at night. It was one thing to die willingly in a glorious Holy fireball, but to be ripped apart slowly and painfully by the jaws and claws of a bear or wolf held a genuine terror for the Arab. He'd never in a million years admit that probably baseless fear to the others, but he was already dreading their first night sleeping in the woods.

Richarde held the terrified Sue Morgan at gunpoint while McBraden joined Grigovich and Aziz in the search for Rod in the baffling greenery of Lake Superior State Forest. The undergrowth was especially impenetrable near the banks of the Betsy River, and McBraden rightfully figured that that was where a man who knew these woods would probably look for a hiding spot.

Although he'd calculated that the man would head into the thickets, knowing that didn't make it any easier to locate him. McBraden knew that he wasn't the expert outdoorsman he let others believe he was, but he'd been hunting deer and grouse in these woods with his dad often enough during his childhood to know that finding anything that was trying to remain unseen was nearly impossible. Most of what he and the others were doing was beating the bush, hoping to pass close enough to their quarry to frighten him into flight. He'd done the same a hundred times in his youth, when the entire group at their annual deer-hunting camp had "run the swamp" in an armed skirmish line.

No such luck, this time. They all listened closely for any sound of flight; rustling leaves and ground duff, snapping twigs . . . It was impossible to move silently through these woods. Anything in motion up to a dozen yards away was sure to reveal itself. On the other hand, something as big as a moose could conceal itself if it remained stationary. And if this guy was armed, the tables could turn on them in a matter of seconds.

McBraden was the closest thing they had to a tracker, according to the stories he told, and that was the prime reason Aziz had chosen him to be a member of his terrorist squad. But although all of them could see signs of something having passed through the greenery, none of them could be sure that any of the disturbances had been created by the man they were after. In the dense, concealing foliage and dust-dry ground debris that wouldn't register a clear boot print, McBraden just didn't have the skills to follow whatever trail their quarry might have left behind.

A sudden explosion of action from the brush revealed itself as a spruce grouse. Aziz yelped audibly at the surprise, but that embarrassment was masked by the booming of Grigovich's Desert Eagle pistol as he fired instinctively at the flying bird. Aziz glared at him with burning eyes, but said nothing. The truth was, he'd nearly fired his gun as well.

They looked hard, but the pine-needle-covered ground registered no discernible tracks of any kind. It took much longer to identify and follow footprints than it took for a fleeing man to make them. McBraden knew enough about tracking to know that it wasn't reasonable to assume that you could trail anything in real-time; it was just too slow an ordeal.

Aziz's unrealistic expectations of his chosen tracker had been fostered by Hollywood movies that were written by people who were themselves inexperienced in woodcraft. They glossed over the finer points of tracking and survival by simply imbuing them with an air of mystery. If a writer couldn't explain the details of how a thing was done, he made it into some sort of mystery that was beyond the comprehension of ordinary humans. With no frame of reference beyond that, Aziz had been easy to convince that McBraden's childhood as a Yooper had somehow made him an expert. The tests he'd put this self-proclaimed master tracker through had all been in an arid desert, where it was child's play to follow the boot tracks of another man.

Aziz mentally kicked himself. McBraden had already proved himself to be less than competent in a wilderness environment. Being a white-bread, American Christian had made him untrustworthy from the beginning, and now the Arab was becoming convinced that maybe he was a liability. Maybe McBraden should become one of the casualties of this mission.

The same thought was occurring to McBraden. When he'd first met the Muslim at a so-called peace rally in Toronto, it had come almost naturally to make himself look like a mountain man to a person he viewed as just an ignorant sand-nigger—that was a phrase his father had been fond of using. Now it was becoming frighteningly clear to McBraden that he was probably judged to be expendable by the sociopath who'd formed this gang of terrorists.

The reality was that whether he liked McBraden or not, it fell to Aziz to deal with this situation. If he wanted to kill anyone right now, it would be Grigovich for his stupidity in having perpetrated the problem in the first place,

"We don't have time for this shit," the Arab said. "There are many ways to draw a scorpion from its hole." He shot Grigovich a glare. "I should fucking kill you right here," he said.

"I'm sorry, Philippe," Grigovich said, hanging his head. Aziz looked at him unfeelingly. The major advantages of having this powerful but stupid man on the team included his dogged loyalty to his leader and his almost natural talent with explosives. The biggest drawback was that Grigovich had a conscience. Aziz did not view that as a positive attribute in this case.

Chapter Nine

The Hunt

McBraden was right. Rod had gone for the river. He knew that even if his pursuers anticipated his strategy, it would be nearly impossible for them to find him hidden there. All he had to do was avoid making an obvious trail. He knew how difficult even the most accomplished tracker would find it to follow the trail of a single animal in these woods, whatever its species. And he knew how easy it was to outdistance anyone trying to follow him.

The drawback to running the riverbank was the same as the advantage; a picket of densely growing tag alders made the terrain impassable in places, and wet ground strewn with their sun-dried leaves made a crunching sound underfoot. He regretted not being able to use the TOPS Power Eagle machete that rode his hip to assist his passage, but the ringing of its blade on wood would've been too loud. Still, thick foliage was an effective sound absorber, and most noises didn't carry more than a few yards.

Rod's pursuers had formed a loose line, as if they were trying to spook a deer that was bedded in a swamp. At one point, the guy who seemed familiar with this area had passed close to where Rod had hunkered down behind a low juniper bush. His mind was made clear and sharp by fear, a fear that was honed by knowing that these strangers with pistols in their hands intended to kill him. Rod instinctively reached down to grasp a stout branch with which to defend himself.

His fingertips sank into the rotted wood beneath the smooth bark of an alder trunk, and he realized the futility of using the pithy trunk as a bludgeon against guns. Instead, holding the dead branch at arm's length so that it wouldn't spin through the air with a whooshing sound, he sidearmed the branch high above the surrounding foliage and into the brush. It landed on the other side of his pursuers, crashing down audibly through the lower limbs of a white pine.

The sound drew the attention of the three men, but elicited no verbal response. The thin man with the narrow mustache and sparse beard held up his left fist, and all movement ceased. Then he spread his fingers wide. In response to that signal, his companions flanked him on either side and sprinted toward the sound. It was impossible to run quietly through that environment, but they made remarkably little noise as they went. Rod wondered at the harmonious way they worked together. That told of training, or at least long familiarity with one another. Were they some sort of outlaw militia group? Maybe a group of sick-minded cultists? Whatever they were, they were dangerous. At least they were moving away from his hiding spot.

As the sounds of his would-be killers faded into the distance, Rod forced himself back to a state of relative calm. His heart was pounding in his chest like a bass drum, and his breathing sounded rough and labored to his own ears. It felt like there was a tight strap across his sternum, squeezing it tightly and making it hard for him to breathe. He closed his eyes, focusing on the splinter of light at the center of his imagination, and then concentrated on returning his respiration to normal. He could hear the three men busting through bush a hundred yards distant, moving away from where he lay hidden on the riverbank. Good. He knew that if he remained motionless, they'd never find him.

After what seemed to be a very long time, but was in fact only a few minutes, the sounds of movement faded back in the direction of where he'd intended to make camp with the class. Rod still didn't move. He'd employed too many tricks to kill whitetailed deer to be lulled into complacency that easily himself. Sure enough, several eternal minutes later, he heard another person moving in the same direction taken by the others. They'd left a man behind, hoping that Rod would be fooled into revealing himself.

He hadn't heard another shot, so he presumed that Sue Morgan was still alive. He'd seen Shawn shot in the chest by two of them, and he was certainly dead. The shot that had echoed through the woods just before Shawn's killers had come charging into the survival camp had most likely gone into Bill Morgan. In spite of himself, Rod began to shake uncontrollably, and tears ran down his cheeks as he was racked with silent, involuntary sobs. His stomach hurt, and he felt like he was going to throw up. Now that the immediate threat to his life had passed, the emotional trauma of what had taken place was exacting a toll from his body and mind. He recognized it because he'd known shock and trauma before, and he knew it was only temporary. It would pass. He forced himself not to retch as he moved quietly out of earshot of the camp.

His backpack and nearly all of his equipment were back at camp with the killers. He took stock of what he had on his person. He had his survival knife, a TOPS Power Eagle 12, with the cargo pouch on its sheath outfitted with a Brunton Tag-A-Long compass, a Blast Match fire making tool, fifteen feet of twenty-pound test-fishing line, and an assortment of fishing hooks contained between two strips of Scotch tape. In one cargo pocket of his BDU trousers was a roll of toilet tissue in a Ziploc bag; in the other, a Ziploc bag containing an assortment of old boot laces and a laminated map of the eastern Upper Peninsula. His right hip pocket carried a disposable butane lighter and a pocket-clip Gerber folding knife. His other pocket had his house keys. On the right side of his belt was a Gerber Omnivore LED flashlight; opposite it, a Leatherman multitool. Around his neck, on a lanyard made from flammable waxed cotton string, hung a Brunton Sight Master compass. His back pocket carried an ESEE survival wallet with his personal identification, and an assortment of survival tools that had come with the wallet—even a polymer handcuff key. He carried no money at all, because he'd never found a use for it in the woods. He felt pretty well equipped for survival, still.

Mosquitoes were becoming plentiful as the day faded toward night. He pulled a handful of feathery-leafed yarrow plants from the riverbank and crushed them between his palms. Then he rubbed the fragrant spicy-smelling juices onto his skin and clothing. The mosquito attacks lessened right away. As he'd told his students, the juices were as effective against biting insects as most store-bought repellents, and remained so for about three days. But when the bugs were determined—as they were immediately following a new hatch—nothing short of being on fire was enough to discourage them.

Now that he was out of immediate danger, Rod began weighing his options. He was a half-day's hike from home, where he could call 911. Cell reception was unreliable out here, and he didn't own a cell phone anyway.

He figured that after he'd convinced the central dispatcher that he wasn't out of his mind or drunk, and a deputy found the corpses, they'd most likely jail him. Being an ex-con, he'd automatically be a suspect in the murders once he'd reported them, and the cops would probably arrest him for his trouble. The thought of being handcuffed and forced to sleep on a concrete slab with slobbering drunks, sociopaths, and career criminals was more repulsive than facing the people who'd just tried to murder him.

While the authorities who ruled Chippewa County took a month to make up their minds about whether or not he was a murderer, the real killers would be long gone. Rod had no reason to expect anything good from local cops. They'd already made it clear that being an ex-con made him an undesirable citizen, and they were just looking for a reason to bust him. Besides, the more he thought about it, the more unlikely it seemed that they'd believe that a bunch of armed guys would just run out of the woods and start shooting complete strangers. Rod had to admit that sounded crazy—even to him.

Chapter Ten

The Killings

Sue Morgan was on her knees, her hands tied tightly behind her back with nylon parachute cord, in front of the campfire that Rod had built. She was clearly terrified, but her brain had retreated into a state of numbed shock. Her shattered mind refused to recognize the horrible realities of what her eyes had just witnessed—and were still witnessing.

Her little brother, one of her most constant companions throughout childhood, and through the most joyous and sorrowful periods of her life, lay unmoving in front of her. His eyes, milky with the white glaze of death, stared upward at blue sky they couldn't see. The right corner of his mouth was wet with drool that was drying in the warm afternoon breeze. She could see the two small holes in the blue plaid material of his shirt, but there was only a hint of congealed blood to reveal that they had gone into the chest beneath. From under his body, though, near his right shoulder, there was a pool of sticky-looking purplish blood. The viscosity of the blood seemed especially awful and surreal to her. Why didn't it soak into the sandy earth? It should soak into the ground, instead of pooling like that.

A pair of denim-clad legs stepped in front of her, blocking the view of her dead brother. Her eyes slowly followed the legs upward to a military-style belt with a brass buckle, then on to a blue North Face down vest hanging open over a green plaid woolen shirt. They finally stopped on the countenance of Philippe Aziz. She shrank from the sight of his face.

Aziz grinned at her reaction to him as he regarded her with the same dispassion one might display when observing a housefly. He liked to see terror in other peoples' faces when they looked at him. It gave him a sense of power that was almost sensual. He craved more of that power.

Aziz knelt in front of Sue Morgan and stared directly into her eyes. "Woman, why are you here?" It was a demand for information, not a question. She gazed at him blankly. Her gaze was upon him, but she wasn't focused on anything.

Without warning, he slapped her hard. Her head spun toward her right shoulder. When Sue's gaze returned to him, her eyes were clear and full of fresh fear. A stream of bright blood welled from the left side of her lower lip and ran down her chin. Then the lip began to quiver and tears flooded from both eyes to stream down her cheeks. Her gaze focused onto his with the intensity of an animal that knew it was about to be killed.

"Please," she croaked in a voice that broke with strain. "Please don't kill me. I have children . . ."

Aziz smiled brightly, almost benignly—he was enjoying this. He spoke to her in a soft voice. "Dear lady, we don't want to harm you. It brings us no pleasure to hurt you," he lied. He laid the back of his hand tenderly against the reddened, wet cheek he'd just struck. "Just tell us about that man who ran away."

Hope sprang into her eyes. The man before her had seemed to sympathize when she'd told him that she was a mother. He hadn't actually shot anyone. Maybe he wasn't like the other three men who stood on the other side of the fire, staring at them with guns in their hands. Maybe this man with the smaller detective-style gun tucked innocuously into his waistband was willing to protect her from those other wicked killers. He seemed to have authority over them, and he seemed more kindly than them. Maybe he'd let her go. Maybe, if she just gave him the information he wanted . . .

Aziz saw the hope come into her eyes, too. Good. That was what he'd intended. Let this pampered, white, American bitch think she was going to go home safely when this was all over. He relished the control he had over this pale, simpering whore of a capitalist. She'd probably be willing to pleasure them all to gain her freedom. The thought made his loins burn and he felt himself becoming erect.

He changed the subject to dispel the physical sensations he was feeling.

"What is your name, dear lady?" he asked as sweetly as he could.

She sniffed back a sob and looked at him with tear-filled eyes. "Sue. Sue M-morgan."

"Sue, I need you to tell me what you were doing here. Who was the man who ran away and left you here all alone?"

It was true, that dirty bastard Elliot had run off and left her here to face these murderers. She sniffed again. "He's a survival instructor from Paradise named Rod. Rod Elliot. I'd never met him before. It was my husband Bill's idea . . ." Her voice trailed off and she started to sob. "Bill . . . Where is my husband? Have you seen him?"

Aziz stifled a grin. He had complete control over this woman now. Surely, she'd heard Grigovich's shot—the 50-caliber had echoed through the woods like a cannon. But she was grasping for the hope that he offered. Not having seen the body, she chose to believe that her husband was still alive.

"Sue, is your husband a brown-haired man wearing Raichle hiking boots and a green Columbia jacket with a hood?"

She brightened. "Yes," she said in a voice that was two octaves higher than normal. "Do you know where he is? Have you seen him? Is he all right? Oh God, tell me that he's okay."

"He's safe," Aziz lied smoothly. "My associates have him. Now tell me about this survival instructor."

"Oh God, he's safe?" Aziz nodded. She continued, eager to please now. "His name is Rodney Elliot. He's a survival instructor who runs Black Bear Survival Adventures on Whitefish Point. I don't know him. My husband made all the arrangements."

"Where is this Rodney now, do you think? Where would he go?"

"I don't know. I don't know. We're not from around here." She looked with terror at Richarde, who had advanced a few steps closer. "Oh Lord, please believe me."

Aziz did believe her. She was too scared to lie. But that didn't make a difference. Without warning, he grasped her right ear in his left hand. Pulling it away from her head, he began sawing it off at the apex of her skull with a Spyderco Native folding knife that he'd drawn unnoticed from his pocket.

Sue Morgan stared at him for a full second with her mouth gaped open, and eyes wide in frozen astonishment. Then the ear came free, and Aziz held it in front of her face, dripping with bright blood. Her emerald stud earring reflected the setting sun from its severed lobe. Then the pain registered, and a scream of agony and primal fear erupted from her open mouth. Her eyes followed involuntarily as Aziz threw the detached ear into the fire, where it sizzled and bubbled on the red coals. She could feel hot blood streaming down her neck. Grigovich and McBraden were staring in horror at what Aziz had done. Richarde seemed unmoved.

Aziz turned away, grinning in spite of himself. Sue Morgan kept screaming and sobbing that she had told him all she knew. Good, this woman's screams were what he'd intended. That son-of-a-bitch survival instructor was doubtless still within earshot, and Aziz counted on his hearing the woman's screams. A man who made his meager living as a small-time survival instructor was probably in that business for reasons other than money.

This Rodney guy was likely an idealistic fool who thought he could make the wilderness a safer place for his clients. That type of man was probably seeking grace from a life that had known considerable misery. He probably needed a reason to feel noble, and he wasn't likely to abandon a woman who'd been in his charge to the likes of themselves. Aziz was counting on this idiot to make some sort of attempt at rescuing her from their evil clutches, and he was determined to see that that attempt was fatal for the would-be rescuer. Either way, his team had to move on to finish the main mission, and the woman was a liability they couldn't afford.

Chapter Eleven

The Evidence

Colyer stopped at the impound yard first before continuing to Whitefish Point. It was an open, rural field on some property owned by an ex-sheriff. Imagine that, he smirked to himself. A bunch of terrorists here in the land of mutually back-scratching good old boys. The retired sheriff raised an eyebrow that the FBI would take an interest in an abandoned boat at Whitefish Point. But he didn't say anything, careful not even to hint that he meant to pick up this cherry piece of nautical equipment for pennies on the dollar at the next auction. He already had some very nice possessions that he'd confiscated from alleged criminals.

Colyer went over the impounded Zodiac meticulously, although his hopes weren't high of finding any meaningful forensic evidence. Deputies hadn't given it the consideration that might be accorded to a potentially valuable piece of evidence, because that's not what they thought it could be. It had simply been lashed onto an open snowmobile trailer with polyethylene rope and driven at high speeds for seventy miles without even a tarpaulin to cover it.

The ex-sheriff was more interested in his breakfast than in whatever this tight-lipped FBI agent was up to—besides, hadn't local forensics boys already gone over the boat? He bid Colyer farewell, and went back into his house, wiping his hands on his shirt front. The mosquitoes were tolerable here in the farmland surrounding Sault Sainte Marie, kept poisoned to manageable levels by agricultural pesticides, but the ex-sheriff claimed that they were eating him alive. It was an irony that most people who lived in—and boasted about—the natural wonders of Michigan's Upper Peninsula always viewed them through a glass barrier.

Like an actor playing detective in an old Sherlock Holmes movie, Colyer inspected the Zodiac's steering and drive mechanisms under an old-fashioned magnifying glass. There were what appeared to be olive-drab polyester or acrylic fibers caught in pinch points at the shifting and steering mechanisms. Probably from gloves. Knit gloves, not the usual latex or nitrile gloves that criminals used to conceal their fingerprints, but the knit-liner gloves used to keep someone's hands warm. Someone who was driving, probably while the craft was at sea. Someone who had cold hands during what was the warmest part of the year around here. Probably a man, and a fit one, judging by the distance the heavy boat had been carried off the beach, but not a local who was accustomed to cold weather.

Using tweezers, Colyer pulled the fibers free and placed them into a Ziploc bag. He couldn't see the old sheriff, but the FBI man could feel his stare from inside the house. He imagined that the retired lawman was in there mumbling derogatory remarks about the stupidity of federal agents, Washington, DC, and outsiders in general. Most people who chose to live in Michigan's Upper Peninsula were less than amicable toward what they considered to be Big Brother. The contradiction of their more-or-less Orwellian paranoia was that small communities often created the very environment they were trying to escape.

Colyer didn't have a lot of faith that the fibers he'd so painstakingly collected were going to be traceable to anything more than a pair of cheap gloves that could be purchased at any military surplus store. Still, he meticulously inspected every inch of the Zodiac and its motor. There was nothing else to be found. Whoever these guys were, they weren't a bunch of kids out for a joyride, that much was certain. There was an aura of seriousness about this whole thing, from the apparently new, professional-quality watercraft to the supercharged motor that drove it. He just knew that there was something he was missing here. But what could it be?

Chapter Twelve

Conscience

Aziz was right. Rod's conscience had forced him to return to where the terrorists had appropriated his camp. From behind a juniper bush fifty yards away, he'd watched in horror as the lean, olive-skinned man who seemed to be in charge of the group had almost casually sliced Sue Morgan's ear from her head. The woman's screams had pierced his brain with a sensation that was much like physical pain to him. He cringed and his body writhed of its own accord as his eyes witnessed the torture from his hiding place, but he made no move to reveal his presence.

Rod had known more than his share of physical pain and mental anguish in his own life, and he never allowed himself to forget that it was probably just dumb luck that he hadn't killed someone in his youth. A brief stint as a drug dealer in his early twenties, before he'd gone to prison, had showed him what some people were willing to do to others for nothing more than a few dollars. He knew how it felt to snap another man's wrist bones under force, and to shatter a femur with a length of water pipe brought down hard. It was a repulsive memory. He shuddered every time he remembered that era of his youth. No amount of money could be worth the inhumane acts he had committed and seen perpetrated over a few grams of cocaine. No forgiveness existed for the agonizing guilt that weighed down his heart every second of every day. So much misery and brutality over a few lousy dollars.

Perhaps just as bad were remembrances of the animals he'd killed. On a sunny knoll in back of his house were interred nearly a dozen dogs he'd euthanized over the years. Living so far from a veterinarian, he'd done the job himself most times, and his mind recoiled at the recollection of every canine friend against whose head he'd put a gun muzzle and then pulled the trigger. Even deer and other game he'd killed for food had taken a little chink from his soul. Maybe he was getting old and soft, but he'd come to realize that with every life he took, he also took part of his own life.

Seeing Sue Morgan mutilated with a knife before his eyes, and having deduced that she was most likely being tortured simply to lure him into surrendering himself to these maniacs, was almost unendurable. The part of his psyche that had driven him to instruct others in the art of staying alive under adverse conditions made her suffering a nightmare for him.

But that same mindset forced him to come to grips with the knowledge that if he revealed himself to these men, his own life would be forfeit. He didn't want to die. He didn't want to never again see the person he loved more than any other human being. Dying was a frightening prospect for him. He supposed it was frightening for most people. The real proximity of death right now made his belly queasy and caused his right eyebrow to twitch.

But Shawn Hennesy and Bill Morgan had already died under his charge. Sue Morgan was still in his charge, so to speak. If he left her with these killers while he went to get help—and probably got charged with the murders of the other two men for his trouble—they'd surely dispatch her before rescuers could arrive. It didn't take much brainpower to determine that these men had little regard for life.

Rod still felt a little nauseous. He knew he had to do something, but his choices were limited. He was no hero—heroism was the antithesis of survival. He felt like crying as he hid like a coward behind his bush. He was torn between a conscience that dictated action and a desire for self-preservation.

Richarde made the decision for him. Reaching with his left hand to undo the button-fly of his cargo pants, the Canadian stepped away from the others to relieve his bladder. Rod watched in horror as Richarde walked directly toward where he hid behind the juniper bush. As the man approached, as if following some sort of beacon, Rod's hand unconsciously went to the hilt of his Power Eagle survival machete.

As if by itself, the twelve-inch blade slid slowly from its sheath, sounding as loud as a manhole cover dragging across concrete to Rod's heightened sense of hearing. His eyes widened in fear as Richarde stepped around the evergreen, hand already reaching into his open fly. Their eyes met, and for a brief moment Richarde froze. Then his opposite hand fell to the 9-millimeter Beretta pistol tucked into his waistband. Richarde drew the pistol, but he twisted its butt outward as he pulled, and the front sight snagged against the fabric of his pants before he yanked it free.

Too late. Rod's Power Eagle flashed upward in a wide arc, and the high carbon steel blade rang as it sank deep into the Canadian's neck, severing his spine, and nearly removing his head from his shoulders. Richarde died instantly. His knees buckled as he fell forward, and for a few seconds bright red arterial blood pulsed from the gaping wound. His head twisted and turned away from his body as it struck the earth with an audible thump. His right foot twitched back and forth spasmodically as his body lay still.

Rod stared in deep shock at what he'd done. He'd killed someone. His mind recoiled from the realization, but the corpse before him was undeniably real. Glazed with death, the eyes stared into the underbrush from a head that was ninety-degrees to its body, attached only by a bloody strip of flesh. Blood still flowed from the severed carotid artery, but became weaker with each failing heartbeat.

Aziz and Grigovich saw it all, saw Rod rise swiftly above the juniper bush and all but separate Richarde's head from his shoulders. McBraden was staring at Sue Morgan, sobbing softly as she knelt before him, still bleeding freely from the wound where her ear had been. All three of them saw Rod turn to look at them with a half-crazed look on his face, and all of them misread his expression as that of a heroic madman.

Aziz was fastest. His Ruger revolver leveled on Rod's torso. The front sight blade settled into the rear sight notch over his sternum. Aziz squeezed the trigger. His aim was good, but the double-action trigger pull was gritty; it caused the barrel to shift slightly right when the hammer rotated back to its firing position. He missed, but the bullet passed close enough for Rod to hear the whipcrack of its passing.

The shot broke Rod from his reverie. Aziz squeezed off another round almost in unison with Grigovich. But Rod was already in motion, and out of sight within three bounds. Aziz pursued. Behind him he could hear the pounding footfalls of Grigovich. It was no use. By the time they reached Richarde's body, his killer was long gone into the thick bush.

"Fuck!" Aziz said, picking up Richarde's Beretta and shoving it under his belt. He stamped his foot and shouted again, louder this time, "Fuck."

McBraden at least had enough sense to stay behind with the whimpering woman without being told to. He had a curious look on his face when Aziz and Grigovich returned.

"Richarde's dead," Aziz said simply.

Except for a slight widening of his eyes, McBraden's expression didn't change. Grigovich checked the position of his pistol's safety and said nothing.

"McBraden, you're supposed to know this area. Tell me what you think about this guy."

McBraden looked at him with a blank expression. He thought fast; Aziz expected something analytical from him.

"I can't be sure, but I think he's an ex-con my dad used to talk about. He said he was a survival expert who was probably a potential domestic terrorist of some sort. My dad didn't like him very much."

Aziz just looked at him. Small-town police officers were the same self-important, pompous assholes whether they were in Afghanistan or here. If this guy was who McBraden said he was, his criminal history was probably one reason why he wouldn't go to the authorities. Outlaws, even retired ones, were always reluctant to go to the law for any reason.

"Regardless, we still have a mission, and we have a time frame."

He walked over to stand in front of Sue Morgan. She was sobbing quietly now, her gaze toward the ground. Blood was still dripping slowly from her chin. She looked up at Aziz. He put his revolver's muzzle to her forehead and pulled the trigger. Her head rocked back with the report, and her hair blew outward, as pink brain matter erupted from the back of her skull. She fell backward and lay still on the ground.

Aziz tucked his revolver back into his waistband as if he'd just done nothing more than dispatch a rodent.

"Okay," he said through lips that were thin with tension, "Peter, you take Paul's load of plastique. Nothing has changed."

Aziz extracted a folded paper map from a Ziploc bag in the cargo pocket of his trousers. "Timmons, lead us to the most direct route to Highway M-28." He looked at Grigovich, "Timmons had one of his old football comrades drop a car for us on an abandoned logging road there, near the junction of M-123."

McBraden nodded. He hadn't known why he was doing it when he called one of his closest friends from high school two months ago and asked him to buy and license a used car for him. That friend was to store the vehicle at his home, and then drop it off at a predetermined location within the state forest. After Aziz had thoroughly checked out the man McBraden chose, the friend was shipped a package containing cash and a small satchel from Canada. The man who bought the car just thought he was doing a favor for an old football buddy, and making a few bucks for it. But the satchel he was instructed to leave in the locked car contained a GPS tracking device, among other things. That way, even if McBraden was dead, Aziz could locate the vehicle.

The idea that he might be dead by now himself had never occurred to McBraden. It occurred to him now as he looked at the map, marked with red grease pencil. He knew the area and its topography. It was almost all Lake Superior State Forest between here and M-28, about twenty-six miles. They had to stick close to the highway because it was bordered by impenetrable swamp along both sides for much of that distance. The route crossed a half dozen two-track dirt roads, but the chance of seeing more than a handful of passing vehicles between here and there was highly improbable.

McBraden nodded. "If we push it, we can do that distance by tomorrow morning."

"What about the bodies?" Grigovich asked, jerking a thumb toward Sue Morgan's corpse.

"Drag them and their gear into the bushes," Aziz replied. "Then cover them all with leaves and branches. We don't have time to conceal them better."

Aziz knew they were going to need to stop and sleep—he'd allotted four hours—but he wanted them to be far from here when they stopped to rest. He scraped sand over the burnt-down campfire with the side of his boot while Grigovich dragged the corpses into the brush. Then he kicked dirt over the bloodstains and pink brain fragments to make them less noticeable. Good enough.

Aziz looked at the two remaining members of his team. His allies in al-Qaeda had agreed to train the infidels for him because the Aziz clan was too wealthy to deny, but the organization had never backed his multireligious team, or even his plan. They'd certainly take credit if the operation was successful, but al-Qaeda wasn't willing to bet on his dark horse before the race was run.

Chapter Thirteen

The Tracker's Wife

Colyer arrived at Whitefish Point in the early afternoon. From his unmarked Dodge Charger, he made a call from his cell phone to Rodney Elliot. People he'd asked regarded Elliot as the most capable tracker in this area. Colyer considered himself to be fairly adept when it came to gathering forensic evidence, but he prided himself on never letting his ego get in the way of doing the job that taxpayers trusted him to get done. A full day had passed since deputies had collected the Zodiac, and who knew for sure how long it had remained hidden in the brush before it'd been noticed? He wanted a skilled tracker to accompany him to the area, even though it was fairly certain that any sign left by the boat's occupants had been obliterated when the craft was dragged away by the Sheriff Department's off-road vehicles.

Colyer had done a quick background check of Elliot on the Combined DNA Index System (CODIS) database. CODIS revealed that the man was an ex-con with such a background that it was surprising he had survived his childhood at all. To Colyer, he looked more a victim than a villain, but a follow-up call to local cops had painted the ex-con as a first cousin to Satan himself. Colyer figured that the truth lay somewhere in between. It usually did.

Ex-con or not, Elliot was generally judged by friends and enemies alike to be one of the most adept trackers in the country. When Colyer called, it was Eliot's wife Shannon who answered.

"Hello," she said, a bit out of breath from running to catch the landline before the answering machine took it.

"Mrs. Elliot, this is Special Agent Tom Colyer of the Federal Bureau of Investigation in Sault Sainte Marie."

The other end of the telephone went silent. Uh-oh, Colyer thought, immediate distrust.

"Yes?" Shannon said.

"Mrs. Elliot, there's no problem at all, but I was wondering if I might speak with Rodney."

"Rod's not here. He's teaching a survival class. He won't be back till next week."

"I'm looking for a tracker to take a look at a scene for me, and tell me what he thinks. Can you recommend anyone else?"

"No, I can't." She sounded genuinely disappointed. "If you just want a tracker, Rod says I'm one of his best students."

Colyer grinned, glad that she couldn't see his surprised expression. "Would you consent to accompany me, Mrs. Elliot?"

When Colyer pulled into the driveway, he was surprised by the neatness of the small house and yard. These were people who took pride in the appearance of their home, something not typical of criminals. He was startled when a pretty, middle-aged blonde opened the passenger door and plopped into the seat next to him. She'd seemed to just appear from nowhere. She was wearing faded denim bib overalls and a light blue T-shirt. On her feet were a well-worn pair of Vasque hiking boots.

"Hi," she said, extending her right hand to shake his. "I'm Shannon." Her grip was strong without trying. This is a woman who does a lot of hard physical labor, Colyer thought.

The drive to Whitefish Point was animated. Shannon pointed out every landmark along the way, and she seemed to have at least one tidbit of information to offer about all of them. She was a lot smarter and more articulate than the FBI agent had expected. He reminded himself to not underestimate this woman.

As they walked the beach past the lighthouse, he noted that there were more tourists here than he'd anticipated. They were sure to have inadvertently wiped clean any traces that might have remained from the people in the Zodiac.

Shannon spotted the place where the boat had been stashed before he did. She pointed to muted grooves in the sand on the shoreline away from the water's edge. "There," she said, "that's where the deputies must have driven onto the lakeshore. This is federally protected beach, so it had to have been the cops." She glanced sideways at him to see if he'd taken offense at her use of the colloquialism. He grinned back; he hadn't.

There were obvious drag marks around the site, and he was pretty sure that looking for clues here among hundreds of footprint impressions was an exercise in futility. He was wrong. Shannon walked away toward the woods a few yards, and announced, "Here, here's where a group of three . . . no, four men stopped."

He looked where she was pointing, trying to make sense of the marks she pointed out to him. She placed her index finger next to depressions in the grass.

"See," she said, "there are four sets of boot prints here. Lug soles. Two are about size 10, but with different traction patterns. One is a lot smaller and narrower—maybe size 8—and the last one is pretty big; size 13, maybe."

Colyer nodded. He could see the disturbances in the foliage when she pointed them out to him, but he had to take her word when it came to describing what they were.

Shannon continued as if he were following her every word. "These flat, pressed-down areas were made by the bottoms of backpacks when they were set on the ground. They put on the packs—see how the boot prints got deeper here?—then they headed off together in that direction." She pointed into the forest.

She had Colyer's complete interest now. "Do you think you can follow their tracks, Shannon?" he asked earnestly, noticing for the first time that her eyes were deep blue.

"Oh, sure," she answered, "four guys with packs can't help but leave clear sign. But I can't commit a lot of time to it. I have sled dogs at home who don't understand when they miss supper. Besides," she said, glancing at the lengthening shadows from the trees, "it'll be dark soon."

He assured her that it was okay. He'd take whatever help he could get for as long as she'd provide it. His curiosity was piqued now, and he was convinced that her ability to follow these guys through the woods could make the difference between finding these four and losing their trail. His attempt to answer questions had only created even more questions. He had to know what this quartet of men was planning.

Chapter Fourteen

Pursuit

Rod had circled back to the campsite just in time to see the slender dark-skinned man shoot Sue Morgan in the forehead. Hidden behind a stand of young spruce trees a hundred yards from the campsite, his traumatized mind replayed the event over and over. He squeezed his eyes shut to block out the image of her brains exploding from the back of her skull, but the vision continued. He felt even sicker than he had before.

He watched in a daze as the burliest of the remaining men dragged Sue's body out of his sight, then came back a few minutes later for her brother. He was a square-faced, blocky-headed man, heavily built and muscular. He looked Russian, or something closely akin to it. It wasn't a cogent deduction on Rod's part, but more of a vague realization in a beleaguered mind that had seen too much, without enough time to digest it.

He sat back heavily against a red pine. The three men returned and rearranged their backpacks. Except for a little smoke from the hastily covered fire pit, there was little obvious sign that anyone had ever been there. The men shouldered their backpacks. The youngest looking of them referred to a map and took a bearing on an old-fashioned military lensatic compass. He pointed into the woods, and the trio set out in that direction.

Rod stayed where he was until his labored breathing eased a little and his chest stopped hurting. He still felt nauseous, but at least his heart didn't feel like it was going to burst from his rib cage.

His digital watch said it was 6:32 PM when he rose unsteadily to his feet and sneaked cautiously back to the campsite. He might need equipment, so the first thing he did was to locate where the killers had hidden the backpacks. He found his own among them, stashed on the mucky riverbank in a stand of cattails. He hauled it up to the dying fire pit, unconsciously avoiding the human gore that lay on the ground, and started going through its contents. He discarded most of the gear in his pack. He needed it to be light if he was going to move faster through the bush than the killers.

In a moment of revelation, he realized with some surprise that he'd already decided to follow these three guys. He grinned bitterly to himself: Why not? What were his options? He dared not go back. The cops would arrest him. They'd eventually turn him loose—probably—but only at their convenience, and only after they'd deprived him of freedom and livelihood for an unacceptable period of time. A single hour in a jail cell was too long.

On the other hand, if he went after these confirmed killers, they'd probably murder him for his trouble. They had guns, they obviously didn't give a damn about human life, and they were three to his one. But they'd killed his survival students, they'd tried twice to kill him, and now he'd killed one of their members. The entire situation infuriated and terrified him on a half-dozen levels. The way Rod saw it, he was between the proverbial rock and a very hard place.

Rod didn't locate the bodies. He didn't want to. He'd noticed where poor Sue and her brother had been partially hidden in a cluster of young jackpines when he'd gone looking for the backpacks. He hadn't taken a closer look because the thought of seeing their lifeless bodies evoked awful emotions in him. He'd never had a weak stomach, but he was repulsed by the corpses of these folks he'd been hiking with only hours ago.

In the end, Rod's pack was nearly empty. He gathered all the granola and fruit bars from his students' packs, and a Schrade Bomb Tech survival knife that he'd provided as part of Bill Morgan's outfit. He might need a lot of calories, and it might be impossible to stop and cook, but he needed high-energy foods that he could eat on the move.

It would be dark in less than two hours. Until then, he'd have little trouble following the clear trail left by three men who looked as if they were in a hurry. They had a destination, and it made sense that they'd follow the straightest line the terrain allowed. He determined after a quarter-mile that the general course direction was south from Whitefish Point.

Referring to his own well-worn, plastic-laminated map, he extrapolated where they meant to arrive. Somewhere on M-28 probably. There were only two highways that crossed the length of the Upper Peninsula, east to west, and M-28 was one of them. There were only two paved roads between here and there, and the only route to M-28 for a hundred miles was a stretch of M-123 that ran twenty-two miles from Paradise. Most of M-123 was bordered on either side by wetlands, tamaracks, and spruce that only moose found penetrable. He couldn't imagine them cutting cross-country through there with heavy backpacks.

Whatever their end purpose, they deemed it sufficient to justify murder and torture. But not robbery—the survival students were on vacation, and the men, at least, were most likely carrying a wad of cash and their credit cards. Historically, most of his male clients were unwilling to leave their money at a stranger's house. Having cash in their pockets made them feel more secure. Nor had they taken Sue Morgan's impressive set of wedding and engagement rings. Or showed any sign of sexual inclination toward the attractive woman. These men had something bigger in mind, some sort of mission.

He followed the clear trail the trio had left until the sun fell below the horizon. Then he took his Surefire Saint headlamp out of his thigh pocket and continued on. The broad arc of its bright LED light illuminated fifty yards around him at its highest setting, but he dialed down its continuously variable brightness to a level that he figured was the best compromise between seeing without being seen himself. Even with an artificial light, three men with medium-heavy backpacks and very heavy feet left a trail that was easy to follow. He made good time.

Chapter Fifteen

Reading Sign

Shannon Elliot was also making good time. Special Agent Colyer had a tough time keeping up with her as she almost scampered through thick, darkened forest that—if the truth be told—gave him a slight case of the willies. He had no idea what might be out there, but she seemed to know every nuance of this terrain. She claimed to be following a trail that he was having more than a little difficulty seeing in places. He had to take her word for it, because he sure couldn't read the signs she told him she was following. It occurred to him that she could just disappear and leave him here, hopelessly lost, any time she wanted to.

The terrain was pretty awful to him, but Shannon seemed tireless. He was glad that he'd had the foresight to wear hiking boots, but his Nike Street Hikers were clearly not the equal of the Vasque boots that Shannon had worn for this outing. She wore a near-empty light backpack with the Coleman logo and the word Exponent emblazoned across its back. He had the feeling that the few items it did contain were essential tools of wilderness survival. Suddenly he felt very vulnerable and very stupid, not the in-control FBI agent he was accustomed to being in every situation.

They came to a dirt track. Shannon pointed to it on her map and said, "Wildcat Road. A two-track that crosses Vermillion Road. It starts on the west side of Whitefish Point Road—the road I live on. It looks like they crossed here. Their trail is heading south."

Colyer looked at the map with her. "They do seem to be on a beeline south, directly away from the lighthouse. Maybe leaving Whitefish Point?" It was a question. He was asking her opinion.

Shannon looked squarely into his eyes—frank and unafraid, a mark of an honest person with nothing to be ashamed of. She nodded in the affirmative.

"Agent Colyer, I don't know who these guys could be, or why the FBI would have such an interest in what they're up to, but there's nothing I know of on Whitefish Point that would interest anyone but a tourist."

He met her gaze and replied honestly, "Mrs. Elliot, I'm telling you the truth when I say that I don't know why they're here either, but I suspect that it isn't to do a good deed."

Shannon nodded, still looking directly into Colyer's eyes. She didn't expect full disclosure from this federal cop, especially since he was basically conducting an investigation based on no more than a personal hunch. Her years of experiences with Rod had shown her that probably most cops were little more than bullies with badges. Rod had always claimed that they'd been the same kids who were shut into lockers and given swirlies in high school, and now they were out to take revenge. From what she'd seen with her own eyes, Rod was more often right than wrong.

But this FBI agent seemed to be a genuinely decent man. He'd treated her with the respect an American citizen deserved, and he'd asked, not ordered, her to help. He didn't bluster and act macho when he was clearly out of his element. So long as he behaved like a real person with her, she'd respond in kind.

She shrugged off her backpack and unzipped it. From inside she extracted a Brunton LED headlamp, and handed him one with the words BLACK DIAMOND on its headband.

"Here," she said, "This might come in handy when it gets dark." She grinned at him and shrugged, "You strike me as a man who thinks there's some urgency here. And you seem to be one of the good guys, so I'm kind of obliged to lend a hand. There's nothing at home that can't wait a few hours."

He smiled, genuinely surprised. "Thank you, Mrs. Elliot. That's a refreshing attitude. I'm not used to it."

She smiled back at him. “De nada,” she said, “and it’s Shannon, by the way.” She looked at the darkening sky. “It’ll be too dark to see without a light in another hour, and I’m not quite as good a tracker as my husband. We’d better get crackin’.”

They followed the men’s trail for another four miles, and then crossed a road that she identified as Vermillion Road. Their quarry had walked down the poorly asphalted road for a hundred yards, and then cut back into the woods on an old logging road. Shannon couldn’t follow their trail on the paved surface, but she calculated that they would follow the easiest route, and her guess that they were headed southward proved correct.

She looked at him and said, “Look, these tracks are almost a day old, and if they’re moving as fast as it appears, we’re probably never gonna catch them on foot.”

Colyer had a feeling she meant that they were never going to catch them so long as he was along to slow them down, and she was probably right. He was convinced of her tracking expertise so far. He had no inclination to doubt her latest assertion.

“What would you suggest?” he asked earnestly.

She looked pensive. “Well, I’d take my truck—it’s closer than your car now—and I’d follow the road. Along the way, I’d stop every mile or so and walk back to the trail to confirm which way they went.”

He nodded. That strategy seemed sound enough to him.

They arrived at her house in ten minutes, and he climbed into the passenger seat of her Nissan Titan. They traveled the length of Whitefish Point Road, stopping every mile to walk back to the two-track and confirm that the men’s trail had continued there.

They reached the campsite on the Betsy River on their second stop. Shannon spent a couple of minutes deciphering the sign she found there. Then her face went ashen. She picked up a clump of what looked like sand and twisted the surprisingly malleable substance apart. After inspecting it for a moment, she dropped it to the ground as though it had burned her fingers. She looked at Colyer with a grimace that was between disgust and horror, and wiped her hands against the legs of her coveralls.

“Oh God,” she said as she continued wiping her hands against her legs. “Oh God, oh God, oh God . . .”

Colyer picked up the fragment she’d dropped so abruptly and rolled it between his thumb and forefinger. He held it to his nose and smelled it. An icy chill ran the length of his spine as he realized that it was a chunk of raw flesh. He involuntarily let it fall to the ground, and he also started wiping his hands against the legs of his suit trousers.

Shannon was already off, tracking like a bloodhound, following disturbances that he saw only after she'd started to trace them. She found the body of Shawn Hennesy first, haphazardly concealed under a pile of freshly broken, jackpine boughs. Then she returned to the campfire and began following another set of drag marks. She gasped audibly when she found the corpse of Sue Morgan at the end of the trail. Even Colyer couldn't stifle a sharp intake of breath at seeing the woman's body with one missing ear.

A look of hardness settled over Shannon's face as she steeled herself for the awfulness of the task at hand. Colyer admired her strength.

"I knew these people," she said. "They were my husband's survival students. There were three of them."

Only then did Colyer notice the dark stains on the ground. He dropped to all fours and held his nose to the sand. It smelled like blood. It had soaked in, and someone had kicked dirt over it, but it was definitely blood.

After an hour of searching the area, Colyer and Shannon found four bodies. Shannon could identify the three survival students who'd been her husband's clients, but the fourth man was a stranger to her. Whoever he was, the man had been killed in as violent a manner as Colyer had seen in all his years as a federal officer. In fact, the whole scene was more terrible than any he'd had the misfortune to investigate.

Shannon was of course relieved to find that her husband wasn't among the corpses. She was shocked by the carnage, but she was bracing up exceptionally well. Colyer spoke into the mini digital voice recorder he took from his button-down shirt pocket, and scratched a few diagrams on his notepad. Then he called Central Dispatch. Cellular reception was spotty this far out in the forest, but the Dispatch operator managed to get his location, and promised to send a four-wheeler with a forensics team.

Chapter Sixteen

The Trek

Aziz's wristwatch alarm woke him from a deep sleep with its steady beeping. He rubbed his gritty eyes with the backs of his knuckles and tried to recall the fleeting dream he'd had about the majestic sand dunes of home. So different from this tangled, green nightmare of forest and swamp filled with mosquitoes and biting flies. They'd had their scheduled four hours of sleep, all three of them, because he didn't think it was necessary to post a sentry way back here in the woods.

Truth be told, he'd had a tough time falling asleep, even with a low dose of Ambien, and he'd awakened several times with a start when he heard some unidentified animal moving in the darkness. After the events of the last twenty-four hours, all of them had trouble sleeping, but only Aziz had been stricken with visions of vicious man-eating carnivores rushing from the shadows to devour his flesh. His fears were unfounded—animals did not typically attack humans—and the educated part of his mind knew that. But like most children, he'd been reared on fables of big bad wolves and killer bears, usually told at bedtime, so that a child was sure to have nightmares about them. And like most modern people who were accustomed to artificial lighting, he had an unfounded terror of invisible creatures lurking in places that were too dark for him to see.

He scratched one of the numerous itchy bumps on his arms. Ironically, the real bloodthirsty animals in these woods had been insects. They'd made the hike here fairly miserable for them all. Grigovich had pulled a fat, blood-engorged tick from his neck—it was one of the grossest things Aziz had ever seen. He hated the bugs here. The Arab had dealt with biting insects before, but not at this level. These were the most prolific, most determined bloodsuckers he'd ever imagined. He slathered on more insect-repellent lotion. This was just one more aspect of America that he hated, and that only made him more determined to fulfill his mission.

They'd made excellent time, thanks to the advanced physical and mental training they'd received from their al-Qaeda handlers in Afghanistan. It had been rough going, especially after sunset, but they'd trained intensively for night navigation. Their al-Qaeda instructors had anticipated traveling through these jungles at night. Night-vision goggles weren't practical for slogging cross-country through tangled undergrowth, but their LED headlamps were fitted with red lenses that allowed terrain features to be seen without causing their pupils to adjust. They could extinguish their lights at a moment's notice without sacrificing their eyes' natural night-vision.

A little more than eight rugged and sweaty hours had passed since they'd left the bodies of their victims partially hidden along the Betsy River. Their route here had taken them across the river, south and west of the village of Paradise, on a mapped snowmobile trail that saw little use during the summer months, and virtually no traffic in any season between the hours of dusk and dawn. Tourists and residents alike avoided the forest itself, sticking only to roads and trails that they could view while sitting on, or inside, some form of motorized vehicle. As predicted, the trio had seen no one.

They skirted the tiny village of Paradise when, in fact, they could have walked down the main street through town as the village was eerily quiet. All forty of the village's residents were fast asleep. Five miles south of Paradise, they crossed the Tahquamenon River. The river was too wide and too deep to cross without using yet another boat, but they were able to stay out of sight along the riverbank until reaching the two-lane bridge that crossed it on Highway M-123. The bridge was located immediately south of the entrance to Tahquamenon Falls State Park, but the park was unmanned by authorities at night. There was little traffic on the remote highway after dark.

They made the fifty-yard dash across the bridge from cover to cover without incident. No traffic was in sight, and for the next seventeen miles they saw only a half-dozen vehicles. Wet, swampy terrain on both sides of the highway for miles at a time was impenetrable to almost any animal, except a long-legged moose. According to McBraden, this was moose and wolf country. They could hear coyotes yapping in the near distance, and the alien sounds sent chills down their spines.

They traveled a muddy snowmobile trail on the east side of the road. A regular, flattened highway of snow kept passable by a grooming tractor in winter, it was a mucky mess in the nonsnow months. The sucking mire was so difficult to walk through in many places that it forced them to travel the road, running for cover whenever they saw headlights bearing down on them from either direction. Once, a dark blue SUV with Michigan State Police markings went by, traveling at a moderate speed because there were a lot of deer, and a few, much larger, and darker-colored moose that crossed this road. As all Yoopers knew, no one drove away from crashing into a three-quarter ton adult moose at highway speed; not even an eighteen-wheeler.

They hiked all night, and reached M-28 just as the first light of dawn was breaking over the forest. McBraden found the two-track where their car was parked by referring to the area maps on his iPad. Aziz confirmed the location of the vehicle on his GPS. They found the plain white Ford Econoline panel van right where it was supposed to be, parked on the side of the track a hundred yards from the highway. The license plate numbers matched his notes, and the fuel tank was full. This was the right car.

The keys were behind the front tire on the driver's side, as instructed. Aziz checked the inside; it held a new-looking spare tire, tire-changing tools, and a satchel shipped to McBraden's friend from Canada by Brenda Waukonigon, containing the tracker transmitter and a fresh change of clothes for each of them. There were four clipboards in the satchel as well, with official-looking, made-up forms about the Mackinac Bridge, and matching pens that read JACKSONVILLE PAINTING on their barrels. Good. The outdoors-style clothes they all wore now had been functional for the trek here, but for this phase of the mission, it would be better if they looked more like tourists.

McBraden's friend had placed the padlocked duffel bag he'd been shipped by United Parcel Service into the van as well. Inside, there was a one-piece coverall for each of them, for when they needed to cover their clothes. Large Helvetica letters on the back of each jumpsuit proclaimed that the wearers were from JACKSONVILLE PAINTING, out of Jacksonville, Florida. Four white hard hats were labeled likewise. Completing the illusion were four tool belts, complete with tools.

They cleaned up with disposable wet wipes as well as the mosquitoes would allow, then changed into their new sets of clothes. The clothes were off the rack from Walmart, purchased for them by Brenda Waukonigon, and shipped in the satchel bag to the man who'd bought the van for them. They fit well enough. Aziz appraised his fellows. They'd pass for tourists all right. Ordinarily, he wouldn't be caught dead wearing a Hawaiian shirt, but in this case, it seemed appropriate camouflage.

"Hang on a second," McBraden said, "I really gotta take a dump."

Aziz grimaced at him. These Americans were such pigs. No couth at all. "All right," he said, "but make it fast. We have a time frame."

Freed of the weight of his backpack, McBraden felt light enough to float off the ground. He hadn't relieved his bowels in more than twenty-four hours. A steady diet of granola bars and MREs and stress had irritated his digestive tract, and now the need to empty his colon had become painfully urgent. McBraden stuffed a partially used roll of toilet tissue into the back pocket of his trousers.

Dawn's first light was breaking through the trees as McBraden retreated hurriedly into the woods, holding the belt buckle of his trousers in both hands. Aziz watched him disappear behind a stand of young spruces, about fifty yards distant. Then he turned away in disgust, not wanting to witness any more than he'd already seen.

Aziz got into the van and inserted the key into its ignition. Its three-sixty cubic inch engine growled to life on the first attempt, and Aziz smiled dryly to himself. There had been enough unforeseen glitches on this mission. Everything was going to go smoothly from now on. He allowed himself a moment of utter satisfaction, imagining how much death and misery his plan was going to cause the Great Satan America.

Grigovich got into the passenger side and closed the door. He turned on the radio and scanned the FM band until he found a song he liked. As Boy George sang about a Karma Chameleon, Aziz looked critically at him. He hated that song, and he hated Brits with almost the same intensity that he hated Americans. Aziz tuned the radio to a local news station. Grigovich scowled at him, because he'd always liked Culture Club, but he said nothing.

After covering a few news items, the announcer proudly proclaimed that this year's Labor Day Bridge Walk promised to be the busiest ever. In two days, the Mackinac Bridge would be cleared of the painters and maintenance workers who blocked two of the four lanes of this length of interstate freeway every other time of year. Two days later was Labor Day, and a record number of people were expected to walk the five-mile span from Mackinaw City at the southern end to Saint Ignace. The walkers would begin at 7 AM, and the governor of Michigan would be the first person across.

After ten minutes, McBraden hadn't returned. It was fully daylight now, and Aziz was getting impatient. He looked at his watch—how long did it take for him to shit? He knew that they were waiting for him. Against his better judgment, he blew a brief blast on the van's horn. He waited a full minute. Nothing. Where the hell was he?

"Okay," Aziz said, his voice trembling with barely controlled anger, "let's go find the son of a bitch." He opened the door and slid to the ground. Grigovich sighed and followed him.

They searched the area, but McBraden was nowhere to be seen. Then Aziz remembered the remark McBraden had made about his parents being participants on the Bridge Walk. Maybe he'd gotten cold feet and run away. McBraden wouldn't have the guts to report their intentions to the police; he knew what would happen to him and every other person he'd ever cared about if he betrayed them.

He would run away, though. That much had been made clear by this spineless excuse of a man. And he would invent a ruse to keep his parents away from the bridge. That alone might compromise the mission. Aziz regretted ever taking him on as a member of this team.

They returned to the van. As Aziz got behind the wheel and started the engine, he fumed. He jerked the shift lever into drive, and pulled onto the highway while throwing a shower of gravel from the rear tires. Wherever he went, whatever he did, McBraden and his whole family would die for this betrayal.

Chapter Seventeen

The Old Tracker

Rod had had little trouble following the trail left by the three murderers. He did have trouble catching up with them, though. They were moving at a fast pace—probably almost four miles an hour—and they took only one break, on the swampy stretch of highway that ran through the state forest, north of Paradise. There, they'd pulled off into the woods and dropped their backpacks. He could see where the long, coarse marsh grasses had been temporarily pressed flat by them and their packs.

It seemed clear that they were making a run down the length of M-123, south of Tahquamenon River. They'd moved during the night, under cover of darkness, and they obviously wanted to avoid being seen by anyone. He could see several places where they'd left the shoulder of the road and pulled back into the woods for just a moment. They hadn't dropped their packs during these brief recesses, which made it look like they were simply avoiding being seen by a passing vehicle.

Rod was feeling his age. He didn't know for how much longer he could keep up this pace. His hips and knee joints were already aching from the strain of hiking with all the speed he could muster for almost thirty miles. His calloused feet and well-worn hiking boots ensured that he didn't get blisters, but both feet throbbed with the memory of every sprain and broken bone he'd ever suffered. He opened his first-aid kit and treated himself to three ibuprofen tablets. He'd been without sleep for almost twenty-four hours, and fatigue was settling onto him like a dark cloud.

But he'd made better time than he'd realized. The night sky was lightening in the southeast when he approached the intersection of M-28 and M-123, where he spied the three men he'd been following jump onto the roadside from the ditch. They looked around furtively to be sure that no one had seen them, and then dashed across. At the woods' edge on the other side, they paused to look around again, and Rod hid himself behind a gnarled, old apple tree at the side of the highway. When they seemed sure no one had seen them, they referenced a map and what looked like a GPS unit. Then, the trio trotted westward to an abandoned logging road, about seventy-five yards from the intersection, and disappeared into the forest.

Rod felt exposed and more than a little afraid as he followed them, yet he was compelled to learn what the killers were up to. The woods were brightening with the coming of a new day as he dashed across M-28. He darted from tree to tree as he approached the still dark, dirt two-track the murderers had entered. He had butterflies in his stomach as he approached the shadowy woods. At any moment, he expected a well-placed pistol shot to ring out and end his life.

He first saw the white van backed into a niche in the red pine forest. The men had the sliding panel door open and were loading their backpacks into it. He ducked behind a large hemlock tree and closed his eyes as he forced his ragged breathing to calm.

When he'd regained his composure, he looked again. He was too far away to hear what they were saying to one another, but the baby-faced one of the bunch seemed anxious about something. Rod grinned in spite of himself when it became apparent that he was displaying a pressing need to evacuate his bowels. The man went off by himself into the woods. He was sort of dancing as he disappeared into the undergrowth, a hundred yards from his friends.

Rod thought quickly. This guy was separating himself from the other two. He was the least dangerous looking of the three, and the one that Rod thought would be easiest to overpower. If he were to make any one of them tell him why they'd so viciously killed his survival students, it would probably be him.

Rod went into predator mode then. Padding as softly as a cougar, he made a wide circle around the men at the van and followed their companion into the woods. The red pines that predominated this section of forest were spaced well apart, so the man had withdrawn well away from his comrades to have some privacy while he did his business. Rod spied him squatting behind a low juniper bush, grunting audibly as he strained to relieve his bowels. A burst of gas erupted loudly from his backside. Rod used the fact that the man was preoccupied with the task at hand to creep ever closer.

When McBraden rose up to fasten his pants, he gasped in panic as a rough hand clamped hard over his mouth, and something cold and sharp pressed against his Adam's apple. He struggled for a second, and felt a stinging pain as the honed blade of Rod's survival knife cut through his skin. He stopped resisting then. Warm blood trickled down his neck. His pants were up, but his 9-millimeter pistol was lying on the ground nearby.

A voice whispered harshly in his right ear, "Make any noise and I'll cut your fucking throat, asshole." McBraden didn't move a muscle. Rod was terrified, but the fear in his voice took on a fearfully vicious tone when he spoke.

Without removing the big blade from McBraden's throat, Rod quickly knelt to pick up the Beretta pistol from the ground. He automatically checked the safety, and then stuck it into his own waistband. Although Rod hadn't liked to hunt for sport for many years now, he'd grown up with guns of all kinds. While he'd never admit publicly to the hundreds of deer he'd killed for his family's dinner table, or how he'd come by his extensive experience, there weren't many firearms that he didn't know how to use.

Rod removed the blade from McBraden's throat and placed it point-first into his lumbar area. "Start walking," he said, pushing McBraden between the shoulder blades. McBraden obeyed, his initial objection silenced by a sharp poke in his lower back.

When they'd gone about a quarter-mile, Rod shoved him hard between the shoulder blades. McBraden fell to the ground on his belly, and Rod sat heavily on top of him. As he straddled the stunned man, he pulled his right hand behind his back and slipped a noose made of old bootlaces taken from his pocket over McBraden's wrist. Then he tied the left hand to the right.

"Over here," Rod said, "against this tree." McBraden complied, his eyes fixed on the point of the big blade that hovered only a few inches in front of his face. Rod tied his hands to the trunk of the tree with another length of bootlace.

Rod ripped open McBraden's shirt, then unbuckled his belt. McBraden had a look of astonishment on his face as the woodsman tugged his trousers off over his boots.

"Hey, what the hell are you doin'?" McBraden exclaimed.

"I have some questions that you're gonna answer, asswipe."

"I'm not tellin' you a damn thing."

Rod grinned in his face, "Oh yes you will. Oh yes you will, you piece of shit."

McBraden understood what he meant almost immediately as mosquitoes began to cover his bare legs and chest. He squirmed and wriggled, trying to shake the biting insects from his body.

"Oh God," he cried, "get them off me! Get 'em off!" Rod shut him up by jamming a piece of his own torn shirt into his mouth.

Rod squatted in front of McBraden and watched dispassionately as the biting insects tortured his captive. He might have felt compassion, but his mind brimmed with feelings of vengeance at the memory of Sue Morgan having her ear cut off. This man hadn't committed that foul act, but he'd been an accomplice, and he was only slightly less guilty than the animal who'd wielded the knife.

McBraden screamed into his gag. His eyes were wet with tears as he squirmed to dislodge the hordes of insects that stabbed him. The stinging and itching were horrible, but combined with the visual stimulus of seeing dozens of bloodthirsty insects crawling over his skin, filling themselves with his blood, made it intolerable.

Rod continued to watch McBraden with black, heartless eyes. He wasn't a cold man, and ordinarily he hated to see any living thing suffer. But he couldn't find it in himself to feel even a shred of pity for this murderous weasel who wriggled in agony before him. Far off through the woods, he heard the honk of the white van's horn. A loud slamming of doors followed, and its engine started. The man's partners had given up on finding him. McBraden heard it too, and he realized that he was being abandoned. He screamed even louder into his gag, his eyes wide with panic.

The van pulled out onto the highway and left in a hurry. Rod grinned maliciously. "That's it, buddy. Your pals've just left you behind. You ready to talk to me yet?" He ripped the gag from McBraden's mouth.

"Y-yes," McBraden answered. He looked at Rod, and kicked his mosquito-covered legs furiously. "Yes, you fucker. Yes, I'll tell you what you want to know. Just give me back my pants."

"In a minute. Talk to me first. Why did your friends kill my clients? Tell me or I'll leave you here till the skeeters drain you dry."

McBraden spilled his guts then, all the while wriggling to shake off the biting insects. Rod listened intently to the whole story of plutonium, dirty bombs, and the Bridge Walk. It was his turn to feel panicked.

"Oh my God," he said softly. "Oh my God. Do you know how many people you'll kill?" He stopped, realizing that this was, of course, the object of the operation.

"That's the point, stupid," McBraden confirmed.

Rod went through the pockets of McBraden's trousers. In his buttoned-down, right-side back pocket was a wallet containing 527 dollars in US currency, and 130 Canadian dollars. The same back pocket also held a passport and a current Michigan-issued driver's license that identified him as Timmons McBraden of Paradise. Rod knew that name. He was a local boy; the son of a retired sheriff who'd never liked Rod. If McBraden knew who Rod was, he gave no sign. There were a few coins from both countries in his right hip pocket, but nothing else.

Buttoned into the thigh cargo pocket of McBraden's pants were two bottles of pills. One of them contained a prescription sleep aid called Ambien—Rod had heard of that drug, but had never used it. The other carried twenty tablets of Dexedrine, a speed-type drug that Rod knew very well from his drug-peddling years. Once handed out like candy by doctors to anyone who wanted them, these had become virtually extinct in the United States in the late 1970s.

"What're these pills for?" he asked McBraden. McBraden looked sullen and didn't answer. He'd passed into the whipped-dog phase of suffering, where his mind simply gave up, and he chose to endure his agony in silence—Rod had seen it before.

Rod sliced the lace that held McBraden to the pine's trunk, and yanked him to his feet by one arm. He didn't give the terrorist back his trousers, but marched him in only his boxer shorts back to M-28. On the shoulder of the highway, he tied McBraden's hands more securely behind his back. Then Rod kicked the back of McBraden's knees so that he fell to a kneeling position on the rough gravel. His pistol was tucked into Rod's own waistband. Its two spare, fully-loaded magazines were in the thigh pocket of his trousers.

It occurred to McBraden then that the man standing behind him might shoot him in the back of his head with his own gun. McBraden squeezed his eyes tightly shut, wondering if it would hurt much.

The same thought passed through Rod's mind as he gazed at McBraden's scalp. But he couldn't do it. The memory of the man he'd already killed, almost without conscious thought, would haunt him for the rest of his days. It was a soul-soiling sin that he could never undo, and he hated that he'd never again be able close his eyes at night without seeing the man's face. No, he couldn't execute this poor excuse for a human being who knelt in front of him, no matter how richly he deserved it.

The first vehicle to approach them was a semitruck loaded with jackpine logs. As Rod figured he would, the driver slowed at the unusual sight of a man at the side of the road in his underwear, but he didn't stop the truck. Following behind him was a late-model Hyundai Santa Fe. Rod flagged him down. The driver was a portly, balding man with a well-dressed, handsome woman of a similar age next to him. Rod opened the driver's door.

"Get out," he said. "I need your car." He shoved the Beretta within inches of the man's nose to emphasize his meaning.

Glenn Hueker was a Yooper, born and raised, and he lived here in this mostly desolate part of the United States because things like this didn't happen around here. His initial response was to take umbrage at being carjacked. But his wife Anna was looking very frightened, and that muted his sense of outrage. Glenn got out of the car with his hands above his shoulders, palms facing Rod, like he'd seen in a thousand movies. Anna did the same.

"You got a cell phone?" Rod asked Glenn.

"Yes," Glenn answered simply.

"Good. Call 911, and tell them that your car was stolen at the intersection of 28 and 123. Tell them you've got a terrorist with you."

The occupants of the Hyundai looked confused at first. Then it dawned on them that Rod wasn't referring to himself, but to the half-naked man who was trussed and on his knees beside them on the shoulder of the road.

Rod handed Hueker all of the Canadian money and all but one hundred dollars of the American money. "This is for your troubles," he said. Then before they could utter a reply, Rod jumped behind the wheel, threw the Hyundai in gear, and sped off in a cloud of dust and gravel.

Chapter Eighteen

THE DESTINATION

Aziz stared intently into the van's rearview mirror. He'd picked up a police tail when he blew through a speed trap at Moran, on M-123. The speed limit changed suddenly from sixty-five to fifty miles per hour for a mere one hundred yards, and there was often a county deputy parked there to enforce it. The cop was two cars back, and Grigovich had noticed two officers in the cruiser. Both those cops would be dead before they reached the van if they decided to stop them.

Fortunately, the cruiser continued on when Aziz turned off on Interstate 75 toward the Mackinac Bridge. Grigovich breathed a sigh of relief and took his hand from the butt of his Desert Eagle. He willed himself to relax and breathe evenly. He wasn't afraid of being shot—he had no doubt that he and Aziz could have taken out both cops before either had time to clear his holster. But they were so close to their objective now, and there had been enough snafus already. They didn't need even one more thing to go wrong.

Aziz felt the same. He glanced at his wristwatch. It was quarter to seven in the morning. Enough time to check into a motel and get some real sleep before they began the tricky procedure of assembling their bombs. For all its power, the C4 plastic explosive they carried was pretty stable stuff. They weren't going to insert the blasting caps or connect the detonators that would trigger them until the bombs were mounted under the bridge's towers. More than one holy warrior had inadvertently blown himself up in recent years in Iraq and Afghanistan, and Aziz wasn't about to add himself to the list.

He drove up to the toll both on the north end of the bridge, and handed the female attendant a ten-dollar bill. While she made change, he engaged her in small talk.

"Are the painters still workin' on the bridge?" he asked in his best Midwestern accent.

She smiled at him, doubtless mistaking his olive skin as Native American, probably from one of the nearby tribal casinos. "When aren't they working on the bridge? The outside lane is closed for about a mile in the middle—you have to drive on the grating—but you have two lanes most of the way across."

She handed him his change, and he put the van in gear. "Thank you, ma'am," he said as he pulled away.

Aziz drove the five-mile span of the Mackinac Bridge a little slower than the posted forty-five mile-per-hour speed limit. A lot of tourists drove white-knuckled across the bridge, petrified at being four hundred feet above the Straits of Mackinac, with only a waist-high rail to prevent them from going into the icy-cold waters below. Seeing someone driving under the speed limit might be suspicious anywhere else, but here it just brought an amused grin to the faces of bridge patrol personnel.

But Aziz wasn't afraid of heights; neither was Grigovich. Their mission demanded that none of them be fearful of working at almost four hundred feet when planting their charges. Aziz was driving slowly so Grigovich could snap photos of painters and other maintenance workers with a digital camera. They'd been sent plenty of reconnaissance information, including photos, by Brenda Waukonigon and a few Middle Eastern sympathizers—none of whom knew about the whole operation—but Aziz wanted up-to-date photos, as well.

As the woman at the toll booth had said, maintenance of the bridge was an ongoing and never-ending process. As she'd predicted, the bridge's midpoint was blocked in the outside lane on both north- and southbound sides, with all manner of trucks and heavy equipment. Maintenance workers were in a hurry to get the span ready for the upcoming Bridge Walk, and especially to make it presentable for the governor.

Security was heightened, but so was activity; there appeared to be less concern for the governor's safety than there was for his approval.

Aziz and Grigovich had made no reservations at any of the motels in the area. That was a wild card in their strategy, but it was probably a safe bet that one of the tourism-dependent hostelries in Mackinaw City would have a vacancy. According to the literature Aziz had gathered on the area, the only times they had been filled up was once or twice during the St. Ignace Auto Show, which had been waning in popularity in recent years, and once in 1995, when the bridge had unofficially been damaged by a tornado, stranding travelers on both sides for almost twenty-four hours. The way that the damage caused by the tornado had been covered up, and the local media squelched, showed that the First Amendment was conditional at certain times. It almost made Aziz giddy to think how his operation would cause the American government to reveal its tyrannical rule over its citizenry.

Aziz didn't want a room at a seedy motel; he wanted it to be mid-priced, busy enough for them to be just faceless guests, but not too expensive for a working-class man to stay there. He found it at the Hammond Inn, a fairly decent-looking place within walking distance of Mackinaw City. More than a dozen cars and trucks occupied the parking lot, even a couple of motor homes. Aziz pulled in to the entrance.

He got out of the van and walked through the frosted-glass front door of the office. Grigovich waited in the van, pretending to be busy with the radio. Aziz noticed a single security camera mounted inside a plastic dome in the office's ceiling when he walked in. No matter; his face wouldn't show up in any of INTERPOL's files. It might later, after he'd done what he meant to do here, but by then he'd have returned to Saudi Arabia as a hero of Islam, and untouchable to America.

The somewhat attractive woman at the front desk was probably in her early forties. Her hair was meticulously coiffed, and her eyes were maybe just a little too accentuated with makeup. There was an excess of concealer around the crow's feet at the outer corner of her eyes. She was trying to hide her age. She appraised his dark skin and Arabic features approvingly, and he smiled at her as warmly as he could. She was hot to trot, probably divorced at least once. He might be able to use those weaknesses to good advantage.

But she was also a motel check-in clerk in a Podunk town that thrived on tourism. If she'd been doing that job for any length of time, she'd probably developed an ear for accents, and an eye for detail that would shame a forensics detective. Applying his best Midwestern accent, Aziz made small talk as he filled out the motel registration as Jaime Johnson.

"What's all the hubbub in town?" he asked, feigning ignorance.

"Why it's the annual Bridge Walk, silly. You mean, you've never been here for that? Why, it's one of the highlights of summer in our beautiful city," she said with noticeable pride.

Her own accent held just a hint of Southern drawl, probably from one of the Carolinas. It was muted by having lived several years in northern Michigan, but Aziz also had an ear for dialects, and to him it was clear. It was also clear that she considered herself a pillar of this community, and she was probably well-informed about local happenings.

"Oh," he said, "I wondered why there was so much commotion on the Mackinac Bridge."

"Oh that . . . They're always working on the bridge, painting and whatnot. They're especially busy now, finishing up for the Bridge Walk. My nephew works there at a toll booth, and he says the state police have been all over it for the last couple of days. The governor is the first one across, you know, and the troopers are making everything confusing."

She held out her right hand. "My name is Becky," she said sweetly. "If you need anything . . ." She looked at the registration card. "How do you pronounce your first name?" she asked, looking earnestly into his eyes.

Aziz smiled a friendly, wide grin that showed his white teeth, "Jaime," he said, pronouncing it "High-me."

"All right, Jaime," she said, shoving her right hand toward him with a big smile. "If you need anything at all, you just let me know, okay?"

He took the hand she proffered, and kissed it with his best affectation of a Hollywood romantic. She blushed. Aziz noted that there was no wedding ring on her left hand. She was probably divorced, and from her flirtatious manner, she was open to romance.

"Thank you, Becky. Do you have a room facing Lake Huron?" It was a question that she might have expected from a visitor. But it was no coincidence that a room facing the lake was also out of sight of the office. He didn't want this busybody taking notes of their comings and goings.

"Why sure, sweetheart," she said, reaching for a magnetic-card room key from the numbered cubbyholes behind her. "Checkout is at 10 AM. Like I said, if you need anything else, you just let me know."

"Thank you, Becky. You can bet I will." There was no one else in the office to see him check in, and he might have need of this woman's knowledge of local goings-on.

He went back to the van. "How'd it go?" Grigovich asked.

"No problem, Peter. The clerk's name is Becky, and she seems to take an interest in everything that happens in this town. She's also on the make. We may be able to use her."

He drove around to room thirty-four. They pretended to be busy in the van until an elderly couple had gotten into their sedan and driven away. Then they quickly took their backpacks inside the room they'd rented.

The room was dark. Aziz didn't want to open the drapes, so he clicked on a lamp between the twin beds. Grigovich threw his satchel onto one of the beds, and unzipped it. The plastic explosive was foil-wrapped in its original packaging. The blasting-cap detonators were isolated in a folding case, each of them tucked into its own recess in a foam liner. The paired blasting-cap wires were carefully twisted together at the ends to short them electrically. If they weren't kept shorted together, even a static spark might set them off, and accidental detonation of thirty pounds of C4 was something he didn't want to even think about.

Aziz opened his own case. Inside were two Pelican-brand, folding plastic briefcases, his own and that cowardly McBraden's. He laid them side-by-side on the other bed and opened them. Each was lined top and bottom with Styrofoam. Nestled securely into recesses in the Styrofoam were two softball-size spheres of fuel-grade plutonium. Each sphere was encased in polyurethane plastic to help prevent radioactive contamination.

Aziz produced a palm-size Radalert Geiger counter. He waved it over the spheres of plutonium. He didn't need to do it; he already knew what the results would be. He just liked to see the radiation that was being emitted by them.

He'd originally wanted to set his charges at the top of the bridge's towers. But the only entrances to the bridge's tower elevators were through oval, submarine-size hatches that were normally padlocked and chained shut. He had thought long and hard about how they could gain access to these portals, but there just was no way to do it without being seen and questioned by bridge authority cops. Even at night, the bridge was just too well lit to get into them unseen. And any use of the tower elevators that carried riders almost to the top was registered immediately at the state police post at the northern end of the bridge.

Instead, he'd opted to mount his bombs to the underside of the bridge. Below the road surface, there was chain-link fencing hung to serve as scaffolding for maintenance workers. Nothing had changed with the loss of two of his team, except that now he and Grigovich had more work to do.

Thirty pounds of C4 placed in two separate bombs between the towers, a little over a mile apart, would collapse at least part of the roadway between them. The plan was to detonate the plastic explosive when the first walkers—including Michigan's governor—reached the second, most northerly bomb.

With any luck, the initial explosions would kill more than a hundred people, including the governor, and cause the hikers in between the bombs to fall into the straits below. The rest would climb over one another in panic. The timing of the explosions would be precise, because the detonating devices were a pair of cell phones; the current that passed through them when they rang would trigger the blasting caps. In the same way crowds of people had become renowned for trampling one another at soccer games and music concerts, Aziz expected them to shove each other over the precipice of the broken bridge by the dozens.

The most glorious part would come later, after they'd triggered the bombs. The powerful charges would turn the plutonium encased in the bombs to aerosol. Heavy particles of plutonium dioxide would then rain down onto the bridge, the cities of Saint Ignace in the Upper Peninsula, and Mackinaw City in the Lower Peninsula. The prevailing westerly winds should carry—or so he had been informed—the radiation as far as Mackinac and Bois Blanc Islands. The real effects of breathing vaporized plutonium wouldn't be immediate, but in a day or so—probably before authorities even thought to check for radiation—there would be an epidemic of radioactive pneumonitis and other respiratory problems. For years after that, there would be outbreaks of lung cancer, especially among the very old and the very young.

Then there were the psychological repercussions. The bridge could be repaired in just a few months, but the radiation would linger much longer, and the terror it inspired would continue for years. No one would be able to drive across the five-mile span without wondering if it were structurally sound, and whatever authorities claimed, travelers would forevermore think of the bridge as being radioactive. Fish from the waters below would be considered inedible, and tourism would suffer a blow from which it'd never recover.

The United States government would probably try to hide the fact that the explosions were radioactive. But two days after they occurred, every media outlet from Facebook to CNN would receive a previously prepared press release Aziz had written about the attack. When Fox News and other media ran their own Geiger counters over the area, they'd indict authorities for trying to cover up a national disaster, and for endangering the lives of tens of thousands of not only Americans, but other nationalities who routinely crossed that bridge. The ensuing finger-pointing would probably extend all the way to congress. Maybe even the president. The thought of causing such chaos made Aziz brim with savage delight.

Chapter Nineteen

Wrongly Accused

Shannon Elliot was visibly shaken from seeing all those dead bodies at the river, but she was also relieved at not finding her husband among them. It was fully dark now, but she'd turned her headlamp to its lowest setting, unconsciously keeping the terrible sight around her beyond view.

"Mrs. Elliot, are you going to be okay? Shannon . . ." Colyer touched her shoulder.

She turned to look at him blankly. Then a fog seemed to lift from her eyes, and she focused on his face.

"Yeah," she said, "I'm going to be okay. It's just that I've never seen anything like this before. This is just so horrible . . ."

Colyer smiled dryly. "Ya wanna know somethin'? Neither have I. This is as bad as I've ever seen."

"Somehow that doesn't make me feel better."

"I still need your help, Shannon. I need to know where these people were headed. I was hoping to impose on you for a few hours more."

Headlights shone from over the hill on the two-track, and they heard the low growl of a powerful engine straining in four-wheel drive. A dark-blue Ford, four-wheel-drive pickup appeared.

Several feet from where they stood, it stopped with a squeal of brakes that struck Colyer like fingernails on a blackboard. A uniformed deputy and a man in blue jeans and a T-shirt got out.

"I'm Jim Thorsen," the man in jeans said, extending his right hand to Colyer. "I'm the acting coroner for Chippewa and Luce counties. This is Deputy Frank Sawyer."

Colyer shook his hand. "I've heard of you, Doctor Thorsen. Glad to make your acquaintance." He nodded to the deputy in recognition, "I've met Frank before."

Thorsen stretched a pair of blue nitrile surgical gloves over his hands as he surveyed the carnage around him. His trained eye took in the dark stains on the sand, recognizing them as blood even by the illumination of artificial light. He noted the fragments of skull and brain tissue near the dead campfire.

"Show me the locations of the bodies," Thorsen said.

"You'd better wait here, Shannon," Colyer told her. "I'll show him where they're at."

Shannon nodded, glad to be left out.

Colyer led Thorsen and Sawyer to where each of the corpses lay. As much as possible, the FBI agent had taken pains to leave the scene just as he'd found it. Wearing a pair of nitrile gloves that he carried in his jacket pocket, he'd removed the wallets from the two men's pockets. The woman carried no identification, but he found a color photo of her and a man posing with three children in Bill Morgan's wallet. On the back of the photo, written in ink, were the names Bill, Sue, Bill Jr., Sarah, and James. The man who'd been nearly decapitated had no form of identification at all. Each of the survival students' wallets had contained credit and debit cards, and several hundred dollars in cash. The motive in these killings hadn't been robbery.

Colyer watched critically as Deputy Sawyer cordoned the area with yellow police line tape. As Shannon had so vividly demonstrated, even someone with formal training in forensic investigation didn't read sign like a skilled tracker. The deputy might be walking over critical information.

When they were out of earshot of Shannon, Sawyer joined Thorsen and Colyer. Leaning close to Colyer's ear, he whispered, "I know that woman's husband. He's got a record; served three years in the joint for dealing drugs." Colyer just looked at the deputy as he continued, "Wouldn't surprise me in the least if he wasn't the one who did it."

Thorsen nodded. "His wife already told you that he isn't among the victims here, and this is his survival class—so where did he go?"

Even though Colyer had to admit that circumstantial evidence made Rod Elliot a suspect, he had to ask, "What do you think happened with the guy who was shot in the chest with two different calibers?"

They'd found two cartridge casings so far, one from a 50-caliber pistol round, and one from a 9-millimeter Parabellum. Both were ejected from automatic pistols, judging by extractor marks on their rims. The 50-caliber matched up with the large-bore wound in Bill Morgan's back. One wound in Hennesy's chest had come from a noticeably smaller caliber, probably a 9-millimeter or a 38, but one round had exited with considerably more hydrostatic shock, leaving a larger hole than the other. The entrance hole in the woman's head looked to be mid-caliber, but the bullet's exit was explosive, denoting considerable power—maybe a 38 Police Positive or a 357.

Sawyer shrugged. "Maybe he had an accomplice?"

They had pieces of the puzzle, but they hadn't fitted them together yet. There had been at least three pistols, and one of them had probably been a revolver. Shannon had told Colyer that none of her husband's students had been carrying a handgun that she knew of. And she said her husband never carried a gun because the laws of this state were almost fascist when it came to ex-cons and any type of gun—even air rifles were illegal. He believed her; she struck him as a good person who didn't lie easily. Nor did she seem to be one of the bad-boy victims he'd seen so many times; he doubted she'd be a woman who took being slapped around or mistreated.

"Motive?" Colyer asked.

"Who knows?" Sawyer said, sounding a little defensive. "Does an ex-con need a motive?"

"Yes," Colyer said, his blood pressure rising. "In this country, a man is supposed to be innocent until proven guilty."

Sawyer's face flushed with anger. Who was this DC, college-boy fed to dispute anything he said? But he knew better than to get into a pissing match with this Boy Scout, so he kept silent.

Colyer was getting a little hot under the collar himself. This beer-bellied idiot of a deputy only confirmed his low opinion of county cops in general. Colyer didn't know what was going on, to be sure, but the whole thing smacked of something far more complex than just these murders. They were only peripheral to a larger crime. Something very big was going to happen very soon—but what?

Another four-wheel-drive came over the hill, a white Lincoln Navigator this time. The sheriff and one of his deputies got out. It was fully dark now, so they lighted the area with their high-beam headlights and a light bar with a row of off-road lamps on the vehicle's roof. Colyer held a hand to his eyes to mute the sudden glare.

The sheriff, a middle-aged man with a full head of graying, brown hair, had been a probation officer when he'd been elected to that position. The sheriff introduced himself to Colyer, but there was no friendliness in his handshake. This was his county, his private domain, and he didn't like federal agents mucking about on his turf. He followed Sawyer and Thorsen to the locations of each of the corpses with his thumbs hooked into his Sam Browne belt, trying to look official. Colyer could see that he was making an effort to hold down his supper as he surveyed the grisly scene.

"Mrs. Elliot," Colyer said, hoping that his display of respect might help to deter disrespect for her from the deputies when they inevitably questioned her, "I'd like to go back to my car now. Would you give me a ride?"

"Sure," she said simply. They climbed into her truck. She started the engine and jockeyed the big pickup between the two police vehicles.

Once he was sure they couldn't be overheard, he said, "Shannon, these deputies think that your husband might have killed those people."

"I know," she said sadly. "I didn't have to hear what they were whispering to figure that out."

"What do you think?"

"Rod wouldn't do that," she said simply. "He has a temper, but he's incapable of committing cold-blooded murder."

"What about the man who was nearly decapitated? That was done with a machete, and survival instructors carry machetes." He stated it as a fact, but he really didn't know.

"Yes, Rod carries a machete for his classes," she answered honestly. "It's a tool; he uses it to cut ferns and grasses, to split wood, to dig holes through roots . . ." She was starting to get angry. "I don't have to justify his need for a machete to you."

"No, you don't, Shannon. Not unless I find out that he's using it to cut people's heads off."

"Well then, I don't have a thing to worry about, do I?" There was fire in her eyes.

"Look, Shannon," he said, resting his hand lightly on her shoulder. "I don't think Rod is a murderer, but the county cops aren't so sure. It would be best for him if I found him first."

"If I know Rod, he's already concluded that the local cops will probably blame him for this. Having decided that, he's most likely following the real killers. That's the only way he's gonna clear himself."

Colyer's cell phone vibrated for attention from his pocket. It was a text message for him to Tx his office in Sault Sainte Marie. He immediately called his office, thinking that it must be urgent for Melanie to contact him here. Oh God, he hoped that everything was all right at home.

Melanie answered the phone. "Tom, I'm sorry to bother you in the field, but the state police post here has been calling every half-hour for the past three hours to ask if you were back yet. I tried to call you a couple of times, but you must have been out of range of the cell tower."

"Sorry, Mel, but I've been in the woods for the past several hours. I probably was out of range for a lot of that time. Who called, and was there a message?"

"It was Lieutenant Perkins, and he just said that he had a lead you might be interested in."

"Okay, thanks, Melanie." He hung up the phone.

They were where Colyer had parked his car. He turned to Shannon as he opened the door to get out of her truck, and extended his hand.

"Shannon, I don't think your husband is a murderer. I want to thank you for the help you've given me today. I hope I can call on you again if I need a tracker."

She smiled, a little meekly, he thought, and shook the hand he offered. "Yes, Agent Colyer, I'd be glad to help you again. Forgive me for getting a little defensive. The cops have never let Rod forget that he did time in prison."

"I promise not to hold his record against him."

"You'd be the first cop who didn't," she grinned humorlessly.

Chapter Twenty

Waiting

Rod kept the Hyundai at a steady sixty-five miles per hour on the forty-five-mile drive to the Mackinac Bridge. He knew that before he reached the town of Saint Ignace on the bridge's northern end, every police officer in the UP would be looking for him and this car. He made it through the village of Trout Lake, eleven miles away, without seeing one. With any luck, the patrol cars in this area would take a half-hour or so to get to the intersection of M-28 and M-123. Then there would be another fifteen minutes until the responding officer issued an All Points Bulletin. He hoped that it was enough time for him to get within hiking distance of Saint Ignace.

He reached Castle Rock Road less than twenty minutes later. It was a dirt road that turned south off M-123 into Hiawatha National Forest, and emerged behind Castle Rock, a rocky outcrop turned tourist attraction on the outskirts of Saint Ignace. Ten years ago, the road didn't even have a name. Today, it was pretty drivable, except when rain turned its clay surface greasy-slick. Many an unsuspecting tourist slid into the woods on one of the road's curves.

For Rod, the most attractive feature of this back way into Saint Ignace was the numerous old logging trails that extended from it. It offered a number of places where he could hide the stolen Santa Fe in case he needed it again.

Rod had no idea where the terrorists had gone, but he knew they wouldn't have gone far. He'd managed to get out of McBraden that their target was the Mackinac Bridge. After all they'd done to get here, there was no doubt in Rod's mind that they meant to go through with their plan.

About a mile from Saint Ignace, he found an old logging road that looked like it hadn't been traveled in months. He shifted the Hyundai into four-wheel-drive and backed up a few feet to make certain the transfer case had locked, then shifted into drive and pressed the accelerator. There were grass-covered, muddy grooves left from the tires of a multiton log skidder that had passed through years ago. The Santa Fe's V-6 engine growled, and the vehicle tipped from side to side in the ruts, but its all-terrain tires clawed through, until the SUV was out of sight of the road.

Rod rifled through the glove box. Most Yoopers carried maps of the Upper Peninsula, in case they had to sort out where some unknown two-track had led them. Sure enough, there were a half-dozen road and trail maps in there. There was also a Colt Hammerless 32 automatic in a leather holster. He drew the World War II vintage pistol from its canvas military-style scabbard and pulled its slide back far enough to show the glint of a brass cartridge in the breech; it was loaded. He slid the magazine out of the butt and thumbed out seven rounds; it was now fully loaded, with one in the chamber. It was a good thing that Rod had gotten the drop on Glenn Hueker first when he'd appropriated his vehicle; the Yooper might have tried to shoot it out with him.

It bothered Rod that he had to presume that the Colt and the Beretta he took from McBraden were already sighted-in. He dared not fire any rounds to confirm that presumption because he didn't have any more ammunition than what was in the magazines. Gunfire didn't arouse much curiosity in the Upper Peninsula, where there were more firearms than residents, but he didn't want to take the chance that someone might get nosy. The fixed, low-profile combat sights on the little Colt weren't made to deliver long-range accuracy, anyway, but it would be nice to know where a bullet would land.

The Beretta 9-millimeter he'd appropriated from McBraden held fifteen rounds in each of its three magazines. With a total of fifty-two rounds for both pistols, Rod didn't think he'd probably live long enough to expend all of his ammunition if it came to a gunfight. The Colt was loaded with plain-Jane, hardball ammo; not especially lethal, particularly in this small a caliber, but it'd kill you if you were hit in a vital organ.

The 9-millimeter was loaded with Winchester PDX1 Defender bullets. Rod knew the ammunition brand and model from the outdoor magazines he'd read. Although he was legally restricted from owning a firearm, he'd fired a few rounds from other peoples' guns while sighting-in for them. For a small caliber, this modern expanding-bullet design was devastating. And the 9-millimeter was renowned for accuracy—if the sights were properly adjusted. He'd seen for himself that an awful lot of pistols and rifles that were being used ostensibly to kill had never been sighted-in, because their owners didn't know how.

He took the big Power Eagle knife off of his belt and stashed it in his backpack. That knife would surely attract interest in the vicinity of any populated area, even in the UP. The Schrade survival knife went in there with it. He zipped the Colt pistol into an outside pocket of his backpack for now, where he could quickly retrieve it if needed. He tucked the Beretta under his belt in back, directly over the hollow formed by his left butt cheek. He'd packed a gun that way in his drug-dealing youth; it was comfortable and secure to carry there, and as quick to draw as if it were in a holster.

Rod hadn't slept in more than twenty-four hours. He was tired, and his joints were telling him, in no uncertain terms, that he wasn't a kid anymore. But he wasn't sleepy, and after the events of the past day, he doubted if he could sleep if he tried. He had the pills he'd taken from McBraden, but there was no way he was going to take a tranquilizer. He was too keyed-up and scared for that. Instead, he swallowed two of the Dexedrine tablets, and decided to hike to the bridge in Saint Ignace. It was about three miles from here. He could walk that distance in less than an hour.

He had no way of knowing on which end of the bridge the two men he was chasing had gone. But he did have the license plate number of the white van tattooed on his brain. They had to come back to set their dirty bombs somewhere along the bridge's span. It made sense that they wouldn't place them together, but wide apart to damage as much of the structure as possible, and to maximize casualties. The towers would be ideal, but getting into them undetected would be nigh impossible.

He pondered the possibilities as he walked toward town. Twice he had to dive into the brush when cars came down Castle Rock Road, but they passed by without seeing him. By the time he'd reached the Castle Rock overpass above Interstate 75, he'd calculated that the most probable bomb locations would be under the roadway. McBraden had doubtless revealed all that he knew about the operation, but Rod doubted that he was the mastermind, and he probably didn't have any more information about the plan than he needed to do his part.

Labor Day was in four days. The state police would clear all maintenance personnel from the span two days before the walk. And for those last two days, the entire length would be under very tight security from the state police and National Guard. The terrorists wouldn't be likely to set a bomb during the final forty-eight hours, so it would already have to be in place. And it would have to be in a location where it wouldn't be found. Under the bridge was the most likely place, high up where most people would be too afraid to spend much time checking nooks and crannies. Today or tomorrow were the best days to get the job done.

If Rod were doing it, he'd exploit the last-minute confusion that naturally went with getting the bridge as good as it could be for the governor's appearance. Every local politician who drew a paycheck from taxpayer money and had designs on career advancement would be trying to orchestrate something to impress the leader of the state. If Rod were doing it, he'd wait until the last day, the last few hours, before authorities cleared the bridge of maintenance workers, when the chaos would be greatest.

A pedestrian carrying a backpack didn't attract much attention in Saint Ignace. The town was a nexus of hiking and recreational vehicle trails, and someone who looked like they'd just come from the woods wasn't an uncommon sight either. Rod walked the entire length of the village from north to south, where the main street intersected Interstate 75 and became US 2. He did the three-mile trek in good time, feeling extraordinarily energetic because of the Dexedrine tablets he'd taken.

He passed every motel, hotel, and boardinghouse in town. There were a half-dozen Ford panel vans that fit the description of the vehicle he sought, but none of them matched the license plate number he'd committed to memory. It was possible that they'd changed license plates, or had even changed vehicles, but he had to look. Who knew? He might get lucky.

At a small parking lot marked BRIDGE VIEWING AREA just off the south side of US 2, he drew a Nikon Monarch twelve-power binoculars from their case on the padded waist-belt of his backpack. He turned the focusing wheel as he surveyed the bridge as well as he could along its five-mile length. The midsection of the bridge was hazy from heat and humidity, and the binoculars' normally sharp optics delivered a fuzzy sight picture. He hoped to see some sign of the white van that was carrying the terrorists, but he knew that was almost certainly just wishful thinking. If they'd crossed to the southern end, they'd be long gone from sight by now. There were just too many motels for him to check in the Lower Peninsula.

He had the hundred dollars he'd kept from McBraden's money in his pocket, so he stopped at a little burger joint along US 2 and ordered a cheeseburger and fries. Again, his rough-looking, bearded appearance and his backpack didn't so much as raise an eyebrow among the staff; these people were used to all kinds. He went outside to an open-air table under a peaked roof in front of the restaurant, where he had a clear view of the Mackinac Bridge. He tried not to appear as if he were starving as he ate his sandwich, but he was feeling that way, in spite of the speed he'd taken. He hadn't eaten since the day before, and now that he had a moment to relax, he was ravenous.

He was also exhausted. The speed was keeping him awake, but he felt as though someone were holding him up by his shoulders. His knees and hips ached, and his feet throbbed. He needed to sleep. He was feeling every year of his age, and he'd pushed his body beyond its threshold; he was keeping himself moving only through toughness now. Rod rotated his shoulders and stretched his neck from side to side as waves of exhaustion washed over him. The Dexedrine was wearing off.

He had enough money left to rent a motel room for the night, but that probably wouldn't be a good idea. By now, there was definitely a warrant for his arrest, and every police officer in the Upper Peninsula was probably eager to protect the population from a survival instructor gone mad. The past two days had seen more excitement than the UP had had in the past twenty years, and cops who were used to nothing more shocking than a rowdy drunk were probably a little trigger-happy over multiple murders on Betsy River.

Instead, he worked his way down to the lakeshore at the Straits of Mackinac on the Lake Michigan side. There were lots of houses there along the shoreline, most of them seasonal residences or inhabited by the elite of Saint Ignace—doctors, lawyers, judges. A rough-looking character like himself would seem out of place there, but it offered a clear view of the bridge, and he didn't plan on being conspicuous, or even seen.

At the lakeshore, he found a copse of poplar trees between two of the typically spacious houses that lined a gravel road. The houses were spaced about seventy-five yards apart, with lots of dogwood bushes growing at the roadside. He found a dry hummock in an undeveloped lot about midway between two of them where he would not be seen by occupants of either house, but still have a clear view of the bridge.

He laid a pallet of dead branches side by side on the ground to prevent his body heat from being absorbed into the earth, and then padded the insulating layer with dried leaves and bracken ferns gathered from the surrounding area. Finally, he covered himself with a layer of ferns that would inhibit his body heat from radiating into the atmosphere while he slept.

He felt secure in this little niche. Using his backpack as a pillow, he snuggled into his sleeping nest. Fatigue washed over him as he fell asleep almost immediately.

Chapter Twenty-One

Paradise

Colyer had driven back to the Betsy River after Shannon dropped him at his car. He'd spent the entire night at the grisly murder scene with state police forensic investigators, trying to piece together what had happened.

He'd decided not to let local and state police agencies know anything more than they already knew; not yet. He'd put together what he thought was a pretty feasible theory, but it would sound crazy to cops who were used to nothing much ever happening in their neck of the woods. And even if local authorities did believe him, there was a real likelihood that they'd do something to tip off the men he was after.

What if the submarine that had been scuttled by its own crew off the east coast of Canada had delivered the four men that Shannon had tracked for him? The Eyes-Only report from the US sub had claimed that the diesel submarine had discharged four men. If these were the same men, where had they come from, and who were they? Money was apparently no object; an undocumented submarine, by itself, denoted millions of dollars spent to achieve an objective that had obviously been deemed worth the expense. Discarding a new Zodiac on the shore of Lake Superior would have been an insignificant expense compared to the money that had already been spent to reach Canada.

Whatever their objective was, it was worth murdering people as well. In fact, the deaths of the people at Betsy River seemed to have been merely peripheral to the main objective. They were acts of convenience rather than an end in themselves. The thought that murder and torture would be committed as easily as it appeared to have been indicated an important goal for the perpetrators, and a potential catastrophe for the United States.

But had the people killed been an active part of the scheme, or had they simply been in the wrong place at the wrong time? It had been easy to determine the identities of the dead woman and two of the men—they appeared to be who Shannon said they were. The third man, the one who'd been more or less decapitated, was a ghost. Colyer hoped that his DNA might reveal who he was, but a cursory search so far had come up with zilch. Fingerprints, face . . . so far the CODIS system had turned up nothing, and INTERPOL was still looking for a match.

When Colyer reached the village of Paradise, within sight of a cell tower, he pulled over and checked the reception of his cell phone. The bar graph was solid. He dialed up Lieutenant Perkins at the state police post in Sault Sainte Marie.

"Hello Tom," Perkins answered. "Are you at your office?"

"No, I'm in beautiful downtown Paradise." The sarcasm was thick in his voice—for Colyer, this collection of decaying buildings was pretty far from living up to its name. From where he sat in his car, he could see the entire village. If he were to tell the people he saw going about their business that multiple murders had occurred the day before, they'd never have believed him.

Perkins seemed to be reading his thoughts. "I know you've been up all night with the forensics guys, but I thought you might be interested in a carjacking that happened early this morning at the 123 and 28 intersection."

"A carjacking here?"

"Yupper, but that's not the part that's really interesting. The middle-aged male who jacked the car at pistol point actually told the victims to dial 911, and then he took off and left them with a fistful of cash and a half-naked man tied up on the side of the road."

"That's weird," Colyer said.

"Yeah, and the man he left them with is Timmons McBraden, the son of retired Sheriff Dennis McBraden."

"And?" Colyer was tired and he was getting a little grumpy.

Perkins noted Colyer's impatience. "And he's been out of sight for the past two years; completely off the radar. Now he's been dropped at the side of the road by a carjacker who fits the description of your ex-con survival instructor, right down to the big knife that he's known to carry."

"Rod Elliot?"

"Yeah. You know who he is? The prosecutor considers him a prime suspect in the murders on the Betsy River."

Colyer bit off a reply. Rod Elliot hadn't killed his own survival students, he was sure of it. But he didn't want to reveal too much of what he thought. Not yet.

Instead he asked, "Do you think he did it?"

"I don't know," Perkins answered. "Doesn't matter anyway. The judge has issued a warrant. We have to arrest him for questioning."

"Okay, thanks for the tip, Jim. I'll follow up on it. Meanwhile, lean on the sheriff a little, will you? Tell him this is a federal case, and the Bureau wants McBraden kept under wraps for now. I'll tell you more when I'm able."

Colyer pushed the end button. It was rude to hang up that way, but he didn't want to give Perkins a chance to ask more questions. He laced his fingers together and leaned the back of his head against his palms. He closed his scratchy eyes and let out a long exhale. God, he was tired, both physically and mentally. He needed sleep if he was going to be effective on either count.

He decided that he'd get a room at one of the motels in Paradise. No sense driving back sixty-five miles to Sault Sainte Marie when nearly all of what he needed to see and do was in this vicinity.

He'd better call Lanie and tell her not to expect him for dinner. He punched his home phone number into his cell. After three rings, the machine picked up, and he left her a message. She'd be disappointed, but being an ex-cop herself, she'd understand. She'd spurned a badge after their relocation to the Upper Peninsula, preferring to be a full-time, stay-at-home wife. It was a decision he heartily agreed with—but she knew that sometimes doing the job meant staying away from home.

Paradise had an abundance of motels for its size, so he snugged his necktie and smoothed some of the wrinkles from his jacket and trousers before checking in to the one he was closest to. When he walked through the door and into the office, he was met by the faint smell of a litter box that needed emptying, and the flowery scent of room deodorizer. There was no one at the desk, so he tapped the desk bell twice. He heard a door open in the back. Seconds later, a balding man of about sixty appeared, dressed in a clean, white tank-top undershirt and faded blue jeans. The clerk wiped his hands on the front of his shirt as he finished chewing a mouthful of his breakfast.

The clerk appraised his suit, rumpled from trying to keep up with Shannon Elliot in the forest, with a critical eye. He seemed to take an inordinate interest in the manner of Colyer's dress; not many people wore suits and neckties in this area, and most of those didn't look like they'd been up all night hunting deer in them.

"Welcome to Paradise," the clerk said. Colyer was glad that he hadn't extended a greasy hand for him to shake. "Can I get you a room?"

"Yes," Colyer answered simply. What'd he think he was there for?

"Okay, I just need you to fill out this card." The clerk slid a small sheet of paper toward him across the desk. It was a boilerplate form that asked the questions every motel asked when it rented one of its rooms. Colyer filled it out as a civilian, never letting on that he was here in an official capacity. The clerk noted that he knew his driver's license and license plate numbers without looking at them.

"How long will you be staying with us?" the clerk asked nonchalantly as he studied the completed card perhaps a little too intently.

Colyer grinned. "I'm not sure yet. Let's take it one day at a time."

"Okay," the clerk said, handing him an old-fashioned room key—no electromagnetic strip cards at this motel. "That'll be seventy-five dollars for the first night. Checkout is at ten. My name is John," the clerk said with a rehearsed smile. "If you need anything, just ring me at the front desk. To get an outside line, you need to dial nine first."

Colyer paid the man and asked for a receipt. The tag attached to the brass key said it was for room thirty-seven, facing Whitefish Bay. Good, that was out of sight of the office, so he'd be spared scrutiny from this obviously inquisitive manager. The manager watched intently as Colyer drove the Charger around to his room.

He had a small bag in the backseat that he always carried on road trips for cases that might demand he spend a day or two away from home. In it were a razor and other toiletries, as well as a change of socks and underwear. Hanging from a hook on the door stanchion between the front and backseats, was a garment bag with a fresh suit and tie. The FBI wasn't understanding of agents who looked slovenly, no matter where they were.

The room was dark and musty smelling when Colyer opened the door, but it was cooler than the outside, which was already growing uncomfortably warm. Colyer laid his garment bag on the other bed, then set his overnight bag next to it. He flopped onto his back atop the opposite bed, and fell instantly asleep.

Chapter Twenty-Two

Bombmaking

Aziz and Grigovich awoke to the bedside alarm clock buzzing at 6 AM. Today was the last day that bridge workers would be permitted to perform maintenance on the structure before everything was cleared in preparation for the annual Labor Day Bridge Walk, less than three days from now. Aziz felt almost giddy with excitement.

They were ready. Aziz's carefully selected and highly trained team of demolition experts may have been reduced to half its size, but they were ready for that, had been ready for it since training in Afghanistan. Satan himself seemed to have frowned on their mission, and everything that could have gone wrong had gone wrong. But Aziz believed that those difficulties had been just tests of his faith and determination. Holy Allah had seen fit to bring them within sight of the goal, nevertheless. They were so close now that nothing could stop them. Allah be praised.

Aziz wasn't ordinarily a devoutly religious Muslim. He'd seldom prayed properly these past few weeks. But this was a special day, and he felt that it would be prudent to ask Holy Allah to guide his hands in the tasks that lay ahead today. He didn't have a proper prayer rug, but the throw rug in the bathroom would have to do. He brought it into the motel's main room and laid it out flat at the foot of the beds.

Then he faced east, toward the rising sun, more or less, and prostrated himself to his god.

Grigovich twisted his knuckles into his sleepy eyes, but said nothing. His bladder was full, and his first function of the day was to relieve himself. He walked to the bathroom wearing only his underwear, and urinated noisily into the bowl, farting loudly as he did. He'd left the door standing wide open. Aziz glared at him from his prostrated position, incensed that his morning prayers had been so rudely interrupted. But he said nothing; it would do no good to give this muscle-bound imbecile a dressing-down, because he was always going to be a simple-minded moron. Aziz would just be wasting his breath.

When Grigovich had finished, he flushed the toilet—his time with Aziz had at least conditioned him to do that much—then he stepped in front of the bathroom mirror to squeeze blackheads that had been erupting on his face since they'd entered the woods. Aziz looked at his companion with disgust, and then went back to his praying. At least he had showered last night. They both had, reveling in the streams of hot water as they rinsed away several days' worth of bug guts, sweat, and grime that had accumulated during their time in these horrible woods. Aziz never wanted to see a forest again.

Grigovich was tenser than Aziz about the events of this day, but it wasn't evident. He hated Americans as much as ever, and he was determined to see this mission through. Richarde had been his friend. Their Arab handlers in Afghanistan hadn't permitted them to consume alcohol, but he remembered several times when they had sneaked off together to smoke opium and drink bootleg whiskey. He'd never much liked McBraden, and he didn't miss him at all, but he missed Richarde. The anger that he felt at having his friend nearly beheaded by that fucking American justified what he was going to do to this country's typically bloodthirsty culture.

Aziz finished his prayers and stood up. Then he went into the bathroom to relieve himself. He closed the door. Meanwhile, Grigovich busied himself with rechecking weapons once again. This he was good at. The fifteen pounds of C4 explosive that each of them carried was packaged in a 50-caliber ammunition box that had been repainted with a flat, black automotive primer. Inside each can, fifteen one-pound blocks of foil-packaged C4 were stacked peripherally around a baseball-size sphere of plutonium.

Inserted equidistantly into the packed plastic explosive at four points were electrically detonated Class B Match-type blasting caps. The detonator wires of each cap were spliced to similar wires on the other three caps, then soldered to a single detonator-switch wire. The two detonator-switch wires terminated at either pole of the ringer circuit in a cellular Tracphone. The Tracphone was turned off, and the wires to its ringer circuit were shunted together with an alligator-clip jumper wire for safety. With all of the generators and electrical equipment that were in operation on the bridge, they wanted to minimize the chances of accidental detonation from spurious, sixty-cycle electrical emissions. When the bombs were placed, only then would they turn on the telephone and remove the jumper clips. When the jumpers were removed, dialing the ten-digit number of the corresponding Tracphone would result in a powerful, radiation-spewing fireball.

Mounting the ammo box bombs to the bridge was simple. In their pockets, they carried big magnets, purchased from a novelty catalog. When they found a suitable place, they'd simply stick the magnet to a bridge support, and then stick the box to the magnet. After that, they'd withdraw to a safe place where they could watch the bridge. At just the right moment—when the governor was within range—either he or Aziz would dial the number of the northern bomb. Right after that, when panicked walkers were fleeing in the opposite direction, he'd dial up the southern bomb. Grigovich smiled when he envisioned the amount of anarchy that would ensue. He wasn't as pathologically bloodthirsty as Aziz, but he loved blowing stuff up.

While Grigovich went over the bombs, and then disassembled and cleaned the pistols, Aziz went out to the van with two plastic magnet-mounted signs. Like their white coveralls, the signs read JACKSONVILLE PAINTING. Brenda Waukonigon had had them made for him before they'd landed in Canada, and they'd been in the duffel when he'd picked up the van. Now he smoothed the signs over the plain panels of the van on either side, flattening and straightening them until they looked just right to him.

When he went back into the motel room, Grigovich had cleaned and reloaded not only his own pistol and Aziz's revolver, but Richarde's 9-millimeter Beretta. An expert with firearms as well as explosives, Grigovich had prudently emptied the guns' magazines and speed loaders, replacing the cartridges with fresh rounds to help ensure that there couldn't be a misfire if they were needed. A lot of soldiers and police had been killed because bullets had worked loose from their crimps, especially on the first round. A loose bullet might allow condensation to enter, causing the first round to misfire. He'd even disassembled the magazines themselves, removing the floorplates, stretching the feeder springs, and smoothing the cartridge follower platforms so they slid against the magazine walls with silky smoothness. With nothing left to do, and an abundance of nervous energy to burn off, Grigovich was polishing the bearing surfaces of each gun's action with a tissue when Aziz walked in.

"Okay," Aziz said, "the van's ready. Let's get our coveralls on."

Grigovich reached into his satchel and shook out his own pair of coveralls. They were laundered, but spattered with paint, and looked as if they'd been worn frequently. After she'd had the JACKSONVILLE PAINTING patches made and sewn onto them, Brenda Waukonigon had spattered the coveralls with assorted colors of paint. Then she'd dragged them several miles down a dirt road while they were tied to the bumper of a pickup truck.

When Grigovich was dressed and ready, Aziz appraised his appearance. He turned him completely around by the shoulders while he looked for any hint that might suggest he was anything but another one of the workers employed to maintain the bridge. Grigovich looked perfect, right down to his worn hiking boots and roughened hands.

"Okay," Aziz said, putting on his hard hat, "now you look me over."

Grigovich obliged. He looked Aziz over head to toe with a critical eye, and, likewise, saw nothing that would indicate he was anything but another bridge worker.

"You look perfect to me, Phillipe," Grigovich said truthfully.

Aziz looked at his wristwatch: 6:32 AM. The sun had fully risen over the water of Lake Huron when he cautiously opened the door to the parking lot and peered outside. As he'd banked on, no one else at the motel seemed to be moving so early in the morning. They grabbed their black nylon satchels and walked briskly to the van. The van's panel door sounded extraordinarily loud as it slid open. He and Grigovich threw their bags inside, and then closed the door with a bang that made them both jump nervously.

Aziz was driving. Grigovich was unconsciously fingering the butt of the Desert Eagle pistol that was tucked into the waistband of his trousers under his coveralls. He kept watch in the rearview mirrors as Aziz wended his way through the streets of the small city toward the on-ramp of the bridge. He was gratified to see that no one seemed to pay any attention to them. Still, Grigovich felt a hard knot growing in the pit of his stomach as they drew closer to the objective.

Aziz was excited, too, but it was almost sexual for him. Nothing turned him on more than the thought of hurting someone. He loved the feeling of being the master over others, and this mission gave him mastery over thousands of the people he hated. It was a delicious feeling to him.

The speed limit on the Mackinac Bridge was posted by a lighted sign. It was different for different types of vehicles, and it changed for different types of weather conditions. A few vehicles had already gone over the bridge's waist-high iron rail—it was never made public, but authorities knew that at least some of them hadn't been accidental. They'd been outright suicides.

Also kept secret from the public were the numerous "jumpers," who'd simply stopped their vehicles in the middle of the bridge, and then jumped over the railing. Their bodies were traveling at nearly two hundred miles an hour when they impacted the surface of the water. At that speed, surface tension made the water seem like concrete, and the effects on a human body were the same. Like a fat bug against the windshield of a car, the abdomen split, and internal organs burst outward with such force that they ripped through clothing.

The incidence of people who drove or jumped to certain death from the height of the Mackinac Bridge was kept strictly confidential. Medical and police personnel were restricted from even commenting about them in private. Some claimed that the press was being controlled through legal threats to keep quiet about such suicides, thereby protecting the claim that the Mackinac Bridge was the safest five miles of interstate in the nation. Journalists who didn't abide by the unwritten law of silence found themselves living under a microscope until they moved away, or their careers were ruined.

Jumpers were the reason that no one, save bridge authority and maintenance personnel, was allowed on the bridge on foot. Absolutely no hitchhiking. No one without a vehicle could reach either side, except on Labor Day. Security was high then, with even a complement of National Guard troops on scene, and all eyes were on the civilian pedestrians, and especially on the governor's party.

There was a small boat in the water below the bridge any time there were maintenance workers afoot on the structure, ostensibly for safety, even though it was common knowledge that anyone who fell from the bridge would die. The boat was, in fact, there to get bodies out of the water immediately, before someone took photos of them. Aziz counted on the people in that boat seeing him and Grigovich when they planted their bombs. In fact, he relished the thought that the boat crew would look right at their executioners from a quarter-mile away, and watch them attach their bombs, without ever realizing what the two men were actually doing.

The day was calm and sunny, with a relatively gentle wind of just fifteen miles per hour. The programmable light sign, just past the on-ramp, cautioned motorists to reduce speed from the posted seventy miles per hour to forty-five—the normal speed limit for optimal driving conditions on the bridge. Aziz drove to the center of the span and parked in the outside lane behind a row of welding company trucks. He left plenty of room between the van and the next vehicle, so he wouldn't be blocked in when he and Grigovich were ready to leave.

They stepped from the van. When they opened their doors, they were assaulted by the din of giant diesel compressors and generators, and the loud, constant hissing of pressurized air. They donned their hard hats, and each of them tucked a clipboard under his arm. They strode officially along the midsection of the bridge, pretending to discuss its construction as they pointed to different components.

They'd been walking back and forth along the bridge for fifteen minutes when Grigovich said, close so that only Aziz could hear, "Christ, doesn't anyone even notice us?"

As if on cue, a black bridge authority pickup truck with a lighted sign in its box pulled up to them. A uniformed officer rolled down his window and asked in a voice loud enough to penetrate the noise, "You guys here to paint the bridge?"

"Yeah," Aziz shouted back with a slight Southern drawl, "we're from Jacksonville Painting. We're here to do an estimate of how much it would cost to prime the underside of the bridge with our patented new polymer paint."

"I didn't receive any notification that you fellas were coming today," the officer yelled, running a forefinger down his own clipboard.

"We weren't supposed to be here until next week," Aziz yelled back. "But with Labor Day and all, our bosses want to get in their bid before the holiday weekend. You probably haven't heard anything about it because they're being real secretive about this new primer our boys have developed."

Aziz handed him a business card printed with JACKSONVILLE PAINTING, COMMERCIAL AND INDUSTRIAL PAINTING and a logo of a paint can and paintbrush. Printed at the bottom was a Jacksonville, Florida, telephone number. If the officer called the number, he'd hear an answering machine message for Jacksonville Painting, followed by an apology that all office employees were off enjoying the holiday weekend. He'd never know that the telephone and answering machine were in a derelict warehouse, in an abandoned industrial park.

"Okay, let me check this out," the bridge cop shouted.

"Officer, we'd really like to get this estimate done and then get the hell out of here and start our holiday weekend. Would you have any objection to us gettin' started right away?"

The officer looked at them skeptically. His eyes took in the coveralls and hard hats, the tool belts and clipboards, the worn look that traveling through the woods had given them—even their boots. He'd worked this mostly idyllic bridge patrol job for six Labor Days in a row, and despite the increased security—maybe because of it—nothing more exciting than a few walkers fainting had ever occurred during the Bridge Walk. Besides, why on earth would two men pretend to be working here when they weren't?

"Yeah, okay," the man in the truck said, "you can get started."

Chapter Twenty-Three

The Interrogation

Colyer awoke lying on his back on the bed, fully clothed, and in exactly the same position in which he'd fallen asleep. Wow, he must've really been tired. He looked at his wristwatch. It was one-thirty in the afternoon. He'd slept for about six hours. That was about the length of time he normally slept. He didn't feel particularly well-rested—in fact, his leg and back muscles were a little sore from trying to keep up with Shannon Elliot in the Lake Superior State Forest yesterday. So were his feet. He really needed a good pair of hiking boots if he were going to be doing that sort of thing.

He felt a need to go to the bathroom. While he was seated on the toilet, he ran his tongue over his front teeth. They felt furry. Then he noticed that his armpits stank, and he felt gritty and covered with grime. He needed a shower.

He turned on the water. While he was stripping off his clothes, he looked into the mirror—the first time he'd looked at his reflection in two days. The man who stared back at him looked different. His face and forearms were scratched in several places. There were bruises on his shins. Itchy mosquito bumps dotted every portion of his body. He was smeared with dirt almost everywhere his skin had been exposed. There was dirt packed under his fingernails, and his face looked grimy and oily in the mirror. He certainly didn't look like a member of the nation's top police agency.

The hot water felt good. He couldn't believe how sore and itchy he was. The freaking mosquitoes had virtually feasted on his body out there. Shannon Elliot hadn't seemed to be more than mildly annoyed. He'd seen people like that before, people who seemed to enjoy some sort of natural immunity, but he didn't know how they did it. Even with a bottle of DEET insect repellent in his pocket, Shannon Elliot seemed to have been less bothered by bloodthirsty insects than he was.

He scrubbed the dirt off his skin with a threadbare washcloth, unable to resist scratching at some of the mosquito bites, even though everyone from his mother to his doctor had always advised against scratching. He wished he'd bought some of that no-itch stuff he'd seen in stores. He ran his palm around his chin, feeling the salt-and-pepper stubble that had sprung up there since yesterday. He remembered when his beard used to be dark brown.

After a good shit, shower, and shave, Colyer felt better. He changed into his spare set of clothes, and he felt even better. He stood in front of the bathroom mirror, as he tightened a dark-blue necktie with broad, red diagonal stripes, and decided that he looked like a proper FBI agent again. He stepped back and admired the image of himself in the mirror. He could stand to lose maybe ten pounds, sure, but not bad for a middle-aged man in any profession.

He had no desire to deal with the curious desk clerk again, so he left the room key in the doorknob lock, and left. As he started his car, he saw the venetian blinds of the office window part ever so slightly, as someone at the desk watched him. He pulled out onto the highway with a wry smile. It was probably driving the locals crazy, trying to figure out who he was, but it was only a matter of time before they found out about the murders at Betsy River.

Now that Colyer had gotten a few hours of sleep, he was thinking clearly again. The submarine last week, the murders at the river, the carjacking, the guy left half-naked on the highway—all of these had to be tied together somehow. Just how they were tied together he didn't know yet, but he'd start with questioning McBraden.

A telephone call to the jail confirmed that McBraden was there, and was being kept in solitary confinement. The judge had set bond immediately, and his father had tried to spring him, but Lieutenant

Perkins had interceded. As Colyer had told him to do, Perkins had informed the judge that the younger McBraden was being held on federal charges, and that any bail she set would be superseded by a federal custody order. The old sheriff had blustered and threatened, but the judge knew better than to overstep her authority, and Timmons McBraden had remained in jail. That type of good-old-boy club was why the FBI had placed an office here in the first place.

Before he drove back to Sault Sainte Marie, he stopped at Glenn Hueker's house to ask him and his wife a few questions about the carjacking. Mrs. Hueker didn't have much to say, but her husband was a veteran of the Vietnam conflict, retired from Chrysler in Detroit, and he had a lot to say. He'd moved back to the tiny community of Hulbert, about thirty miles southwest of Paradise, after his retirement a decade ago. He'd been born there, and had moved back there, he said, because this kind of shit wasn't supposed to happen in the UP. He was angry, and he wanted Colyer to know it. He gave a detailed description of the carjacker, and it sure sounded as if the man had been Rod Elliot.

What Hueker didn't divulge was that there had been an unregistered, 32-caliber Colt automatic in the glove box of the Santa Fe—Hueker's wife had let that little bit of pertinent information slip. Hueker, of course, didn't want to incriminate himself to a federal agent, but his wife had prudently—and responsibly, Colyer thought—worried that an unrecorded handgun, in the possession of a man who was clearly of a criminal bent, might come back to haunt them, legally and morally.

Colyer was glad to have that information, because he wanted to know what kind of armament Elliot might have in his possession. But he wasn't about to get in an uproar over an unregistered handgun. It hadn't been required to register handguns with the federal government until 1968, when liberal politicians, in a knee-jerk reaction to the assassination of Robert Kennedy, had circumvented the Second Amendment in the name of national security. Congress had required all American citizens to register their handguns, which, until then, could be bought by mail, and, of course, most gun owners had flatly refused. The result, in Colyer's opinion, was that the politicians had made an entire generation into felons with the stroke of a pen, and created a black market for guns that existed to this day. There were politically minded agents in the FBI who might have arrested this war veteran on federal felony possession charges, but Colyer wasn't one of them. He had bigger fish to fry, in any case.

After leaving the Huekers, he drove to the jail in Sault Saint Marie, where he requested to speak with Timmons McBraden. The undersheriff came to the Booking Room to meet him. Colyer had never had occasion to meet the short, chubby, and abrasively self-important man before, and he didn't like him right away.

"I'm Undersheriff Emil Borden," he said, extending his hand. Colyer accepted the handshake reluctantly.

"I'm here to speak with Timmons McBraden," Colyer told him.

"I'm sorry," the undersheriff smiled, "but you can't talk to him without having an attorney present. He hasn't been able to afford one himself, and we're waiting for the judge to assign a public defender. It'll be a couple of days before that happens, I figure. The court docket is full right now."

Yeah, Colyer thought, and in a couple of days you'll have found some excuse to move him to another holding facility. He was getting a little fed up with these back-slapping, good ol' boys acting like he was a bastard cousin who'd be best kept in a closet. He'd better establish his position with this self-important little man right away.

Colyer leaned close to Borden, so that he wouldn't be overheard by the several turnkey deputies who were trying very hard to eavesdrop.

"Listen you cocksucker, you're impeding a federal investigation, and if I have to call in agents to move McBraden to Guantanamo Bay, I'll make certain that you go with him in belly chains for interfering in a case that bears on national security. Now take me to his cell."

Borden's eyes grew wide in astonishment. No one talked to him like that in his jail, not in his county. He opened his mouth to rebuke this fat-mouthed federal agent, and then clamped it shut so abruptly that his teeth clicked. He saw something in Colyer's eyes that said he wasn't just making an idle threat.

"Follow me," Borden said, taking a ring of heavy brass keys from a clip on his belt.

Colyer followed him down a hall past the jail's Control Room, past the curious eyes of several deputies. He stopped at a welded, steel door with a square-foot pane of half-inch tempered glass mounted in its center. Borden opened the door, using one of the big brass keys on his ring, and led Colyer down a long hallway to a row of single-prisoner cells with sliding doors made from steel bars.

McBraden was reclining on a steel rack atop two jail mattresses—prisoners typically got one. He was munching from a bag of Doritos, while he listened to a small radio. On the floor next to him were a Coca-Cola and a bottle of antihistamine lotion for his bug bites. Colyer grunted and looked sidewise at Borden. None of these things were allowed to ordinary prisoners.

"Thank you, Undersheriff Borden. I'll call out when I'm ready to leave."

"I should stay here with the prisoner . . ."

"I'll call you when I'm ready to leave, Undersheriff."

Borden got the message. McBraden's eyes flickered with fear for a moment, when the undersheriff turned and walked out the door, leaving him alone with this plainclothes cop, who apparently had no special consideration for the fact that he was the son of Sheriff Emeritus McBraden.

"Mr. McBraden, I'm Special Agent Colyer of the Federal Bureau of Investigation. I'm here to ask you a few questions." Without giving any indication that he did, Colyer noted that there was a video camera mounted up high on the wall behind him. Everything he said was being watched and recorded by the deputies in the control room.

"Mr. McBraden," Colyer said through the bars, "why are you here?"

McBraden looked him in the eye and said with assumed anger, "Because some asshole pervert kidnapped me and left me half-naked on the side of the highway. I'm the fuckin' victim here . . ." He knew what Colyer was asking, but he was purposely being obtuse.

"Where have you been these last couple of years, Mr. McBraden?"

A furtive look came into McBraden's eyes for just a moment, but he hid it with angry posturing. "I'm not tellin' you a fuckin' thing, G-man."

Colyer ignored the blustering pretense. "There's no record of you having been in this country for the past two years. No contact with your family, no phone records, no Social Security deductions, no one remembers you, no nothing. Where have you been, Mr. McBraden?"

McBraden looked scared now. How much did this fed know?

Colyer picked up on the doubt in McBraden's eyes. The agent was bluffing, but McBraden couldn't know that. He pursued that line of questioning.

"We know you've been in Canada, Mr. McBraden. Who are your friends?"

"I don't know what you're talking about."

"Yes, you do. You're a suspected domestic terrorist, son. If you don't start talking to me, I'll have you transferred out of here so fast you won't have time to blink twice. You'll be having supper tonight at Guantanamo Bay. The Marines have a little more persuasive way of getting you to talk to them there." He winked at McBraden, as if sharing a secret.

McBraden knew what he meant. He knew about waterboarding. His trainers at al-Qaeda had put him through simulated interrogation in Afghanistan. He knew about sleep deprivation; he knew about finding the deepest, darkest horrors in a man's mind, and then applying them through psychological means, until even the toughest subject cracked. They broke everyone. No one went through the interrogation simulation without cracking. McBraden had broken down like a baby after three days. It was one of the most awful memories in his life, and the thought of repeating it for real scared the hell out of him.

"I wasn't doing anything wrong," McBraden said. His eyes were downcast.

He was weakening. He'd started to make excuses. This man knew all about interrogation procedures, yet he'd never served a day in the Armed Forces of the United States.

"So what's it gonna be, son?" Colyer pushed. "You want to talk to me, or a bunch of mean-ass Marines who actually like hurting people?"

"Okay," McBraden said, "I don't need to be tortured. I'll tell you what I know. But promise me that you'll protect my mom and dad. You've got to promise me that first."

Chapter Twenty-Four

Hitchhiking

Rod awoke with the whine of mosquitoes humming in his ears. He wasn't bitten too badly—he had a knack for sleeping through bug bites, anyway. He didn't know exactly how or when he'd acquired such an ability, but, at some point, mosquitoes had decided that he wasn't one of their favorite meals. One theory was that a person's body chemistry changed after relentless bug attacks, and that seemed to be as good an explanation as any. When bugs had a choice between a gnarly, old woodsman and nearly anyone else, they almost always bit the other guy.

He'd been having a terrible dream. His shell-shocked brain refused to recall its details, but he remembered that it had been filled with blood and suffering. For a moment, he lay where he was, wondering whether the blue sky above him or the awfulness that lingered in his mind was real. An ice ball, once again, formed in the pit of his bowels when he realized that the parts of the dream that he could recall weren't a nightmare; he'd crossed a line from which there was no turning back: He had killed a person.

He unburied himself from the pile of leaves and loose foliage that had kept the night chill from his bones, and looked at his watch. He'd overslept. Damn this old body of his! Every injury he'd ever known was coming back to haunt him with a painful vengeance. It was already seven o'clock in the morning, and the late summer sun was high. The men he was looking for might have planted their bombs by now, and be gone. He didn't know what to do about it, even if they had. He didn't even know what his next move should be.

He thought again about calling Shannon. He'd thought about calling her many times since leaving the Betsy River. But if he called her, the cops would probably track down the call, regardless of where he called from. Even he knew that it wasn't like in the movies; tapping a phone line was as simple as throwing a switch, and authorities could get an instant lock on the source of any phone call. Especially if they were already monitoring his home phone, and he was certain that some agency or another was doing that by now. He remembered wryly, not so long ago, how the feds had crossed their hearts and promised the American people that they wouldn't listen in on cell-phone calls.

He scanned the bridge through his binoculars, glad for their twelve-power magnification. "Get big glass, and get the best glass you can afford," had been the advice of the Nikon dealer who'd sold him these Monarch 12 × 42 roof-prism binoculars. It was advice that he'd never regretted.

There were three white vans on the bridge, but none of them exactly matched the one he was looking for. One was clearly a Chevy—he could make out the emblem on its grill—but he was too far away to make out the license plate numbers of any of them. One of the other two vans could be the van he'd seen back in the woods when he'd nabbed McBraden, but both had signs on their sides. The van he'd seen there hadn't been marked. They might've applied a decal, or maybe they switched vehicles. Or, maybe the men he was looking for weren't even on the bridge. And, maybe the man he'd captured in Hiawatha National Forest had been telling him a tall tale to escape the mosquitoes.

But even supposing the man had been telling the truth, it wasn't Rod's job to stop the bombers. It wasn't even his responsibility; this country hadn't been especially kind to him at any point in his life. Besides, he wasn't an antiterrorism expert. And he damn sure wasn't a hero! In fact, he was probably the villain in all this in the law's eyes. They'd never believe him, even if he did go to them, and would doubtless prosecute him as an accomplice, anyway.

He'd had a lot of time to ponder his situation, and there was just no way out of this for him, that he could see. Supposing he was cleared of the murders of his survival students, the hard truth remained that he'd killed a man. And he'd killed him in a grisly and undeniably gruesome manner. He'd also stolen a car at gunpoint. With his criminal record, he'd definitely be considered guilty until proven innocent, and nothing in his experience with the criminal justice system made him think that he might be found not guilty in a so-called court of law.

But he couldn't let these terrorists literally get away with murder; they'd made it personal. They'd murdered and tortured people who'd entrusted Rod with their lives—the guilt from that weighed heavily on his conscience, no matter how he tried to rationalize it. Then they'd tried to kill him. Twice. Now they were intending to kill thousands of innocent people, including the governor of this state, and he didn't know why. None of this made a lick of sense to him. But then, taking any life without good reason had never made sense to him.

No, he was no hero, but he wasn't able to let this pass without at least making an attempt to stop it. But how to get onto the bridge? Pedestrians weren't allowed. He knew he'd recognize the two men if he saw them, but he had to at least get close enough to see their faces; that meant getting onto the bridge on foot.

There was a busy truck stop on US Highway 2, near the on-ramp to the bridge. Lots of truckers stopped there for a good meal, while on their way north or south. Rod was hungry, anyway, and that seemed a likely place to catch a ride.

The truck stop was filled with customers, when Rod walked in through its glass front door. The smell of fried potatoes, eggs, and bacon made his stomach growl, and the aroma of fresh-brewed coffee reminded him that he hadn't had any for days. No wonder he had a headache. Rod seated himself at a booth, and took a menu from the holder in the center of his table.

He'd barely opened the menu, when a thirtyish brunette with short, permed hair and a name tag on her dress that identified her as Candy approached his booth. She held an order pad and an ink pen poised to write. She asked if he wanted coffee.

"I sure would, Candy. Black, please. And I'd like an English muffin." He pointed to an item on the menu.

"English muffin and coffee," Candy repeated, scribbling on her order pad. "Coming right up. Would you like cream cheese on the muffin?" He shook his head no.

"By the way, Candy," Rod asked with a smile, "are any of these truckers headed south across the bridge? I need to hitch a ride across to Mackinaw City with someone."

It wasn't an uncommon request. She heard the same from lots of hitchhikers. "I'll ask around," she said. "There's probably a driver in here who'll oblige you."

"Thank you, Candy. I appreciate it."

Barely a minute had elapsed before Candy brought him his coffee in a covered Styrofoam cup and said, "See that man paying his bill at the cash register? That's Hank, and he said that if you leave right now, he'll give you a ride as far south as Pellston."

Rod glanced at the cash register, where a big-bellied, forty-something man motioned him to come along.

"Coffee's on the house," Candy smiled at him through cigarette-stained teeth.

"Thanks anyway, Candy," he answered, picking up the coffee and sliding a five-dollar bill onto the table. "It's worth it to me."

Rod hurried over where Hank was waiting at the door.

"Howdy," Hank said, extending his right hand. "Name's Hank, and I can take you as far as Pellston."

"Hi Hank, I'm Rod," he said, taking the trucker's hand. "That'll be fine. I sure appreciate it."

Rod followed Hank to a International Cabover in back of the restaurant. They climbed in, and Hank fired the powerful diesel engine. He shifted the transmission into two-high, eased out the clutch, and they started rolling across the parking lot. Hank looked both ways at the exit to the highway, then wheeled the truck into a wide, right turn and pressed down on the accelerator.

"Where ya headed, Rod?" Hank asked idly, as he ratcheted through the gears.

"Petoskey," Rod lied. "I've got relatives there."

Hank guided the big rig expertly into the semitruck tollbooth at the entrance to the Mackinac Bridge, and paid the toll. He pulled away, muttering about the increasing cost of using this thoroughfare, the rising price of diesel fuel, and unfair taxes on truckers in general.

Before they'd reached the center of the bridge, Rod was scanning the maintenance vehicles parked at its center through his binoculars.

Hank thought that was curious, but he didn't think it was worth conversation.

There it was, the Ford van he was looking for, and it was wearing the correct license plate. It had signs on it now, though.

They reached the center of the bridge, a hundred yards past where the suspect van was parked, and Rod said abruptly, "Hank I've got to get out here."

Hank look surprised. "I can't stop in the middle of the bridge," he objected.

"You don't have to stop, just slow down . . . let me jump out."

Rod made the decision for him by opening his door and starting out.

"Wait a minute," Hank exclaimed, stepping on the brake. It was an automatic response, something anyone would have done if their passenger threatened to jump from a moving vehicle. Rod was counting on that, and it was all the pause that he needed. The eighteen-wheeler was still moving at about fifteen miles an hour. With his backpack in one hand, Rod leaped forward from its running board onto a pile of painter's canvasses. He sure hoped they weren't covering anything sharp and hard.

They weren't. He landed on the piled tarpaulins with enough force to knock the air from his lungs, but the impact was soft. He rolled onto his feet with an agility that he didn't know he still possessed. Only two of the workers had actually witnessed his stunt, and they looked astonished.

"Quick!" Rod said in an even voice that was loud enough to be heard over the racket of running machinery. "Get everyone off this bridge right now. There are two guys planting a bomb on it right now. Get off immediately."

As he might have guessed, the two men just gawked at him. They didn't move. Rod snatched the hard hat off one of their heads, hoping that this might make him stand out less among the bridge workers. The hard hat was too large, it fell down over his ears. He held it in place against the perpetual wind, then he ran over to the white van he'd seen through the windshield of the truck.

The license plate matched, all right, but the side of the van read JACKSONVILLE PAINTING now. He peeled back one corner. It came off easily. Magnetic.

Rod asked the workers, one after another, if they'd seen anyone from Jacksonville Painting. The fifth person he asked said yes, they were under the span on chain-link fencing that was kept suspended there as a sort of scaffolding to support bridge workers. The worker said that they were down there doing some sort of inspection or something. He pointed south; one of them had gone down there.

Rod ran to where the man had pointed, not knowing that Aziz was closer, almost beneath his feet. Rod had a fear of heights, and his stomach was filled with butterflies just standing on the roadway this high above the Straits. But his natural fear of falling to his death was countered by a fear that tens of thousands of people might die if he didn't do something to stop these terrorists. He had to act, even if it cost him his life. He prayed fervently that it wouldn't.

Among the bridge workers, news of a bomb was slowly beginning to spread. His announcement hadn't caused a sudden panic, but rather a creeping fear. Some workers were already gathering their personal property and departing in company vehicles. As some left, more followed. Bridge patrol trucks were driving back and forth, the officers in them stopping to question departing workers about what was going on. Several times, he heard someone repeat the word "bomb."

Nobody seemed interested in what Rod was doing when he clambered over the bridge's guard rail. He was keenly conscious of his lack of a safety harness as he dropped onto the chain-link safety net. Rod's stomach did somersaults when he landed on his hands and knees, staring at the Straits four hundred feet below through wire mesh. When he looked up again, it was straight into the face of Peter Grigovich.

Grigovich was preoccupied with mounting his ammo-can bomb to the inside surface of an I-beam under the bridge's roadway, and keeping one eye on the safety boat below while he worked. The two-man crew of the safety boat typically paid no attention to the bridge workers above them, unless one hit the water. Then their job was to get the dead man or woman out of the water before someone had a chance to photograph the grotesque spectacle. Right now, the crew members were listening to a baseball game, and they'd barely glanced his way. Grigovich figured they wouldn't be able to see the details of what he was doing clearly through the chain-link mesh below him anyway.

Grigovich's task was made easier when some sort of commotion happened on the roadway above. The two workers who'd been on the mesh with him, forcing him to pretend that he was busy inspecting the structure, left in a hurry after receiving a message over a walkie-talkie.

Because of the din of machinery, he couldn't hear the message that had caused them to clamber topside, but he was glad for the chance to accomplish his task unobserved.

Then, this man with the loose-fitting safety helmet dropped onto the mesh just as he was applying the magnet to a main support. Grigovich didn't hear him, but rather felt the impact of his landing on the chain-link under his feet. Rod's hard hat had fallen over his eyes from the unstable force of his landing. He struggled to retain his balance while lifting the bill of the helmet from over his eyes.

Both men stared at each other for a brief moment as recognition set in. Grigovich was a powerfully built man, and Rod would be clearly overmatched in a hand-to-hand confrontation. With no time to strategize, Rod dove forward and tackled Grigovich at his waist. Both men tumbled off their feet and onto the mesh. Grigovich grasped Rod in a headlock; he was so strong that Rod feared he'd break his neck. Grappling with Grigovich was clearly a bad idea. Before the Bosnian could inflict serious damage, Rod grabbed his testicles and twisted. Grigovich was obviously stronger, but forty years of gripping an axe handle had left Rod with the forearm strength to crack walnuts in his bare hands.

The nuts he was cracking now were considerably softer. Grigovich howled and punched Rod hard between the eyes before he let go. Rod saw a bright splinter of light, and he felt hot blood run from his nose onto his upper lip. Both men rolled to their knees, then rose shakily to their feet. Both realized the futility of hand-to-hand combat on such unstable footing. Grigovich unzipped his coveralls and grabbed for the Desert Eagle pistol tucked into his waistband. Simultaneously, Rod reached under his jacket for the 9-millimeter stuck in his own belt.

There was no time to sight properly, but both men brought their guns to bear and fired instinctively from the hip—almost in unison. The bullets might have hit their marks, had it not been for the unstable mesh beneath them. The sudden motion caused both men to fire wide, and knocked Rod off his feet. The Beretta pistol slipped from his grasp when he bounced against the chain-link.

Grigovich grinned maliciously as he carefully drew a bead on his enemy a second time. Rod rolled onto all fours; his eyes went wide with fear, and he could almost feel the thud of a bullet as he waited for it to impact his body. Rod grabbed the chain-link tightly to get leverage and rolled his body out of line with the Bosnian's gun muzzle. His motion caused the chain-link to become a wave under Grigovich's feet, and he, too, fell onto his back.

As he struggled to regain his feet, the attempt hampered by his refusal to let go of his pistol, Rod sprang forward. He landed directly on Grigovich's body, and he heard the man exhale forcefully as the wind was knocked out of him. There was no time to retrieve his pistol. Or to reach the 32 automatic inside his backpack. Instead, his hand went instinctively to the Schrade Extreme survival knife on his belt, under his jacket. Without realizing he'd done it, Rod unsnapped the knife's retaining strap and drew the shiny, silver 420 stainless-steel blade.

Grigovich had just enough time to assume a look of horror before the blade sank hilt-deep into the soft spot of his solar plexus. Rod's full weight was behind the blow, and the stiletto-style blade easily pierced Grigovich's heart, stopping at the solid mass of his spine. Rod as quickly jerked the blade outward, and the backward-facing serrations along the spine of its blade tore bits of flesh and gore out with it. Grigovich started to scream in acknowledgment of his death, but the sound subsided to a gurgle of blood. Grigovich stared into Rod's eyes, and his last thought was that this must have been what Brenda Waukonigon felt before dying on Aziz's blade.

Rod just stared back in horror as the life went out of Grigovich's eyes. This was the second man he'd killed with a knife in as many days. Once again, he hadn't meant to do it; it was simply an automatic act of his subconscious. He'd reacted from pure survival instinct. For just a moment, Rod lay atop Grigovich's corpse filled with remorse, wishing with all his soul that he could undo what he'd just done.

The commotion must have attracted attention from above, because he felt a vibration on the chain-link, and when he turned, there was a bridge patrol officer behind him. The officer was wearing a safety harness, and he wasn't prepared for the sight he encountered. The officer reached for his holstered weapon, but the speed of his draw was slowed in that position. Rod, spurred by fear, and still in self-preservation mode, dove forward before the officer could draw, grabbing his safety harness in one hand. The other hand pressed the tip of his survival knife hard against the underside of the officer's chin. The silver blade was smeared with fresh blood.

The officer's eyes went wide, and he put his hands in the air, his gun still in the holster but unsnapped. On his other hip he wore a Taser.

"Take it easy, dude," the officer said. "We can work this out."

Rod grinned in spite of himself at the bridge cop's obvious law-enforcement training. It was amazing how easily telling lies came to these fucking servants of the people. Letting go of the officer's harness but keeping the knife pressed hard enough to convince him not to resist, Rod deftly flipped the Glock 40-caliber out of its holster and over the edge of the chain-link. Then he did the same with the Taser.

Real fear came into the cop's eyes when he was disarmed. He felt truly helpless now. Rod added to his insecurity by handcuffing the officer's hands behind his back with his own handcuffs.

Next, Rod conducted a quick search for the bomb that he knew was there somewhere. He didn't have much time to find it; that was pretty clear. And he didn't know what it looked like; he wasn't sure he'd recognize a bomb even if he saw it. If he did locate it, what did he know about disarming any explosive device? His entire strategy consisted of throwing the thing into the Straits below.

The bridge cop made the decision for him. He started screaming, "Help! Help!" at the top of his lungs. He was heard over the racket. A moment later, several faces appeared, peering over the railing.

Rod resheathed the Schrade and automatically snapped its retaining strap—even without giving it a conscious thought, his knife was his most valued survival tool. Then he picked up Grigovich's Desert Eagle and the 9-millimeter Beretta he'd dropped. He held one in each hand for only a moment before tossing the Beretta over the edge. Fifty caliber was better than 9-millimeter, and he might need all the stopping power he could get. He found two loaded spare magazines in one of Grigovich's pockets, the same way he had with McBraden.

"Look," the handcuffed cop said, still spouting police academy rhetoric, "you can't just walk away from this. Give yourself up now, and maybe we can work something out."

Rod just grinned at him humorlessly, and then climbed over the man, and shimmied up the cop's harness rope to the bridge railing. Nearly all of the few people still left on the bridge had witnessed what had happened below, and none of them was willing to be a hero against a man who was armed, and who had already killed someone. They were painters and welders by trade, and the armed bridge officer someone had summoned had apparently been subdued by this killer.

Rod was aware that the people who were keeping their distance from him feared him, but there was at least one more terrorist on the loose, and he was the most dangerous of the four. He'd never forget that man's face, the face of the killer who'd mutilated, then murdered, poor Sue Morgan, and who'd tried twice to shoot him. This man, whoever he was, needed to be exterminated for the good of everyone. Rod had never felt that way about another human being, not even in his felonious youth, but this man had to be stopped—permanently.

Chapter Twenty-Five

Planting a Bomb

Aziz drove to the second bridge tower, almost a mile from where he'd dropped Grigovich, without incident. The bridge authority officer, who'd stopped them when they'd first arrived, was probably sidetracked by all the preparations that were being made for the governor's appearance, less than twenty-four hours from now. Aziz had no doubt that he'd called the number for Jacksonville Painting, and that he'd gotten the answering machine—he wouldn't have been much of a cop if he hadn't done at least that much. But with all the uproar the day before the annual Bridge Walk, he probably wouldn't have had the time, or the inclination, to follow up as thoroughly as he might have under normal circumstances.

Aziz descended from the bridge's second tower to the chain-link scaffolding below the roadway without attracting attention from anyone. Every person seemed busy working his or her own agenda, and no one paid him any mind. Even the trio of men who were spraying primer onto the underside of the structure didn't give him more than a second glance. He hoped Grigovich was being equally ignored.

The three men spraying primer were probably curious, but the respirators they were wearing, and the clatter and hiss of compressors, made normal conversation impossible. Aziz pretended to be inspecting the bridge supports until they all left to take a break topside, then he went to work.

First, he found a niche in a main support I-beam that was out of sight, in a place on the beam's opposite side that couldn't be seen without actively looking for it. It was a portion of the substructure that had already been freshly painted, and not likely to be seen again in the next twenty-four hours, unless someone were actively looking for the bomb he was going to plant there.

Aziz opened the ammunition box's lid, exposing the foil-wrapped C4 that surrounded the sphere of plutonium at the container's center. From an inside pocket in his coveralls he removed a small, foam-lined plastic box containing four match-type, electrically-detonated blasting caps, their detonator wires carefully shorted together to prevent accidental detonation.

Using a screwdriver from his tool belt, Aziz punctured the foil wrap of the plastic explosive near the four corners of the ammo can. He drove each hole about three inches deep. Then, he gently inserted the four blasting caps into each hole, so that only their detonating wires protruded. He carefully separated the wires, then twisted them together, one wire from each cap, in two sets of four. Finally, he twisted the bared end of a six-inch length of wire to the ends of each set of detonator wires, then wound the opposite ends of the two wires to a pair of screw terminals that had been electrically connected to the ringer of a Tracphone cellular telephone.

Aziz was sweating; he didn't like this part. He'd assembled and planted dozens of explosive devices—mostly IEDs for use against American military personnel in Iraq and Afghanistan—and he'd never gotten past having a case of anxiety whenever he armed one of them. More than a couple of his childhood friends had vaporized themselves during this critical stage of the process, and it scared him to think that he might join them one day. He recalled a class he'd taken in college, probability analysis, which had taught him that the more times someone performed any task, the greater the likelihood of a mistake. Every bomb he set brought him closer to the inevitable, and that frightened him.

When he'd made all the electrical connections, he turned on the telephone and placed it atop the blocks of C4 in the box. He closed the lid and latched it securely. The last step was to mount the six-inch-square, novelty magnet in his pocket to the bridge support, and then simply stick the ammo can onto the magnet. After that, all it would take was a phone call to the Tracphone's number to cause detonation. Aziz grinned to himself; ten little digits were all that it would take to destroy thousands of unsuspecting Americans.

That reminded him to call Grigovich, to see how he was progressing with setting his bomb. He was gratified to see that the bar graph on his phone showed near-maximum signal strength. He should have no trouble triggering the bombs whenever he wanted from anywhere.

Grigovich's telephone rang and rang. Aziz counted the rings; after five of them, it was answered by a male voice that didn't belong to his partner. "Hello," the mystery voice said. When Aziz didn't answer, the voice said, "Who is this?"

Aziz pushed the END button immediately. That stupid Bosnian bastard had been caught. He was compromised. The entire mission was compromised. It was a matter of time before they found the other bomb, if he'd even been able to plant it. Now that the authorities were sure to be alerted to a potential threat, they'd scour the entire structure until they found the ammo can.

The survival instructor was behind this; he knew it. He regretted everything that had happened on the Betsy River. Not because he felt remorseful for any of the killings—he'd kind of enjoyed that part—but because of all the trouble and delay that had come from it. This mission had been so well planned; it had cost so much in time, training, and money; and then it had begun to unravel from the seams as soon as they'd reached Whitefish Point. And all because Grigovich had been so stupid; his trigger finger had always been quicker than his mind.

Grigovich might also have been mentally dim enough to simply give himself away—that was why he'd been teamed with Richarde when they'd begun. He didn't think that was what had happened, though. He was more inclined to think that this was all the doing of that survival instructor. If there was one aspect of this rapidly disintegrating mission that he did regret, it was having missed the son of a bitch when he'd had him in his sights. This survival instructor might be ex-Special Forces or something. He was good. Or maybe he was just lucky. Whatever he was, he'd ruined the best-laid plans of Aziz and his team of highly trained experts.

Fortunately, Aziz had a backup plan for everything. He'd come here to kill Americans, and by Holy Allah, he was going to kill Americans.

Chapter Twenty-Six

Ignored Warning

Rod Elliot wasn't ex-Special Forces. He wasn't ex-law enforcement. All he could claim to be was an ex-con. Before that, as a teenager, he'd served a year in the United States Navy as a gunner's mate technician. That was at the end of the Vietnam War, and he'd only joined the navy because he was afraid the draft would be reinstated, and they'd take him for the army. When the war ended, the navy was only too willing to let him out voluntarily with a general discharge.

Aside from having a natural talent and some training with firearms and ordnance, he didn't feel like he was anything special. Quite the contrary; he was feeling very much like a broken-down, old woodsman. His joints and muscles ached, and he felt very tired. Some of it was, no doubt, a result of coming down off the Dexxies, but he felt every year and every trauma of his life today. He'd been pushing himself beyond his body's limits for three days now. Not only was he physically played out, but he was mentally traumatized from the blood that was on his hands. There truly was blood on his hands, literally and figuratively, and it wouldn't wipe off.

There was also blood on his face. The big man he'd killed had hit him as hard as he'd ever been slugged. When he'd gingerly touched the bridge of his nose between a forefinger and thumb, the pain had been excruciating. It was probably broken; he could already feel pressure from both eyes swelling. At least the swelling had slowed the blood gushing from his nostrils.

Despite his pain, Rod almost laughed at the way everyone on the bridge backed away from his approach when he climbed up. Of course, he did have a 50-caliber pistol stuck into his waistband. He opened the driver's door of a four-wheel-drive Dodge utility truck, unopposed by whomever it had belonged to, and threw his backpack onto the passenger side.

He didn't know which way to go, and he didn't have a destination in mind, but he knew for sure that he was toast if he stayed here. An ex-con survival instructor, who'd killed at least one man with a knife, overpowered an officer of the law, and who was heavily armed. Geez, his situation was growing worse by the hour. Based on what their computers told them, the cops would shoot him down like a dog.

Then he spotted the white panel van he was looking for. Its headlights faced southward, toward him. There was no front license plate—they weren't required in Michigan—but he recognized the JACKSONVILLE PAINTING logo on its side; it was the same logo he'd seen on the big terrorist's coveralls. A man climbed up from below the roadway. He swung himself over the railing and loped toward the van's driver's side door. Even at a distance, Rod recognized him as the last terrorist.

The bridge cop below was still shouting, but his words were unintelligible over the racket of machinery that had been left running. Rod leaned out the truck window and raised his own voice to the handful of people who were still on the roadway. There were always a few idiots who refused to evacuate until it was too late.

"Get off the bridge. There's a bomb somewhere down there." He jerked a thumb down toward the roadway. "Somebody call the bomb squad."

About half the people still on the bridge ran in a panic for their vehicles when they heard the word "bomb." The other half just stood still, staring dumbly—like sheep. Rod shook his head in disbelief. He was reminded of the crowd of gawkers who'd ignored the warnings to stay back, and then had to flee for their lives when the first World Trade Center tower collapsed. Rod shook his head again. Pathetic. He doubted that anyone here would report the bomb.

He started the Dodge one-ton. Its big V-8 engine rumbled to life immediately. He pushed the stick shift into first gear and let out the clutch fast enough to make the rear tires squeal. Workers who'd remained on the bridge scattered out of his path as he wheeled the truck over the steel median, and into the northbound lane. Near the tollbooths at the bridge's north end, he could see flashing lights. State police and bridge authority vehicles were blocking traffic into or out of the Upper Peninsula at the tollbooths. But they weren't actually doing anything; they were just blocking the road.

They probably had orders to shoot him on sight, but still Rod shifted his stolen truck through its gears as he sped toward them and the terrorist. The terrorist must have seen him too, and he accelerated out of his parking place to head southward, coming toward Rod fast in the opposite lane. As they neared each other, Rod tried to think of the best way to stop the white van. He had to do something fast, so when there was a hundred yards separating the two vehicles, Rod cranked the wheel hard left; the Dodge bounced over the raised median and into the van's path.

It didn't work. As soon as Rod had committed himself to driving across the median, the driver of the van had done the same. Rod was still fighting the wheel, trying to regain control of the lumbering truck, when the van passed him, heading south in the northbound lane.

"Goddamn it," Rod cussed. He pulled the steering wheel hard right again, and braced himself for a bouncing ride over the median. This time he lost control, and both drivers' side tires impacted the curb. The truck went up on two wheels, and a chill ran down his spine as he looked over the guard railing.

When the truck fell back onto all four wheels, Rod gunned the accelerator. His asshole felt puckered, but soon his fear had evolved into anger. He was scared, and that made him mad. When he caught up with that son of a bitch in the van, he was gonna kill him.

The road was clear, but there was a bridge authority truck and a squad car from the Mackinaw City Police Department parked across the exit to Interstate 75. Two more squad cars blocked the exits leading into Mackinaw City.

Rod wasn't surprised when the white van he was pursuing accelerated into the bridge authority truck and the squad car, parked nose-to-nose like they were posing for an adventure movie. The heavy Ford Econoline van split the roadblock easily, probably making both of the blocking vehicles undrivable, and then kept going. Rod flew through the opening a second later, sideswiping the squad car again. He couldn't suppress a grim chuckle; the fleeing officers actually had the audacity to look surprised that their roadblock had failed.

It wouldn't be so funny next time, he knew. The small-town police had been caught by surprise. When they regrouped, it would be in force, and with blood in their eyes. They'd been caught off guard and embarrassed this time. But now, they'd likely be out for revenge as much as justice.

The white van peeled off on the first exit it came to, and headed down Trailsend Road, toward Big Stone Bay on Lake Michigan. Before it got to Lake Michigan, the driver turned abruptly onto a dirt two-track that led to French Farm Lake. Rod knew this road from many years ago, and he knew this section of Mackinaw State Forest. At least he used to. He hoped it hadn't changed too much in the past few years.

The narrow roller-coaster road they were on split up ahead; one fork went to a primitive campground on the east end of French Farm Lake, the other ran the length of the lake to a beaver pond and a creek at its western end. To the south was Carp River, a beautiful little tributary of nearby Carp Lake, where he'd camped many times in his youth. Whichever fork the terrorist took, it was a dead end.

He was glad the road came to a dead end, because the heavy suspension of the big Dodge he was driving didn't allow Rod to drive as fast as the van he was chasing. The terrorist was pulling away from him, but he couldn't drive any faster; he was bouncing into the truck's ceiling now. The van took the right fork, the long one leading back to the beaver dam. It was more than three miles long, if Rod remembered correctly. Michigan's Department of Natural Resources had filled in the mud holes he remembered, so that even cars could negotiate that two-track. Even so, his top speed driving it was no more than ten miles an hour.

In the van, Aziz smiled to see his pursuer steadily becoming smaller in his rearview mirror. With one hand, he withdrew a cell phone from a button-down shirt pocket under his coveralls. He pushed the speed-dial button, and then punched a single digit on its keypad.

Chapter Twenty-Seven

Murder on the Bridge

Colyer had been driving back to the Sault when his car radio informed him that there was a commotion on the Mackinac Bridge. In fact, it sounded like it was a goddamned disaster. Radio traffic was, of course, cryptic, to help stymie the hundreds of citizens who routinely monitored police calls on a Radio Shack scanner.

It didn't appear that Central Dispatch was all that clear about the details, anyway, but the woman on the mike seemed agitated. Whatever was happening had caused enough uproar to close the bridge to all traffic. That alone made it a big deal.

Colyer rummaged through the Charger's glove box for the magnetic-mount red strobe that identified his vehicle as a police car, and stuck it to the roof. He seldom used the thing; he hoped that it still worked. The light responded with bright flashes of red when he plugged it into the receptacle. He stuck it onto his roof and sped toward Saint Ignace. He looked at the digital clock on his car's CD player; almost 2 AM. It would be another forty minutes before he got there, even if he drove like a madman, and a deer or moose didn't jump out in front of him.

During the long drive, Colyer mulled over again what had happened so far, trying to put it all together into a cogent picture. It had all begun with that unusual incident with the diesel submarine off the coast of Canada, he was certain of it. The abandoned Zodiac boat at Whitefish

Point probably had something to do with whoever the submarine had delivered to the east coast of Canada. The abandoned Zodiac also had some connection to whoever had committed the murders on the Betsy River. But what was Rod Elliot's connection to all of this?

Colyer tended to think that Elliot's part in all of this was purely incidental: He'd simply been in the wrong place at the wrong time. But local police seemed to have a hard-on for anyone who'd done time in a penitentiary. A belief that he'd be blamed for what had happened would cause a man to avoid reporting what had happened, and Rod's silence wasn't helping anyone put together an intelligent picture of what was going on. Colyer really needed to know what Rod Elliot knew, and why this survival instructor should have apparently taken up with the men who'd landed on Whitefish Point.

Or was he pursuing them? If that were the case, then why? Colyer's time with Rod's wife Shannon hadn't led him to believe that the man was any kind of hero. If anything, he was a bit antisocial and introverted; a man who'd seen enough trouble in his life to want to avoid more. Not the kind of man who'd risk his own life by chasing after known killers.

Unless he thought he had a good reason. Maybe he was trying to clear himself. Maybe he believed that he was in a corner. No man was more dangerous than when he thought he was cornered, and no man was more likely to act illogically than when he could see no way out of a predicament. That sounded like a profile that might fit Rod Elliot's behavior. If Elliot thought that he had nothing to lose, he could be a danger to outlaw and lawman alike.

When Colyer arrived at the Mackinac Bridge, the scene he encountered was one of sheer anarchy. Interstate 75 was roadblocked at the first exit to Saint Ignace on the northbound side, and all the tollbooths at the bridge were blocked by police vehicles. He was stopped by a state trooper there for just a moment, but the trooper acknowledged his ID without an argument, thankfully. He suggested that Colyer could find a place to park at the visitor center. Colyer took his advice. Then he stepped out of the Charger to take stock of the situation.

"Who's in charge here?" he asked a state trooper who was hurrying by.

"Captain Jameson. Over there," the trooper said, pointing his index finger at a tall, gray-haired man who looked to be in his mid-sixties and stretched thin at the moment. He was surrounded by lesser-ranking officers, who all seemed to be asking him questions at the same time.

Colyer walked over and introduced himself, brushing past the crowd of querulous troopers. There appeared to be no time for politeness, and rank had its privileges.

"Captain Jameson, I'm Special Agent Thomas Colyer of the FBI," he said, extending his right hand.

Jameson shook his hand, glad to be interrupted, and sorry, for once, to be the person in charge. "I'm Ed Jameson, Agent Colyer. How can I be of service to the FBI?"

"Just bring me up to speed about what occurred here, sir," Colyer said.

Jameson told Colyer what he knew. It wasn't much. He related the story of the failed roadblock; how the two vehicles that had managed to smash through it had then eluded the rest of the surprised police long enough to disappear, probably onto one of the many side roads that led into Mackinaw State Forest. How at least one of the escapees had stabbed a man to death on the scaffolding below the bridge's roadway. Jameson described the horrific stab wound in detail, the way there'd been bits of the victim's heart muscle found outside the wound on the man's clothing. Jameson seemed more than repulsed by the nature of the crime.

Colyer was thinking more clearly—or maybe he was just more calloused from what he'd already seen in the past twenty-four hours. He requested to see the body, which had thankfully already been removed from the scaffolding—Colyer really hated heights. No one had identified the victim yet, but they were sure that he wasn't on the list of maintenance personnel who were cleared to work on the bridge. How he'd gained access to the scaffolding under the bridge, what he'd been doing there, and why he'd been killed were some of the questions Jameson and his men were looking to answer.

Jameson led Colyer into the state police plaza at the northwest end of the bridge. There, in a conference room turned temporary morgue, was the body of Peter Grigovich, laid-out, naked on a collapsible Stryker cot. Colyer pulled back the purple sheet that covered the cadaver's head and inspected the single knife wound in its chest. Jameson was right; it was a terrible and obviously fatal wound. At one of the narrow edges of the wound, flesh had been pulled outward.

Colyer tried to envision the blade that would have caused such a wound. It would have had backward-facing serrations along the blade's spine. This type of serration would resist being withdrawn when it was stabbed deeply into flesh. Yet, it seemed to have penetrated easily. Not a dirk or dagger that was designed for use as a weapon. Maybe a survival-type knife, one with a serrated back that was meant to work as a saw.

It also didn't fit the profile that the victim had been stabbed only once. Most knife murders, both premeditated and crimes of passion, involved multiple stab wounds. Whether he (or she) meant to be so precise or not, the single stab wound in this man's chest was perfectly sited to cause immediate death. It had probably been inflicted by someone who knew how to render the victim harmless with one blow.

"Well?" Colyer looked up. Jameson was staring into his eyes. He seemed genuinely anxious to hear the FBI agent's thoughts.

Colyer replaced the sheet. He looked pensively at Jameson.

"Well, it was efficient, no doubt about that. The assailant seemed to know what he intended to accomplish."

"You think it was premeditated, then?"

"I think it was intentional. Do you have any idea of what the motive might have been?"

"No," Jameson said, looking at the floor. "We haven't even identified the body yet. What we do know is that he wasn't cleared to be where he was when he was killed."

"Was there anyone with him?"

"There was one man, middle-aged, gray beard. He overpowered the bridge patrol officer who rappelled down to investigate, and then he escaped in a welder's truck. We're pretty sure he was driving one of the vehicles that ran the roadblock. We think he's the one who did the stabbing. We know he's armed and dangerous, but we don't have an identity on him, either."

The man that Jameson was calling armed and dangerous was Rod Elliot, Colyer was sure. And this man laid out on the cot before him was almost certainly one of the men who'd landed at Whitefish Point. He didn't have enough evidence to make more than an educated guess about anything, but it was pretty clear to him that Elliot wasn't in cahoots with these guys.

"I'd like to inspect the site where this man was stabbed," Colyer said.

Jameson nodded compliance, and led him out of the room. Colyer was glad to leave; this room was starting to give him the proverbial creeps. They walked outside the building and Jameson said, "I'll see if I can find an officer to drive you onto the bridge. That way you'll go right to the correct place . . . it'll save you having to look for it."

The scene he'd wanted to investigate revealed itself to him almost as soon as they'd walked out to the parking lot. As Colyer and Jameson watched in astonishment, the far tower was engulfed in a ball of red flame and black smoke. The roadway around it heaved upward in a massive wave, as if it were flexible, and then shattered into huge chunks of asphalt and steel that flew outward and upward from the structure. Trucks and cars flew upward in slow motion, and then tumbled back downward into the Straits below. He saw the bodies of people fly outward, too, and his gut wrenched as he watched them cartwheel downward to the water. Then the shock wave and noise hit them, traveling at the speed of sound. Colyer could actually feel the heat of the blast on his face, felt his hair blown back from its force. The earth trembled under his feet, and he took a step backward from the push of a tremendous shock wave.

"Oh my God . . ." Jameson stuttered.

"Holy fuck," Colyer exclaimed in spite of himself.

Winds cleared away the smoke in less than a minute, leaving a scene of carnage and destruction that was only too visible to Colyer from more than two miles away.

"Oh my God," Jameson repeated.

Screw waiting for an officer. Colyer ran up to a patrol car and ordered the officer to get in and drive him to the scene. The officer, with a dazed look on his face, looked askance at Jameson. Colyer shoved him out of the way and seated himself behind the steering wheel of the already running car. He threw the transmission into gear and punched the accelerator pedal. The cruiser's powerful V-8 engine responded with a low growl and a squeal of rubber on asphalt.

Chapter Twenty-Eight

Through the Woods

Rod heard the explosion from more than five miles away. Even in the deep forest, it rumbled and shook the earth with a vibration that he felt through the truck's steering wheel. The boom sent a chill like ice water down his spine because he knew that one of the bombs that McBraden had told him about had exploded. That was the sound of people dying, and knowing that filled him with a remorse equal to any he'd ever known.

When Rod caught up with the van, it was abandoned at the end of the two-track. He remembered the years before the Department of Natural Resources had decided to improve this road with bulldozers to make it more accessible to the telephone workers who maintained the underground line it paralleled. Before that, it had required a pretty gnarly four-wheel-drive to reach this dam, where French Farm Creek exited from the lake's western end and drained into Lake Michigan. It was ironic that now a car could not only get through, it could actually outrun a truck because its whipped-cream suspension absorbed bumps more gently. Rod rubbed the back of his neck; he'd probably gotten whiplash from bashing his head into the Dodge's ceiling so many times on the way here.

He didn't pull up next to the van. As soon as he'd broken into the clearing where it was parked, he jammed the accelerator to the mat and braced himself against the steering wheel. The brush-guarded, front end of the truck hit the van on its side, crushing the panel door and actually pushing the vehicle sideways onto two wheels. If the man he was chasing had hopes of hiding inside and ambushing Rod when he pulled up, Rod wanted to throw a monkey wrench into that strategy.

Almost before the truck had stopped moving, Rod was out the door with the 50-caliber Desert Eagle in his fist. Using the truck door for concealment—he knew that a bullet would punch right through it—he waited several long minutes while he scrutinized the van and the woods around the parking area intently. He'd taken too many deer to make the mistake of being the first one to expose himself. He kept the gun's Tritium sights in front of his eyes wherever he looked, his trigger finger ready to squeeze off an aimed round at anything that moved.

Nothing moved. Not in the van, not in the woods. Robins resumed their chirping, and frogs started croaking again. He let out a long exhalation—how long had he been holding his breath? He ran around to the opposite side of the van and jerked the door open, ready to shoot anything that stirred inside. No movement. Whoever had been inside had left; Rod hoped that there had only been one person.

The van had been pushed a foot sideways when he'd rammed it. The tires on the driver's side were still about two inches in the air. When he looked at the ground, he could see where the driver had opened the door and jumped out just before Rod had arrived. The grass had twisted under the man's feet as he spun about and ran for the woods along the North Country Trail. There had been only one person in the van. That made him feel a little better; the last two days had taken a lot out of him, and he dreaded taking on multiple opponents.

The trail beyond French Farm Creek was hiking only, and as such, it wasn't used much—there weren't a lot of backpackers in a world of dirt bikes and ATVs—so the man he was chasing couldn't avoid leaving a discernible trail. His would probably be the only tracks on it.

Rod studied the trail closely for about fifty yards, almost willing it to reveal personal characteristics about the man he was tracking. One hundred-forty pounds, size 9 shoe. The tread identified the boot as a Timberland Chorocura hiking boot—not top of the line, but definitely a boot that he'd recommend for the backcountry; Rod had a pair of them at home. The man's stride showed a tendency to walk heel-toe, typical of someone who spends a lot of time walking in the city, on flat surfaces. He lacked the loose, duck-footed gait of an experienced woodsman; he occasionally caught his toe against exposed tree roots and other natural protuberances. His rearmost heel came down first, and he rolled straight forward onto the ball of his foot when he walked; he was off-balance, unused to rugged terrain.

There was a difference in the depth of the boot prints from when the man first disembarked from the van, and when he shouldered his bag. About thirty pounds, maybe a little more, Rod figured. Pretty heavy for a clumsy shoulder bag in the backwoods, and especially if the objective was to move fast away from pursuers. Rod's own full-size backpack carried everything he needed to survive indefinitely, and it would have tipped the scales at less than twenty pounds. This man was loaded heavy, and Rod doubted that he was lugging food and shelter. He cringed to think what the man might be carrying.

He seemed to know where he was going, too. After a quarter-mile of meandering generally southward, the trail intersected another that ran east and west. The woods were swampy and shaded back there, but Rod's pursuee didn't miss a beat, he turned right without a pause. He wasn't running blindly; this guy knew where he was going, and he doubtless had a plan. He must've had a map. Or maybe he was from around here; Rod didn't like the thought of that.

After another quarter-mile, he made a hard left, onto the North Country Trail. Three miles from the Carp River. Almost no one hiked this hilly, swampy trail, even though that was the purpose for which it existed. Most locals were afraid of it, because if you needed medical assistance in the middle of it, you were going to wait a while. It was routinely patrolled at either end to keep dirt bikes and ATVs from tearing it up, but the miles in between were mostly ignored by authorities. Hardly anybody wanted to chance running into trouble that far back in a wilderness.

The guy Rod was following was moving fast. Too fast. Rod could barely keep up with him, let alone catch him. The going was made slower because he had to be constantly alert for any sign that the man he chased might have left the trail to lie in ambush. Rod had killed more than a few whitetails along this trail; if it were easy to ambush a deer, it would be doubly simple to bushwhack a man. That was the greatest danger of man-tracking, and it had happened more than a few times. A tracker who trailed any dangerous or wounded game needed to keep his attention divided, yet keenly focused on his surroundings at all times.

The plus side was that this guy would almost certainly stick to the trail; the woods were thick here, and there was no access to the Carp River until he'd nearly reached Cecil Bay Road, where it crossed. There was nothing but a scattering of houses along Cecil Bay Road for miles in either direction. He seemed to have a map of the trail system, judging by his apparent sureness, but he was miles from what most people would consider civilization. Where was he going?

The call of crows echoed from up ahead, and a flock of the big, black birds rose above the treetops about a mile down the trail. They'd probably been feeding together, probably on a deer carcass, when something had suddenly spooked them. If Rod had been a betting man, he'd wager, two to one, that the birds had fled at the approach of the man he was chasing.

Then the tracks abruptly turned off to the right, deep into the swamp. The sight prompted Rod to dive off the trail on its opposite side. His stomach felt tight as he lay prone behind a moss-covered knoll. The 50-caliber was gripped tightly in his sweaty fist as he peered into the shadows. At any second he expected a fusillade of bullets to come his way. He watched and listened carefully, because it wasn't impossible that an attack could come from behind him.

When nothing happened after several endless minutes, he crept quietly through the shaded woods parallel to the trail for about fifty yards, keeping to cover as much as he could. Nothing. No movement or noises that were out of the ordinary; just the sounds of squirrels and birds going about their business without regard to a foreign presence.

He'd been had. The man's footprints came out of the woods and back onto the trail just a few yards ahead of where he rejoined the path himself. The man Rod was pursuing had used this ploy to delay him and to lengthen his own lead. He must have feared that Rod was catching up to him. He seemed to be tiring.

Back on the trail, Rod pushed himself even harder to regain the precious few minutes he'd lost. His whole body hurt, especially his feet and hips. He'd been pushing himself hard, and his strength had long ago been expended. All that he had left was a toughness borne of many years of knowing increasing pain from arthritis and a generally aging body. He popped two more of the Dexedrine tablets he'd appropriated, and added three ibuprofen caplets to take the edge off. He washed them down with the last swig from his water bottle. He shook the emptied container balefully; he had to find water soon. He was sweating like a pig, and a bladder infection was the least he could expect from dehydration.

When the man's tracks turned off into the woods again, Rod made a quick decision to ignore them, counting on the action to be another trick. He broke into a clumsy lope; his feet ached, his knees hurt, and his hips sent sharp pains through him at every step. He wanted to get some distance from the point where the tracks turned into the woods, just in case this wasn't just another attempt to slow him down.

Rod gambled wrong this time. He caught a movement from the side of trail opposite where the tracks had gone into the woods. It was followed by a flash of light and the report of a gunshot. Rod felt the bullet hit him, heard the thud of it hitting something solid. He felt no pain, but he fell to the side of the trail, opposite from where the bullet had come. He rolled purposely to the trunk of a large white pine, and got to his knees behind the trunk. His left hand still gripped the 50-caliber; he hadn't lost the gun.

A man burst from the bushes and onto the trail. His feet pounded the dusty path, raising small clouds as he ran fast in the direction he'd been going before he'd laid this ambush. Almost by itself, Rod's pistol pointed at the fleeing man and squeezed off a round. He missed, and the running man disappeared around a bend in the trail.

After the man had gone, Rod wondered how badly he'd been wounded. There was no pain, but he'd heard and felt a bullet hit him. He'd never been shot before, but he'd read accounts of people who'd received serious, even fatal gunshot wounds without feeling any pain. He unshouldered his backpack, and then ran his hands over his entire body, feeling for wet spots, and looking at his hands from time to time. He found no blood. It appeared that he hadn't been hit at all.

But the bullet had struck something. He looked at his backpack. Sure enough, there was a neat, round hole in one side of the main sack where a bullet had entered, then a frayed, outward hole on the other side where it had exited. Casualties inside the pack consisted of his first-aid kit and the blade of his Power Eagle survival knife. The blade hadn't broken, but there was a hole through its sheath and a circular mark on it where a bullet had impacted.

For just a moment, Rod counted his lucky stars. Then anger replaced fear; this was the third time this murdering son of a bitch had tried to kill him in the past two days. Rod didn't know where he was heading, or if the Mackinac Bridge had been saved or not, but this guy was a stone-cold killer, and he'd ruined Rod's life. He needed to be put down as much as any rabid animal.

Chapter Twenty-Nine

Aftermath

When Colyer braked the cruiser as near as he dared to the broken edges of the bridge's roadway, the scene was ugly and chaotic. Dead bodies littered the roadway, some with missing limbs, many burned black. As awful as the scene before him looked, he couldn't help thinking that it could have been far worse if the bomb had detonated in the midst of the Labor Day Bridge Walk. He came to the awful realization that that was when it had been intended to go off. He didn't know why yet, but this explosion was premature; something had forced the bomber's hand.

Several police officers were already on the scene, trying to bring order to a situation that couldn't be brought to order. He turned as the scream of an ambulance siren warned of its approach to the tollbooths at the bridge's northern end. A patrol car backed up to let it through. The ambulance slowed down only slightly as it shot through the tollbooth. It sped along the broken bridge's roadway and stopped about ten yards from where Colyer had parked. Colyer wondered just how much the explosion had damaged the substructure. Could the added weight of emergency and law-enforcement vehicles cause more of the roadbed to cave in?

As if to answer his unspoken question, a hundred square yards at the bridge's center gave out with a low groan and broke free, plunging toward the Straits below, taking a half-dozen vehicles with it. It struck the water with such an impact that Colyer could feel the vibration through his feet. He watched in horror, praying that there hadn't been people on that section when it collapsed.

Another cruiser squealed to a stop next to Colyer's, and Jameson jumped from the passenger door.

"Oh my God," he said yet again. "What the hell happened?"

Colyer just looked at him and didn't answer. It was obviously a rhetorical question.

Without a word, Colyer got into the cruiser and drove back to where his own car was parked. He drove the Charger, its roof-mounted light still flashing, back to within a hundred yards of the edge of the caved-in roadway. He exited the car carrying a small briefcase, which he sat on the hood of his car. Inside the case were a number of forensic instruments, like a tape measure, pocket microscope, and instant glue for raising fingerprints. On a hunch, he removed a small rectangular device that resembled a large, handheld calculator and turned it on. A lighted panel of digital numerals appeared. He faced the direction of the explosion and waved the instrument through the air in front of him.

The Geiger counter went wild. Its digital display showed a variation of radiation that measured from several hundred micro-Sieverts to more than a thousand. One Sievert was enough to cause a victim's gums to bleed and his hair to fall out. More than one Sievert could be fatal. The effects became worse the longer a victim was exposed.

Colyer knew that this situation had to be handled prudently, and by someone with more political horsepower than he wielded. Right now, though, he was thinking more as a human being than as an FBI agent when he decided that his first priority was to get everyone off the bridge. Including himself.

Colyer turned to Jameson and said, "Captain, we have to get everyone off the bridge. Right now."

"Why?" Jameson asked, looking into Colyer's eyes suspiciously. "What do you think is going to happen? Is there another bomb?"

"I don't know," Colyer answered truthfully. "There might be. In any case, I'm assuming responsibility for this incident until someone who outranks me arrives on the scene. And, right now, I want everyone who's still alive off this bridge."

Jameson knew that Colyer wasn't telling him the whole truth. He'd been a cop for more than twenty years, and he hadn't bucked his way up through the ranks by having dull instincts. The state of Michigan had been granted full authority over the operation and upkeep of the bridge itself, but this was also an interstate highway, and the explosion was clearly an act of terrorism. That put it squarely under the jurisdiction of the FBI. He could get into a pissing match with Colyer about who was in charge now, but it wouldn't do him or his career any good. Egos aside, Colyer seemed to know something about this that he wasn't willing to talk about.

"Okay," Jameson said, "I'll put the word out for paramedics to just get the injured off the bridge as soon as possible. How about the dead?"

Colyer looked him in the eye. "Leave 'em. I want every person who's been on that bridge since the explosion to go straight to the hospital, and I want them to stay at the hospital, even if they weren't injured by the explosion. That includes me and you. Close every road leading into Saint Ignace and Mackinaw City from twenty miles away, and man those roadblocks with officers brought in from beyond that distance."

Jameson wasn't stupid. This FBI man was saying that he wanted everyone who'd been exposed after the blast to be quarantined. That meant that this was more than just a terrorist bombing. It was a "dirty bomb," and it had spread some kind of chemical, biological, or nuclear contaminants. It was then that he noted that the device in Colyer's hand was a Geiger counter.

"All right, Inspector," Jameson said with a look of worry. "I'll put the word out for everyone to evacuate to the hospital and stay there. I won't say why, but there'll be a lot of questions from my men who want to go home after their shifts."

"Please just trust me on this one, Captain Jameson. You can draw your own conclusions, but I'm not at liberty to divulge more than I've said. Not yet."

"Just tell me one thing," Jameson said, still looking into his eyes for some sort of clue. "Is there a reason I should tell my family to get out of Saint Ignace?"

"No," Colyer answered, "they'll have to stay here and report to the hospital with the rest of us."

Jameson pulled his cell phone out of a breast pocket and punched in a number. While he was passing along Colyer's instructions, Colyer called Washington on his own cell phone. First, he laid the iPhone into a scrambling device and plugged it into a port in the bottom of the phone.

His boss in DC didn't waste time. When Colyer told him what he knew, and what he thought he knew, the conversation took a dead-serious turn. The Bureau had been anticipating this type of dirty bomb attack for years, and the only real surprise was its location—no one had even considered the Mackinac Bridge as a potential target. Now, in hindsight, it seemed so ridiculously obvious . . .

Colyer didn't speak to anyone except his immediate supervisor. He didn't need to; his encrypted report was digitally recorded so that it could be passed along to the joint chiefs and the president. That this had happened was a matter of national security, and it went beyond top secret. The bombing was serious enough in itself, but if the American people were told that they'd been terrorized with a radioactive weapon, there might well be a nationwide panic.

There was no way to cover up the fact that the Mackinac Bridge had been bombed; too many people had seen it happen. And, although casualties from the explosion had been considerably less than they might have been, too many people had died. Official protocol dictated that the bombing be made public, and the emergency management team that already existed in every county had to be called in to implement a predetermined plan.

That wasn't going to happen, not in real life. Already, the fear that every bridge in the country could be similarly targeted was likely to disrupt commerce at a national level. If the citizens who kept the United States in operation on a day-to-day basis thought that there was a possibility that they might be irradiated too, they'd doubtless change their ways of life. Phobias and paranoia would abound; many Americans would quit their jobs to flee to remote locations, depriving society of the necessary services they rendered. Truck drivers would stop delivering goods, factories would lose employees who produced those goods, and consumers would stop buying—a survivalist-type who moved to a cabin in the woods wasn't likely to purchase new carpeting or a luxury car. It was imperative that John Q. Public not be made aware of what Colyer's Geiger counter had revealed. Not yet.

Whatever story Jameson had told his troopers and the medical personnel on the bridge, it was working, because nearly everyone had gotten off the structure. Colyer watched as ambulances and police cruisers alike took the exit into Saint Ignace, where they'd all report to the hospital to undergo testing and decontamination procedures.

Captain Jameson approached him and said in a low, conspiratorial voice, "Well, Agent Colyer, we got the word to everybody, and the bridge should be completely cleared in about ten minutes. I had to field a lot of questions, but nobody knows the whole truth. Come to think of it, I don't know the whole story myself—think you'll be able to enlighten me about what the hell happened any time soon?"

Colyer grinned at him humorlessly. "As soon as my bosses say that I can, Captain. Any word on the tallies of dead and wounded?"

"Twenty-seven confirmed dead, and thirty-three wounded. We're expecting to find as many as a dozen more bodies, but I'd say we got off easy. The explosion was probably from a military-grade, high explosive, rather than a homemade fertilizer bomb. Very powerful, and not very large physically; picked up cars and threw them like softballs for fifty yards. Probably anything within twenty-five yards of ground zero was vaporized. The boys in forensics think that the bomb might have been planted under the roadbed."

Colyer jammed both his hands into his pockets and exhaled forcefully through pursed lips. He knew that in the grand scheme of things, it could have been worse, but it couldn't have been worse for the people who'd died in the initial blast. For them, the world had ended today. Whether the death toll had been a dozen or a thousand, it would've made no difference to the people who were fatalities, or their loved ones.

Chapter Thirty

The Trail

It was getting too dark to see clearly when Rod decided that he wasn't going to catch up with the man he was trailing. Using the headlamp in his backpack was out of the question, because all the other guy had to do was wait for the light to come down the path, and then shoot an inch below it. That would end Rod's pursuit quickly enough.

The pain in Rod's joints had become almost excruciating. Overexertion and the fact that he was taking speed to provide artificial energy had a lot to do with that. He was too damn old to be teaching survival classes, and he was, for sure, too old to be chasing terrorists through the woods. He still had the iron weight of fear in his gut from the bullet that had come too close to hitting him. By God, he was no hero, but his hatred for this murderous son of a bitch, a man he'd never met, was becoming boundless. Rod didn't want to die—and he knew that this man wouldn't hesitate to kill him at the first opportunity—but something more intense than his own self-preservation was driving him.

Rod dared not strike a fire. He really wanted one, not just for warmth, but for the cheer and bug-repellent properties it provided. The mosquitoes in this swamp were thick and voracious tonight. He'd found some tansies growing in a low, wet depression along the way, and he'd stuffed a bunch of the plants into his pocket in anticipation of the night. He pulled them out of his pocket now and rolled them between his palms until they'd become a wet, pulpy mass. Then he applied the spicy-smelling plant juices to his face and hands. The onslaught of mosquitoes lessened immediately, and he knew they'd be deterred for hours to come. He shoved the mass of crushed plant material into a breast pocket to further discourage the bugs.

He hoped that the man he was after had stopped for the night. And he hoped that the mosquitoes were eating him alive, too. When he recalled what this slimeball had done to poor Sue Morgan, no amount of pain and suffering were great enough for him.

At least he had his headnet. It was a simple homemade, baglike affair he'd sewn from a yard-size piece of no-see-um netting. Worn over his head—Shannon liked to kid him about hiding his face by wearing a bag over his head—it served not only as an effective barrier against bloodsucking insects, but as an excellent diffuser of bright sunlight when he was snowshoeing. It was also ideal camouflage when he hunted deer.

As the sun set, Rod was getting hungry, and he thought it would be wise to carbo-load before the night chill set in. He rummaged around in his backpack for another snack bar, only to be disappointed to find that he'd already eaten them all. He sighed. Time to get into survival mode. He dropped down into the wet lowlands at one side of the trail and put on his headlamp. He pointed the light at the ground and adjusted the LED to its lowest setting.

Before long, he'd located a patch of blue violets. He pulled the small succulents up and ate them where he found them. There was also a patch of common plantain; a little stringy when eaten raw, but palatable enough. He wished he was closer to the river so he could fish and catch crawdads, but then he'd also need a fire to cook the parasites out of them. Oh well, so long as he staved off hypoglycemia, he was halfway through the night.

After more than thirty-five years in the woods, Rod wasn't scared of the dark. Ordinarily, he could tell what species of animal was moving about in the woods just by the sound of its passing. But these weren't ordinary circumstances, and every noise made Rod jump. Every sound from the darkened woods became the harbinger of a bullet aimed at his heart. Maybe it was the Dexedrine he'd been taking, but he couldn't get to sleep. His nerves were frazzled, and every joint in his overworked body ached.

Chapter Thirty-One

Darkened Woods

Aziz was having a tougher time than Rod. Like most people, he was scared of the dark—even if he wouldn't admit it—and he was doubly frightened of spending a night alone in the shadowy, moonless woods. In his stressed mind, every noise was the sound of the killer survival instructor taking careful aim at him. Or maybe getting ready to pounce from the shadows with a razor-edge knife. He'd seen this maniac bastard all but behead Richarde, and he was pretty sure that he'd done-in Grigovich as well. Maybe he'd even gotten McBraden. This survival instructor was as crazy as those portrayed in the movies, and these woods were his turf. He could probably take out Aziz any time he wanted. He was probably laying in the shadows right now, just waiting for the time of his choosing.

Aziz was hungry and thirsty. He had a shoulder bag with fifteen pounds of C4 in an ammo box, wrapped around a ten-pound sphere of plutonium, but nothing to eat or drink. He didn't even have a flashlight, and the moonless night was black as pitch. He couldn't see the trail, and this green, mosquito-infested nightmare was the most horrible place he could imagine. If he got out of this alive, he'd never leave his beloved desert again.

But Aziz wasn't done yet. His best-laid plan had gone wrong from the start, but he had a number of backup and alternate plans, and he was nothing if not versatile. Mackinaw City had attracted a number of Muslims from Middle Eastern countries in the past decade, and while most of them were devoted American citizens, there were a few friends of Islam that he could count on for support.

It was his intention to return to Mackinaw City while it was filled with police and other civil servants, and thousands of tourists who'd become trapped there by the destruction he'd caused to the Mackinac Bridge. They'd never expect him to return, these stupid Americans, and they'd especially never suspect him to plant a second bomb. It was a given that they'd have a roadblock on every route into Mackinaw City, but it should be easy to infiltrate the village on foot. Posing as a tourist, he'd plant the second bomb in the Mackinac Point lighthouse tower, east of the Fort Michilmackinac tourist attraction. There, it would shower the crowded village with radiation. With any luck, he'd kill more than a hundred people with the initial blast, and contaminate thousands more with fallout for years to come.

The going was very slow on this black night, and the cursed mosquitoes were relentless. He itched everywhere. Convinced that he wouldn't be needing it again, he'd discarded his insect repellent, along with numerous other items, in a dumpster at the motel in Mackinaw City. He wished he had it now. Several times, he walked off the trail, and had to feel with his feet to find it again. He wanted to run; maybe if he were moving faster the mosquitoes wouldn't be so bad. But if he broke into a run, he'd go off the trail again, maybe injure himself. The last thing he wanted to do now was to poke his eye out on a tree branch.

A glint of reflected starlight up ahead caught his attention, and he heard the sound of running water. It was the Carp River. It had to be. There was no other water within miles of here. He could just make out the shape of the wooden, pedestrian bridge that crossed it, and the gleaming stars reflected in the running water below it. A quarter-mile past it was Cecil Bay Road, an asphalt ribbon that led to US Highway 31, which ran northward into Mackinaw City.

But first he had to slake his terrible thirst. He'd been craving an ice cold Coca-Cola for the past three hours, imagining the burning of its carbonation against the back of his throat as he guzzled the brown liquid. He tried to lick his lips now, but his mouth felt as though it were filled with cotton balls. Unable to see clearly, he stumbled down to the river's edge and fell onto all fours, his hands in the cold, running water. He lowered his mouth to the surface and sucked greedily until his stomach was filled.

When he rose again, his thirst was gone and he felt much better. Almost refreshed. He tried not to think of all the aquatic parasites he'd just ingested. He was very tired, but filled with a renewed determination to reach Mackinaw City before dawn. The mosquitoes were unbearable here anyway, and that provided extra motivation.

He crossed the footbridge and followed the trail to Cecil Bay Road with no trouble. When he reached the asphalt, the mosquitoes were fewer and more tolerable. He breathed easier, even though there was no doubt in his mind that the crazed survival instructor he'd shot at earlier in the day would try to follow—Aziz was sure his bullet had missed its mark. The man might be a skilled tracker, but surely even he couldn't follow footprints on pavement.

Aziz encountered a dozen cars before he reached US 31 at the end of Cecil Bay Road an hour later, but they'd all been easy to evade by simply ducking down into the grassy ditch. Several times, he'd heard a rustling back in the woods, and once a deer had crossed the road in front of him, but he was becoming less frightened by unseen animals in the shadows.

There was no traffic at all on US 31. He hiked to the intersection where it merged with Interstate 75, and spotted a roadblock manned by one squad car and two officers from the Mackinaw City Police Department. They were preoccupied with their own worried conversation about being quarantined. Aziz skirted them in the woods at the roadside with ease.

Dawn was breaking over Lake Huron, but even though it was well before normal business hours, Mackinaw City was bustling. The normally quiet community was filled with people who'd become stranded there by police order. Restaurants that normally closed had stayed open all night, and they were busy, as was the town's only bar, and all of its motels. The village was inundated with police officers and a few resident National Guard members in uniform, but the influx of strangers who weren't permitted to leave was defeating any attempts at heightened security. Once again, Aziz's dark pigmentation caused him to pass for Native American, and no one gave him a second glance.

He made his way to one of the few remaining public telephone booths and pretended to be looking up a phone number. In actuality, he was looking at a street map of the city. When he'd found the address he wanted, and committed its location to memory, he dialed a cell phone number that wasn't in the telephone book.

"Welcome to Jada's Bait Shop," a female voice said. "How may I serve you?"

"Are there any tarpon in O'Neal Lake?" Aziz answered.

"No sir, tarpon are a South Atlantic species."

"I see. What kind of bait would you recommend for them?"

"Sir, maybe you'd best come here to see for yourself. Do you know where we're located?"

"Yes," Aziz said, "I can be there within twenty minutes. I'll walk over."

"How will we recognize you?"

Shit! Aziz suddenly remembered that he was still wearing coveralls. He self-consciously turned his back to the telephone, away from the sight of any passersby who might recognize the logo between his shoulders.

"I'll be wearing a blue-and-white-flowered Hawaiian shirt with khaki Dockers slacks. I have dark hair and a goatee."

"We'll see you in about twenty minutes," the voice on the phone said. The line went dead.

Aziz quickly slipped into a public restroom near the telephone. It was empty except for one man washing his hands. Aziz kept his back to him as he stepped into a stall, latching the door behind him. He unzipped the coveralls and stepped out of them. Beneath, he was dressed as he'd described himself on the telephone.

He unlocked the stall door and cautiously looked outside. He was alone in the indoor bathroom, so he quickly stepped over to the swing-top wastebasket and stuffed the coveralls inside. Then, he stood at the sink and looked at himself in the mirror. His face was dirty and scratched from his trek through the woods, and there were itchy mosquito bumps all over his body. He splashed water over his face to wash off some of the trail grime and blood. He didn't have a comb, so he wetted his hair and smoothed it back with his palms. He tore off a section of brown paper towel and used it to dry his face.

Aziz stepped back and studied himself in the bathroom mirror. He tucked in his shirt and smoothed the most major wrinkles out of his pants legs. Satisfied with the man he saw in his reflection, he pulled open the door of the public restroom and stepped out onto the sidewalk.

The sun was above the horizon now, bathing downtown Mackinaw City in a golden light that made the village look as quaint and as enticing to tourists as it had been designed to be. But this was no ordinary day, and these weren't typical tourists. Some people were hurrying, as if they had someplace to be, but some were just milling about as if in a daze. The ferries to and from Mackinac Island were still in operation, still selling tickets and taking fares from people who were, in reality, going nowhere. Even the fudge shops were open with their wares arranged attractively behind large-paned windows facing the sidewalk.

There were dozens of uniformed police, firefighters, and paramedics to be seen, and a few camouflage-clad National Guardsmen armed with obsolete M-16 A2 rifles. The show of force was pathetic, thought Aziz. These officials had no idea what they were protecting against, and from what Aziz could see, most were venting their frustrations by bullying the citizens they were sworn to protect. It was the same in every country he'd ever been to.

Aziz put his bag over his shoulder, stuffed his hands in his pockets, and began walking nonchalantly away from the downtown area. He didn't want to attract any attention to himself, but he was extremely conscious of the assembled bomb that was swinging from a strap over his shoulder. In his imagination, everyone was curious about it, even though no one seemed to give him a second look. They were, in fact, too busy trying to understand what had happened to make them prisoners in this suddenly overcrowded community. In this crowd, he was just one more confused, displaced tourist.

City blocks weren't as consistent or straight in Mackinaw City as they were in larger cities, but as near as he could calculate, the safe house Aziz had called from the pay phone was a little over a mile from the downtown area. As he'd told the woman he'd spoken with there, he could be there in twenty minutes—if no one delayed him. That didn't look like it would happen, but so many unforeseen problems had come up, he was ready to expect anything.

Chapter Thirty-Two

Mackinaw City

It was about midnight when Rod reached the bridge over the Carp River. He spent several minutes in the shadows before he crossed the bridge, listening for any sound that might reveal an ambush. He'd be a sitting duck in the middle of the twenty-yard-long footbridge between the rails and with no cover. After several long moments of silence, he sprang from the shadows and loped across the bridge. His footfalls echoed hollowly against its wooden planking, each one sounding like an invitation to shoot him. He made it across, and then squatted in the darkness for several more minutes, listening intently.

When he was sure that nothing was there that wasn't supposed to be, Rod knelt at the river's edge. He splashed cool water over his face to rinse away some of the crusted blood and grime. The water felt good. His nostrils were filled with congealed blood, and he was pretty certain the cartilage in his nose had been broken. It felt like there was a bump in it that shouldn't be there, but the pain that shot through him when he tried to wiggle it was excruciating enough to convince him to leave it alone. Rod pulled a LifeStraw ultralight water filter from his pack and filtered enough water to slake his thirst.

When he'd finished washing his face, he walked the short distance to Cecil Bay Road. It was still very dark, but he couldn't see or hear anything out of the ordinary, just frogs, fireflies, and the ever-present mosquitoes. Now, Rod had to determine whether the man he was pursuing had gone right toward Cecil Bay, straight across the road into the state forest along the North Country hiking trail, or left toward US 31.

He put on his headlamp and pointed it at the ground. There had been several people through here within the past two days, but the tracks of the man he was following were easily identifiable from the rest: They had the sharpest edges and were on top of the previous imprints. The high contrast provided by Rod's headlamp made it easy to see where gravel on the shoulder had been displaced when the man had twisted on the ball of his right foot as he turned toward US 31. When he'd stepped onto the pavement, sand granules that had been clinging to his hiking boot fell away to leave a partial outline of his sole. That was it; the man had headed toward the highway.

Rod hiked as fast as he could toward the highway, his joints objecting at every step. He made it to US 31 in a little over an hour, just as the first dawn of a new day was lightening the eastern sky. There had been no foot traffic at all on the highway, and it took only a few minutes of careful searching to find his quarry's footprints on the gravel shoulder, heading in the direction of Mackinaw City.

Rod was reminded of the old axiom about criminals returning to the scene of the crime. That had never made any sense to him personally, but it sure looked like that was what this guy was doing. He was certain that the earth-shaking boom he'd heard when he was chasing the van on the two-track to French Farm Lake was a bomb detonation. What else could it have been? But if that were the case, surely the terrorists had done what they'd intended to do. If this guy he was now trailing was the last of them, as he appeared to be, maybe he just wanted to get away. But it would have made more sense to head south, where the population was denser and it'd be easier to disappear. Security around Mackinaw City would be high right now, wouldn't it?

Was it possible that the murderer intended to blow up something else? Maybe he had some other terrorist act in mind. Or maybe he had friends in Mackinaw City who'd get him out of the country. That probably made the most sense, because there didn't seem to be a hell of a lot left in this area that would be considered a worthwhile terrorist target.

Rod was surprised that there wasn't more traffic on the road. In fact, the highway was downright desolate—no cars at all. That was weird, and a little spooky. Traffic here was usually moderately heavy all of the time, day and night. But he didn't see a single car all the way to Mackinaw City. On the outskirts of town, there was a police car and a roadblock on the freeway. No doubt about it, that had been a bomb that he'd heard go off. The damage must have been pretty extensive for authorities to have closed the highways.

He had no trouble slipping past the roadblock by going around it through the woods. In Mackinaw City, he saw lots of cops and National Guardsmen in uniform. They were apparently there to provide at least the illusion of enhanced security, but Rod didn't have to think too profoundly to conclude that it was mostly for show. There was no way the authorities could know who was or wasn't there. The town was jammed with people who weren't from the area. Every restaurant or bar in town was filled to capacity, and there were hundreds of folks walking the sidewalks or just sitting on the curbs, talking. The authorities who were ostensibly providing security seemed mostly lost themselves.

Ironically, Rod's backpack and disheveled appearance made him fit right in with the crowd of tourists who'd found themselves stranded in this little town. Rod was sure that there was an All Points Bulletin out for him, but he doubted he'd be recognized. His reflection in a store window as he passed was a little shocking; his swollen nose and black-ringed eyes made him hard to identify among the multitude of other injured people.

Besides, these cops had bigger fish to fry—even if they didn't know what they were. Rod openly asked around on the street about what was going on, and before an hour had gone by, he was up to speed about the events of the past twenty-four hours. Everyone was eager to tell what they knew. It was probably cathartic for them. There was plenty of conjecture, but if half of what Rod was told was true, he was more convinced than ever that the killer he was trailing was one of the most dangerous people he'd ever meet.

But Rod had to find him before he could stop him, and that was looking to be a daunting task. Rod didn't know where to begin. He suddenly felt very stupid, and very disheartened. He shrugged his backpack off his shoulders and sank heavily onto one of the public benches that lined the main street of the town. He was exhausted. He ached all over, and his nose hurt like hell from the hammer blow Grigovich's fist had landed on it. All he really wanted to do was rest. He was at the end of his proverbial rope, and he didn't have any idea what his next step should be. He decided to call Shannon. He needed to talk to his best friend. There were still a few pay phones around the north woods where cell coverage was often spotty, even nonexistent.

Shannon accepted the charges almost before the operator could ask.

"Oh baby," she said, "where are you? I've been so worried."

For just a second, he pondered the pros and cons of revealing his actual location, and then it occurred to him that he really didn't give a damn. The cops were probably listening in right now, and they'd zeroed in on his location as soon as the number connected. He was sure they already blamed him for the murders on the Betsy River.

"I'm at a pay phone in Mackinaw City," he said. "The bridge is closed, and from what I've been told by people on the street, there was a helluva bomb that went off there yesterday."

"It's been on the news," Shannon answered. "And it's worse than that: They just announced this morning that the bomb was a dirty bomb. It wasn't nuclear, but it spread radiation all over—you're probably in it right now. The news didn't say how bad it's supposed to be, but any amount of radiation can't be good."

"I was afraid of that. I heard the explosion, figured it had to be a bomb. Didn't know it was radioactive, though."

"Rod, they're blaming you for the murders on the Betsy," she confirmed. "I saw your boot prints at the scene. Please tell me you didn't have any hand in killing them."

"Do you have to ask me that?"

"No," she said, sounding a little ashamed of herself. "I don't. But I wanted to hear it from your lips."

"I did kill one man there, though," he said with genuine sadness. "But he was a stranger; never saw him before. He had a gun, and he would've killed me. I killed another man on the bridge yesterday. Same circumstances."

"Oh God, baby, I'm so sorry." Shannon might have asked such a question for her own peace of mind, but she knew in her heart that the man she loved wasn't capable of murder. The only way he would have done the things he said he'd done was in defense of his own life.

"Listen, sweetheart," Rod said. "I'm betting somebody is tapping our phone. Our conversation is probably being recorded right now, and if so, they've got a fix on where I'm calling from. I've gotta make this short."

"Okay," Shannon was all business now. "The sheriff's department seems to be blaming you for murdering your survival students, but there's an FBI agent named Colyer who told me that he thinks you're innocent. Colyer wants you to turn yourself in."

Rod snorted cynically. "Yeah, don't they always?"

"I think Colyer might actually be a good guy, and I wouldn't deal with anyone but him if I were you. The sheriff and his deputies have you convicted of murder already."

"All the more reason not to turn myself in, don't you think?"

"Yes," she said with a deep sigh, "I do think. What're you going to do?"

"I'm not going to go into detail because I figure our phone is tapped—and I'm not too sure what my next step is myself—but I do know that there's one more terrorist out there. I think he's the head honcho behind all that's happened, and I think he's still really dangerous. I've tracked him to hell and back, and I think he's here in Mackinaw City right now. I don't know where."

"How will you find him?" she asked more or less rhetorically.

"I don't know," Rod answered. "I just don't know. It'll be pure luck if I do. Maybe I'll get lucky."

"Take care of yourself, please. I love you, Rod."

"I love you too, baby. I miss you something awful. I'll call when I can. 'Bye."

"G'bye, baby." Rod got away from the pay phone as soon as he'd hung up the receiver. He withdrew to about a block away, where he could watch the location without being noticeable himself. Sure enough, in about ten minutes, two uniformed city police officers nonchalantly strolled over to the telephone Rod had used, approaching from either side. They confirmed what he already knew: His movements were of interest to law enforcement, probably at the highest level, and his home telephone line was tapped. They could get a fix on any telephone he used to call home in just seconds. But there was still the human factor, the delay between knowing his location and getting an armed human being to that location.

Now that he was in the city, Rod had no idea where the terrorist had hidden himself. Maybe he had a motel room. Maybe he had a sympathetic friend who lived here. Hell, maybe his was one of the faces in this crowd roaming the sidewalks this morning. Rod was sure that he'd recognize him if he saw him, though; the face of that killer was forever etched on his brain.

The crowd hadn't milled for long before a National Guard pickup truck with a bullhorn attached to its roof began ordering everyone who had a home or motel room to get back to it and await evacuation to a decontamination center in buses driven by uniformed officers. Everyone who didn't have a place to go was to report to the open space at the waterfront, where an impromptu refugee center had been constructed, complete with porta-potties, a soup kitchen, and sleeping cots—all under big tents. The place looked like it was hosting some sort of festival. But, in reality, martial law was being imposed, and all persons were to evacuate the streets to await transport.

Rod looked at his watch. It was a little after 11 AM now. The imposition of martial law would inhibit the terrorist as much as it did him, but he was betting that it wouldn't stop him from getting away or from doing what he'd planned. This guy, doubtless, made a science of finding chinks in his enemy's armor, and he'd find a way to do what he needed to do, no matter how many personal freedoms were restricted under the mantle of increased security. Besides, even normal people would now act furtive and suspicious, as if they were doing something wrong; people always behaved that way when they were being scrutinized by Big Brother. Unfortunately, that wouldn't make it any easier to spot the real terrorist.

Chapter Thirty-Three

The Sniper

Benjamin "Biff" Katz took off his black cotton ball cap and used it to wipe the sweat from his brow. He liked the image and the perks that went with being a state police SWAT sniper, but this type of duty took all the romance out of it. He'd been here manning a plank scaffolding suspended under the southern end of the Mackinac Bridge since 7 AM.

Directly below was the entrance to the Fort Michilmackinac tourist center, which was, almost unbelievably, doing a booming business in spite of being quarantined and having a limited audience. Almost none of the people who went inside the building below him even looked upward to see the sniper over their heads. He peeled back the Velcro cover strap that protected the crystal of his wristwatch and sighed. It was just past ten o'clock now, and he was roasting in the sun, uncomfortable, and bored out of his mind.

Biff was twenty-nine years old, he'd been married to his high school sweetheart for the past four years, and he'd been a Michigan State police officer for five years. He held a Bachelor's degree in public safety from Northern Michigan University in Marquette, but sometimes he wondered if he hadn't wasted his shot at an education by choosing such a limited career. Being a state cop was pretty prestigious in itself, and he was a natural when it came to handling a rifle. This job was tough on a wife, though, and there wasn't much chance for advancement.

Still, his years in civil service probably weren't a complete waste. If he kept his nose clean and didn't make a lot of waves, he was entitled to a shot at a political office, maybe even the state senate. He was one of the good guys, he thought. He was a servant of the people, and he liked to think that he deserved the respect that should be accorded a state trooper.

He had earned the nickname "Biff" from the way he described steel silhouette targets that he "biffed" when he knocked them over at long ranges. Around here, he was considered the best, but he'd tested his mettle against the big boys at Camp Perry in Ohio a couple of times, and he really didn't want to talk about the experiences he'd had there. It sort of irked him that the best rifle and pistol shots in the world had always been civilians. Still, he'd found his comfort zone. He'd rather be a big fish in a small pond than the other way around.

Biff checked the safety mechanism on his Winchester Model Seventy bull-barreled rifle for the thousandth time, making certain that it was engaged—he'd never had an accidental discharge, and he wasn't going to have one today. Like many urban police snipers, he'd opted for 243-caliber, instead of the more publicized 223 or 308. The 243 was hair-splittingly accurate, and although he'd never shot anyone—and hoped that he never would—he wanted to have every advantage if he did. A gunfight was one contest in which he definitely didn't want to place second.

But actual sniper work was unglamorous. He knew that most of a sniper's job consisted of long hours behind a weapon, "glassing" some point of interest through binoculars or telephoto camera lens, maybe never firing a shot. But actually doing that was maddening. He couldn't even listen to a radio or watch TV on his iPhone. He had to stay focused on the area he was charged to watch.

He positioned himself behind his Steiner binoculars again and scanned what he could see of the south side of the bridge. It looked so different with the center of the span missing. He'd grown up with the Mackinac Bridge as part of his local culture, and to see it in ruins was just surreal. How many times had he crossed that span? How many times had he driven his family across for vacation? He shuddered to think that this might have happened while those he loved were crossing.

His binoculars were mounted to a short Gorilla Pod, whose ball-joint construction allowed its articulated legs—and whatever optical device was mounted to its baseplate—to be firmly affixed to just about any object. His Olympus 14.0 megapixel digital camera was similarly mounted about a foot away, and it was also affixed to a Gorilla Pod. This outfit was rugged, and it let him pick up and change location in under a minute.

He gazed through the binos until he began to get sharp pains in his brow line. Just another of the sniper's laments. Worse than the long hours spent behind camera, binoculars, and riflescope was the realization that he probably wasn't going to see anything anyway. The deed was already done. What terrorist would be stupid enough to return to the scene of *this* crime?

Chapter Thirty-Four

Command Center

Colyer answered his cell phone on the third ring. He'd been sleeping, sitting upright in his Charger in the welcome center parking lot at the northeast end of the bridge. It was uncomfortable as hell, but it was a lot quieter than the state police post across the highway, where a never-ending stream of vehicles was coming and going. Every motel and hotel from here to the Soo was filled up with stranded travelers. Even the truck stops and rest areas were filled beyond capacity. As one redneck had put it, there wasn't enough room to fart without a dozen people smelling it. After spending several hours at the hospital, where he was hosed, showered, tested, and finally dressed in ill-fitting but nonradioactive clothes from the resale store in Saint Ignace, he'd spent the night here in a parking lot.

Colyer pushed the TALK button and answered groggily, "Hello?"

"This is Ed Jameson. Elliot just called his wife from a pay phone in Mackinaw City."

"And . . . ?"

"And we sent two men to that location, but it's safe to say that he's long gone by now."

"Did you call his wife?"

"Yeah, she says she told him you wanted him to turn himself in. We have the entire conversation recorded. She did say that. He didn't sound like he thought that would be a good idea."

"Humph," Colyer said, "I wouldn't expect that he would."

"The governor has declared Emmet and Mackinac Counties to be Disaster Zones, and we've begun to implement martial law. We've got a recent photo of Rod Elliot, and we're circulating it among officers and military police. We'll find him."

"Keep me posted," Colyer said, and then hung up. He wanted to talk to Elliot, too, but Rod Elliot wasn't the prime suspect in this case, not from his perspective. The way Colyer had it figured, even if they caught Elliot, they wouldn't get anywhere toward solving this case. Oh sure, the prosecutor would hang it on him just to have something to show for their efforts, but an international terrorist living the simple, meager life that Rod and Shannon Elliot had been living for the past ten years didn't fit the profile. And it was unreasonable to believe that he might've been a part of the sophisticated planning and huge expenditure that had been required to accomplish the bombing of the bridge. Especially not without his wife knowing something about it, and she obviously didn't. No, Rod Elliot wasn't the driving force here; he was just caught up in it somehow. The state cops weren't just barking up the wrong tree; they were in the wrong forest.

Forcing himself awake, Colyer drove to McDonald's to get a large cup of black coffee. Most businesses in Saint Ignace were still running as usual. Ironically, some of them were enjoying increased revenue as a result of the bombing and subsequent imposition of martial law. He then drove to the waterfront, where Moonlight Lines had committed a ferry to transit the Straits between the peninsulas. He needed to get to Mackinaw City, because if Rod Elliot was there, he had a hunch that the real terrorists were there, too.

The ferry was named the *Moon Beam.* It was a sixty-foot, catamaran-style boat that was touted as the fastest of ferries. The *Moon Beam* didn't carry anything but passengers and luggage; it was designed for transport to Mackinac Island, where motorized, wheeled vehicles were prohibited, so Colyer had to lock up and leave his Charger at the docks. He'd borrow a police cruiser when he got to Mackinaw City.

The catamaran made the five-mile distance between Saint Ignace and Mackinaw City in about fifteen minutes. Most of its passengers were uniformed police officers and National Guard personnel of varying ranks. There wasn't much conversation between them; they seemed to still be in a mild state of shock.

And, of course, there were the obligatory assholes, a handful of large-mouthed, testosterone-filled civilians who'd either been up all night getting stoned and drunk, or had sucked down a blunt and beers first thing that morning. They were ostensibly talking among themselves, but loudly enough so they could be overheard.

"Yeah," one young man with a shaved head and an unshaven face announced to his buddies, "when we find out who bombed the bridge, we're gonna fuck them up."

"Yeah, America, Dude," said another, his camouflaged overshirt open so anyone could see his T-shirt said KILL 'EM ALL, LET GOD SORT 'EM OUT.

There was a round of high fives. Colyer just stared out to sea, not wanting to look at these miscreants that he had taken an oath to protect. At some point in every day, he wondered if he'd made the right career decision. He was wondering that now. When he looked around him again, he was pretty sure he saw the same thought in the minds of most of the people in uniform, too. Maybe the America of today didn't deserve protecting.

All that aside, he was an FBI agent, and he loved what he did, because in some small way, he was making the world a better place to live. He would've felt the same way if he'd been a priest, a school teacher, or a plumber. It was in his nature; he derived satisfaction from taking something that was bad, and turning it into something good.

The bump of the ferry making contact with its dock broke his reverie. As soon as the crew extended the gangplank, he was onto the wooden walkway. Several marked and unmarked police vehicles waited in the parking lot. A state police sergeant with a photograph of Colyer's face in his left hand walked over to him and said, "Inspector Colyer?" The sergeant extended his right hand, and Colyer shook it. "I'm Sergeant Wilson from the Petoskey post. I volunteered to come here, and I've been assigned to be your driver."

"Why in hell would you volunteer to come into a radiated zone? You know you can't leave now?"

"Yes sir," Wilson said, "I know that, but I figured that I at least might be able to do something more valuable than chasing speeders and arresting drivers for having a beer with dinner."

Colyer grinned. "Let's hope that we don't get more than we bargained for."

They drove to the Mackinaw City Municipal Building on Nicolet Street, where a command post had been set up. Inside, it was crowded with desks, long folding tables, and personnel from every law enforcement agency in Michigan; National Guardsmen; and a few feds from Washington, DC. There were even a handful of state representatives and senators making an appearance for appearance's sake. There were maps all over the walls, laptop computers on every desk, and every other person was talking or texting on a cell phone. One wall was lined with full-face, N94 respirators.

"Agent Colyer?" Colyer turned to see a hand thrusting toward him. "I'm Dave Williams, the Emergency Services Coordinator for Emmet County. We're glad to have you onboard."

"Glad to be onboard, Dave. What do we know?"

"So far, we know the Mackinac Bridge was bombed. We hope to find out by whom and what their long-term objectives might be very soon."

"Okay, keep me in the loop, will you Dave?" They knew jack. The bustle of this command post consisted mostly of keeping patrol cars on the road, transporting radiation victims to the nearest hospitals in Petoskey and Cheboygan for decontamination, and establishing a pecking order.

Colyer laid his large attaché case on an open spot atop a folding table and got online with his Toshiba laptop. He turned to Wilson. "Sergeant, I'm looking for information about a 2008 or 2009 Ford E-150 panel van, marked with a logo that says JACKSONVILLE PAINTING. It's a phony company, but the driver of that van gave a bridge officer a business card and phone number just before the bridge blew. He didn't get a license plate number."

Wilson nodded, jotting the information quickly in a spiral note pad.

"Next, I want you to get me everything you can find on the Dodge utility truck that ran a roadblock on the south end of the bridge at the same time that van did—here's the license number of that truck; it's registered to B and B Welding, and it's beige in color." He handed Wilson a scrap of paper with the truck's identifying information. "If you find anything about either vehicle, no matter how seemingly insignificant, I want to know."

"Oh hell," Wilson said, looking at the paper Colyer had handed him. "Two vehicles fitting both those descriptions were reported out at the dam on French Farm Creek early this morning. A bass fisherman found 'em. The truck was smashed into the side of the van. Nobody was around, though. Sheriff department just figured that it was probably a couple of drunk kids in stolen vehicles. They had them towed back here, because the usual impound lot is beyond the containment boundaries. They're investigating it."

"Shit!" Colyer exclaimed. "I hope they at least printed them." Wilson shrugged, it wasn't his case. "Take me to them," Colyer said.

The impound lot was a grassy field a mile west of Mackinaw City. When Colyer ran the police report, he saw that both vehicles had been dusted for fingerprints, and the prints from the stolen truck had been identified as Rod Elliot's. The two sets of prints lifted from the van, which had been rammed hard in the side by the truck, remained unidentified at this point.

Colyer ran his Geiger counter over the inside surfaces of the van. It showed several hundred micro-Sieverts of radiation. Not a lot, but certainly more than normal. Aside from that, the van was clean. Too clean for a work van, but being too clean didn't insinuate criminal activity in a court of law.

While he was searching the pickup truck, Colyer's cell phone rang. It was Dave Williams from the command post in Mackinaw City.

"Agent Colyer? You said you wanted to be kept in the loop . . . This might not mean anything, but the city janitor just reported finding a set of coveralls marked JACKSONVILLE PAINTING when he was emptying the trash in the public restrooms here. Out of curiosity, we ran a Geiger counter over them, and the forensics boys say that they're radioactive. Not dangerously so, but a lot more than they should be."

Colyer got a chill. "Listen, Dave, that probably means the man we're looking for is in Mackinaw City right now."

"You mean Rod Elliot?"

A sudden flush took Colyer by surprise. "No, you idiot, not Rod Elliot. I mean whoever blew up the bridge. The person driving the first vehicle to crash the roadblock on the bridge ramp."

"Not Rod Elliot?" Williams asked dumbly.

Colyer took a deep breath. "Listen close, Dave. Rod Elliot is involved in this mess, but he's probably not the bomber. In fact, I think Elliot might be on our side, and he's after the bomber, same as us."

"Oh," Williams said, his mind trying hard to change and assimilate this new and contradictory information. He'd heard from other officers that Colyer wasn't a team player, and now he wondered why he was trying to convince him that this known murderer might be innocent. What was this game Colyer was playing?

Colyer picked up on the coordinator's confusion and disbelief, and he knew he was getting nowhere. These guys had a target in mind, and they were zoned in.

"Listen," Colyer said, "I want you to put out the word that if Elliot is spotted, he is not to be harmed. We need his testimony, and I want you to consider him a necessary witness for the prosecution. He is not to be harmed. Do I have your word on that?"

"Yes," Williams said, "you have my word."

Chapter Thirty-Five

Business as Usual

There seemed to be little real change to business as usual in Mackinaw City. The only noticeable difference was that traffic was now restricted to police and military vehicles, and there was a loosely enforced curfew that required everyone to remain in an assigned location for at least the next ten hours. Most residents and business owners knew each other, and were treated as comrades by local authorities. Most tourists seemed to ignore the curfew. In fact, the gift stores and the usual tourist traps were busier than ever. Everyone seemed to want a souvenir of the disaster, and prices rose to reflect demand. Aziz shook his head in disgust.

The buses to and from the hospital decontamination centers in Cheboygan and Petoskey were running throughout the day and night. Once a person was declared radiation free, he or she was free to leave the quarantined zone; but the cleansing process was untested, having never been used before. There were innumerable wrinkles that made it deucedly slow, and there weren't enough buses to handle the transportation demands.

When Aziz emerged from the safe house, he was showered, rested from a four-hour nap, and dressed in new clothes. Like almost every American community, Mackinaw City harbored Friends of Islam, people who would offer safe haven and succor to dispossessed freedom fighters like himself. Aziz carried a coded list of them in his wallet so that he could find safe harbor from the authorities, even a vehicle, no matter where he went. Many of the most helpful weren't even Islamic; they were just discontent with the American government, and they spanned all ethnicities and walks of life. He grinned inwardly; American citizens, in general, were more concerned with free-range chickens, peanut allergies, and undrinkable tap water than they were with a potential terrorist living next door.

Aziz had changed the carrier for his bomb from a shoulder bag to a Jansport daypack provided by his host; it should be easier to carry and less noticeable among the backpack-wearing tourists and bicyclists here in Mackinaw City. Still, a cursory inspection by a curious National Guardsman would reveal the daypack's contents to be suspicious, even if the ammunition can weren't identified immediately as a bomb, so Aziz kept the Ruger revolver tucked into his waistband where he could reach it quickly. He still had no intention of sacrificing himself in a fireball if that were avoidable, but he did mean to use this last bomb. Its cost had been high—both in terms of money spent and in lives lost—in getting it here.

The sidewalks of Mackinaw City were crowded with people who were afoot, visiting restaurants to get their daily meals, and just meandering in and out of gift and other shops. The fudge shops were doing a handsome business, and, Aziz thought wryly, that it was no wonder that Americans were the fattest people in the world. Many pedestrians were carrying backpacks, usually by only one strap slung over a shoulder the way they'd seen cool actors do it in the movies, and just about everyone carried a satchel or bag of some type. He was just one more apple in the peck, and no one seemed to pay him any mind.

His plan was to enter the Fort Michilimackinac tourist site at its entrance directly under the ramp leading onto what was left of the Mackinac Bridge, and then nonchalantly stroll over to the old Mackinac Point lighthouse tower that stood to its left. Visitors were permitted to ascend the long spiral stairway that led up to the beacon room of the tower, but relatively few wanted to exert themselves enough to make the climb to its glassed-in pinnacle. There, at the top of the lighthouse, he'd arm his bomb, and leave it, still inside the daypack.

When he was past the blast radius, safe from shrapnel—he figured about a half mile—he'd hit the speed-dial number on his cell phone that would trigger it. The explosion should take out much of downtown Mackinaw City, killing hundreds, and injuring hundreds more, while a fresh aerosol of plutonium contamination would taint dozens of square miles for decades to come. The devastation might be greater than he'd dared hope for, now that authorities were inadvertently trapping people at ground zero. In the mass confusion and hysteria that would ensue, it should be easy for him to slip away.

Chapter Thirty-Six

Pure Luck

Rod's nose throbbed painfully. It was still bleeding a little from his having shoved two pencil-size sticks as far up his nostrils as he could stand, and then smacking the bridge hard between the heels of both hands. It was an old football player's remedy for realigning the bridge of a broken nose and opening occluded nasal passages. He'd read about the process in an antiquated first-aid handbook, but never had the occasion to actually try it until now. He was glad that he'd done it out of sight inside a bathroom stall, because the pain had been blinding, and it had made him yelp out loud. He'd almost lost consciousness; but after spending a minute to recover from the tunnel vision and intense pain, his rostrum was straight again. He wiped a trickle of blood from his upper lip with a piece of tissue paper and plotted his next move.

Along with thousands of other displaced people, Rod headed to the waterfront refugee camp. He was never going to find a single man in this vast crowd. What was he thinking? Rod's heart sank like a rock to lodge heavily in the pit of his stomach. He was done for; the sheriff's department and the prosecutor would only be too happy to hang all the murders and the bombing on him; they needed to blame someone, at least to save face in the press. The real mastermind behind all this mayhem would simply disappear and strike somewhere else, while Rod served the rest of his life in prison for that man's crimes. He'd be blamed for the murders he'd committed, as well as for those he had not. But at least the authorities would have their demon to parade before the public. That was all that really mattered to them, anyway.

Rod was almost at the line waiting to sign in at the refugee camp when his attention was grabbed by a familiar-looking man with a day-pack walking across the street. He blinked and looked again. No way. It was the terrorist that he'd been following. His mind wasn't playing tricks; he'd remember that murderer's face from the Betsy River for the rest of his life.

The terrorist wasn't heading for the refugee camp, though. In fact, he was heading away from it, in exactly the opposite direction. Why had he returned to the area?

Most disturbing, what was he up to? Rod had to know. He crossed the street to follow the terrorist. Rod didn't want to get too close, he didn't want the younger and more able man to spot him and make a break for it. In his present condition, Rod was pretty sure who the winner of that footrace would be.

Maybe it was the hunter in him, but Rod had an unfathomable desire to learn what the man was up to. The National Guard truck was still patrolling the streets, blaring its amplified message for citizens to vacate them. The warnings went largely unheeded by diners and shoppers anxious to take home a memento. It would take a while until the warning became a threat, enforced by troops. Rod decided to disregard its message, as well. He let the terrorist get a one-block lead, and then followed as carefully as he was able.

The man Rod was stalking seemed to window shop in each store he passed by. But he wasn't looking at himself or the merchandise on display there; he was studying his surroundings in the reflection. He turned completely a couple of times, as if suddenly remembering to look back at something. This guy was cautious; he was expecting to be tailed. His backward glances weren't overly suspicious to a casual observer, but it might make anyone who was overtly following give himself away. It almost worked; Rod almost jumped behind cover when the man turned to look back. But Rod had taken many a deer by walking past the critter when it thought he hadn't seen it, then turning to shoot the animal when it had let its guard down. He was sure the Arab hadn't recognized him, but he figured him for a clever man. Rod wasn't about to underestimate him.

When the man stepped into the entrance to Fort Michilimackinac State Park, Rod turned down a side street. Safely out of sight, he leaned against a wooden fence and closed his eyes. God, he was tired. It was a given that he had to follow the terrorist into the park, but first he wanted to at least attempt to envision what his objective might be. Rod had been a step behind the entire time, and he couldn't help but feel some of the blame for the devastation that was visible to him even now. He felt a cold hollow in his heart when he gazed on the sight of the broken bridge for the first time after the bombing. It must have been a powerful explosion to have done so much damage.

Of course. That was it. This guy had the second bomb McBraden had told Rod about in the backpack he was carrying. He meant to blow up Fort Michilimackinac. No, that wasn't it. Who would even care if he blew up an old wooden fort? From what Shannon had told him when he'd called her, the bomb was probably dirty. The terrorist would want it to detonate in a place where it would do maximum damage. He'd want to plant it somewhere up high, where prevailing northwesterly winds would carry radioactive contamination as far as possible.

Old Mackinac Point Lighthouse would be the place to plant a dirty bomb, Rod thought. Just east of the Mackinac Bridge, it was a popular tourist attraction. The old lighthouse keeper's quarters had been kept just as they were a hundred years ago, complete with a nicely made-up brass feather bed, and a fully dressed mannequin in uniform seated at an oak desk. The quarters were attached to a beacon tower with fifty-one steps. About eighty feet in the air, Rod figured.

It had been several years since he'd been there himself, but he recalled that although there was a paid tour guide, the building was often left unlocked and open to the public. It would be easy to leave a backpack bomb in the beacon room, where it might not be discovered for a couple of days—especially in the chaos that existed on both sides of the Straits right now.

Rod still had about eighty of the one hundred dollars he'd confiscated from McBraden. The ticket counter inside the entrance under the bridge was still taking money from tourists, and there seemed to be no shortage of visitors who wanted to get in. Most of them weren't interested in seeing the usual sights; they just wanted to get an unobstructed view of the broken suspension bridge, heedless of the radioactive dust that they were undoubtedly breathing.

The authorities would surely close this place to the public within the next day, Rod thought, but profit was king in these small, tourism-oriented communities, and they were making hay while the sun shined. Besides, what was a little more radiation in a town that had been quarantined anyway? Rod didn't know who he thought was most pathetic, the business owners who placed profit above their own safety, or the tourists who would've fought each other to be closest to a mushroom cloud.

Chapter Thirty-Seven

Fooling the Fools

Aziz was surprised to see that the ticket counter inside the welcome center under the ramp that led onto the Mackinac Bridge was operating as if nothing had happened. Judging from the number of tourists who were present, his bomb hadn't affected them at all. He knew otherwise, because the talk on the street in Mackinaw City had been predominantly about radiation and what its effects on the population might be. Yet these people didn't seem at all concerned that they were exposing themselves to probable lung cancer; they were actually paying to get closer to the source of radioactive dust. These Americans were nothing if not lasciviously greedy.

The employees inside the welcome center were easily discernible from the tourists because they were dressed in eighteenth-century period costumes. After pretending to browse racks of postcards and other paraphernalia for several minutes, he approached the ticket counter and spoke to a middle-aged woman wearing a frilled bonnet and a gingham dress. Her contemporary, metal-framed eyeglasses ruined the illusion she tried to portray.

"Hi," he said, flashing her a bright, toothy smile.

"Hello sir," she replied, "what can I do for you today?"

"I've got a thing for lighthouses," he answered with an accent that would have been traceable to southern Ohio. "A friend told me that I can't miss seeing the old Mackinac Point Lighthouse. And," he added with a wry grin, "it looks like I'm going to be here a while."

"Yes sir," she replied with assumed sympathy, "I'm sorry for the inconvenience. We're all still in shock over this terrible act of terrorism."

Aziz faked a cough to hide his amusement at this woman's obviously canned attempt at public service. She would probably apologize for the inconvenience of an asteroid strike. Anything to keep those tourist dollars flowing into her cash register. By Muhammad's beard, what would it take to panic these damned people?

"The tour guide for the lighthouse didn't come in today. His brother was one of the bridge workers who passed away when the bomb went off. He called in sick."

This was surreal. This woman was divulging private information about employees to cover the failings of her business. Aziz hid his contempt.

"Darn," he said, "this was going to be one of the highlights of my trip to the north country. I really wanted to see that lighthouse," he said wistfully.

"Oh," she said, leaning closer and looking from side to side as if confiding a secret to him, "you can still see the lighthouse. The door to the ladder leading to the beacon room has to be kept locked for insurance reasons, but you can view the keeper's quarters. The outer door is unlocked."

"Hey," Aziz exclaimed with feigned Midwestern enthusiasm, "I'll be grateful for what I can get. It would be nice to get a few pictures from the beacon room, but I'll take it."

"I'm so sorry, hon. But at least you'll have the place mostly to yourself. I don't think more than a dozen people have gone to that side today. They all go to the fort side."

"Thank you," Aziz said with a grin.

He walked to the east exit and went out. The woman was right; there were four people, two preteen kids and an adult couple who were probably their parents. They didn't seem to be interested in the lighthouse, they were taking digital photos of the bridge, as if it were the tourist attraction they'd come to see. Aziz grinned at them as he passed. They half-smiled back nervously, as though embarrassed to be photographing memories of a disaster.

Aziz never looked up or looked back to see the SWAT sniper suspended above his head. Neither did the family of four, who headed back into the welcome center when Aziz came out. In fact, Biff the sniper barely paid any of them more than a passing glance, either. He didn't expect trouble, and everyone he'd seen today looked boringly harmless.

When he reached the lightkeeper's quarters, Aziz found the door unlocked, just as the woman had said it'd be. Once inside, with the door closed behind him, Aziz did look back, scrutinizing the open space around the building through its glass. It was then that he spotted the sniper on a scaffold suspended from the underside of the bridge. Worth noting, but not a hindrance to his plans. He should be able to plant the bomb and make good his escape without the sniper ever being the wiser. At least not until the millisecond when he was killed by the explosion; that thought made Aziz chuckle to himself.

Aziz listened carefully for a full minute before he was convinced that there was no one else inside. Then he turned his attention to the door that opened onto the spiral stairway that led to the top of the lighthouse tower. From the wallet in his back pocket, he took a pick and a tension bar. By maintaining torque against the lock cylinder, he was able to depress its five locking tumblers one at a time, and hold them there under pressure until the cylinder was free to turn. After less than a minute of fiddling, he felt the lock cylinder rotate. He tried the doorknob; it turned freely, and the door swung open.

The stairs rang with a hollow, metallic sound as he ascended them. Light shone in from windows in the wall of the tower, illuminating the otherwise dark staircase. He was slightly out of breath when he reached the top. He was bent over at the waist, trying to get his wind back, or he might have seen that another man had exited the welcome center, and was approaching the lighthouse at a fast walk.

Chapter Thirty-Eight

Showdown

Rod watched as the man he was pursuing entered the welcome center, under the Mackinac Bridge. He counted off two minutes on his wristwatch before heading for the entrance himself. Just before he reached the door, he saw the man through the chain-link fence that separated the parking lot from the park. Like Rod had calculated, he was exiting the east side, and was walking toward the Mackinac Point Lighthouse. He still had his backpack, and Rod was willing to bet that it contained an explosive device similar to the one that had already devastated the bridge.

He forced himself to remain calm as he paid the middle-aged lady behind the counter the admission fee required to see the lighthouse. She explained to him that access to the beacon tower's staircase was denied because there wasn't a tour guide on duty today, and she seemed a bit surprised that he didn't express more interest in that fact. Indeed, he didn't seem to be all that interested in the lighthouse in general, although he clearly felt an urgency about getting to it. In light of the terrorist bombing that had occurred yesterday, Rod's behavior seemed to be more than a little shifty in her perception.

Rod picked up on the woman's suspicion, and he knew that it was well merited. He was exhausted, he looked like he'd gotten as little sleep as he had, and his clothing was dirty from miles on the trail. He looked pretty scruffy. But there was nothing he could do about that. She handed him a cardboard ticket and told him to have a good day, but Rod could see that he'd established a germ of apprehension in her mind. He departed the welcome center a little more purposefully than he should have, anxious to find the terrorist before he could trigger another explosion. The closer he got to the man, the more certain he became that that was his objective.

In his hurry to get to the lighthouse door, he also failed to see the SWAT sniper stationed over his head. But Rod's brisk pace and the backpack he carried didn't escape the sniper's attention. A lot of people wanted to see the old lighthouse, but not many of them were in a rush to gain the experience.

As he'd been told, the door leading into the living quarters was unlocked. He turned the knob slowly and entered cautiously. He closed the door behind him as quietly as he could, keeping its doorknob fully turned and its latch retracted until the door was fully closed, then releasing the tension against it slowly to allow the latch to seat into its recess with as little noise as possible. As the door slipped almost silently shut behind him, Rod turned his attention to the adjacent room, which held the door to the tower stairway. He crept into the room silently, listening for any sounds of movement.

He thought he heard footfalls ring against the wrought-iron stairs that spiraled upward to the beacon at the top of the tower. The stairs were behind a door that Rod had been told would be locked, but as he continued to listen, he was sure that someone was climbing them even now. It had to be the terrorist, and his reason for getting to the top was absolutely clarified in Rod's mind now. He was planting a second bomb.

Rod tried the door that opened onto the staircase, but the terrorist had locked it behind him. The lock and the key that fit it were manufactured by Schlage, and the keyhole accepted the same blank as Rod's house key. Employing a trick he'd learned years before, during his own time in state prison, Rod slid the house key from his pocket into the keyhole in the doorknob. He kept a constant, firm clockwise torque against the doorknob while simultaneously applying force in the same direction with the key as he slid the key's teeth back and forth to depress the tumblers inside the lock cylinder. The concept was easier to explain than the action was to accomplish. He'd learned it from a fellow prisoner who could open almost any lock in just seconds using only a bent paper clip.

Rod had never had that convict's adroitness with locks, but he understood the principle. It took him a couple of minutes to locate and depress the lock cylinder's tumblers, especially since he was trying to do the job while making no noise. After a few attempts at wiggling and jiggling, the lock cylinder gave, and the doorknob turned. The door opened, and Rod stepped warily into the tower room, his gaze drawn fearfully upward, the Desert Eagle 50-caliber clutched in an already sweating palm.

♦ ♦ ♦

The first explosion from Aziz's 357 Magnum rang off the wrought iron stairway before Rod had climbed even five of the fifty-one steps above him. Aziz was a practiced marksman, but the gritty double-action trigger pull of his revolver was causing him to pull slightly to one side, and trail dust that had penetrated the revolver's inner workings didn't make it smoother. He cocked the hammer for the next shot, but shooting past so many obstructions was more difficult than merely shooting targets at a gun range.

This redneck bastard who'd followed him all the way from Whitefish Point had been doggedly trying to drive him insane the whole way. And now the asshole quite literally stood on the ladder that was Aziz's only avenue of escape. How in hell had he gotten the locked door open? Aziz meant to kill this irritating infidel. He fired twice more, and again the slugs were deflected by some part of the metal stairway that lay between them. He could hear them whining as they ricocheted off the brick walls of the tower silo. Caution was thrown to the winds, displaced by pent-up fury as Aziz recalled how this son of a pig had used a short sword to nearly decapitate Richarde in the woods at the Betsy River. He fired twice more, not even seeing a clear target this time.

♦ ♦ ♦

Rod was no hero. He ran out of the tower after the second shot and stood pressed against the wall of the lightkeeper's quarters, breathing heavily. Sweat beads dotted his forehead, and his chest heaved as if he'd just run a mile. He'd seen the man just as he'd fired the first round; the gun was a big silver revolver. It looked like a cannon to him. He'd fired four—no, five rounds. Rod tried to think how he might use that knowledge to his advantage, but that still left one round unfired.

He heard the clinking of spent cartridges as they rattled down the stairway. The guy upstairs had just reloaded, probably from a speed loader that replaced all six shells at once. Rod wasn't going back in there.

Still, he couldn't let this murderous son of a bitch get away, either. Rod's will to survive argued that it wasn't his responsibility to bring this evil man to justice; that was the job of people who made a lot more money than he did. Besides, Rod had his own eggs in hot water. Why should he even care what this terrorist had done to a state whose laws prohibited him from ever voting or owning a firearm? It wasn't his fight.

But this *was* his fight. The man above him had made it his fight when he'd maimed and killed everyone in Rod's survival class. He involuntarily squeezed his eyes shut tight at the memory of seeing Sue Morgan tortured, and then simply shot through the forehead like a pig going to slaughter. When he opened his eyes again, they were wet with tears. Yes, this was his fight; maybe his alone. This wasn't a man on the stairs above him, but a dangerous, rabid parasite who needed to be removed from this world for everyone's sake.

Rod wiped his eyes on a dirty sleeve until his blurred vision became clear. He still didn't fancy exposing his body, so he adopted the spray-and-pray technique that grunts had used in Vietnam. He shoved his pistol arm through the staircase doorway and fired blindly upward. He spent a full clip with no apparent results. He ejected the magazine and replaced it with a full one. He snapped the pistol's slide back and chambered a new round. Then he emptied that magazine the same way.

The noise made by the 50 caliber was deafening within the confines of the brick silo. Rod's ears were ringing loudly when the pistol stopped firing and he changed magazines for a third time. During the intermission, he heard the roar of the terrorist's revolver returning fire, and it occurred to Rod that it would be his luck to be hit by a bullet as it careened off the walls. He slapped the last magazine into the butt of the Desert Eagle and started firing upward into the tower again. The gun fired five times then went empty—it was a short magazine, and Grigovich hadn't loaded it to capacity.

Shit. Now Rod's stomach went cold. He was unarmed except for his knife, and his hand went to its hilt automatically, even as the old axiom about bringing a knife to a gunfight forced its way through his mind. The revolver roared twice more, and Rod pressed against the wall to one side of the doorway. His luck was holding per usual; in the heat of the moment he'd expended all of his ammunition, and the enemy was still firing.

Then he remembered the little Colt 32 in his pack. He'd forgotten that he was still wearing it. He unclipped the belt and shrugged off the shoulder straps. The gun was in an outside pocket. He found it in the second compartment he looked in, and hope washed back into him as he held the pistol in his hand. It felt puny compared to the big Desert Eagle, but it was a whole lot more comforting than his knife in this situation. Rod stuck his arm into the tower silo again and pulled the trigger. This time, he'd count the rounds he fired, and save at least one in case he needed a close-up, aimed shot.

The first round didn't fire; the firing pin hit the cartridge's primer with a dull click. Who knew how long this gun had ridden in the Hyundai's glove compartment without being fired? Rod had seen that problem before. He jacked the slide back to eject the dud, and chambered the next round. He stuck his arm back into the silo and fired one round.

This time, he was rewarded with the sound of something falling down the stairs. Without thinking, he stuck his head through the doorway to see, and stared right into the muzzle of the other man's revolver, fifteen feet up on the stairway. The bullet hit Rod low in his abdomen. It felt like he'd been punched hard in the stomach. Rod fell back against the doorjamb as the hiking boot Aziz had thrown down the stairs clattered to a halt.

Before the terrorist could fire again, the low sights of the Colt appeared before Rod's eyes, and yellowish flame spat from its barrel. Its first shot hit the welded-pipe railing that Aziz was using to rest his gun hand. The Colt kept firing of its own accord, and at least two of its bullets found their mark in their target's chest. Aziz curled into a ball and fell down the stairway to its bottom, where he lay sprawled face up with staring eyes that could no longer see. Incredibly, the man had numerous bullet wounds that ranged from superficial to mortal. How he'd continue to return fire was a mystery.

Rod fell back against the door jamb, feeling more tired than he'd ever felt in his life. He felt his back, and was horrified when his hand felt a large, bloody hole where the 357 bullet had exited. Unless he got to an ambulance in the next ten minutes, it was probably a fatal wound. In that case, he thought wryly, it *was* a fatal wound. His only regret was that he wouldn't be able to embrace his beautiful wife just one last time. Tears sprang to his eyes at the thought of how much she'd endured to be at his side throughout the years, and he suddenly felt very lucky to have known the love of such a great lady for even a day.

Still clutching the Colt in a hand that seemed to be losing its grip, he turned the knob on the outer door and stepped out into bright sunlight. He blinked his eyes against the glare, and thought that maybe, just maybe that nice lady at the ticket counter would call an ambulance, and he'd live through this.

Then something he didn't see slugged him hard in the middle of his chest. He sat down hard on the grass as his eyes blinked, trying to comprehend what had hit him with such tremendous force. Rod's ears vaguely registered the echoing report of a high-powered rifle, and his half-blinded eyes saw the sniper, a hundred yards away, cycling a fresh round into the action.

"I'll be damned . . ." Rod said aloud. Then he fell onto his left side and the world went black around him.

Chapter Thirty-Nine

Parting

The March air was cold and driven by a stiff wind as Colyer stopped at the tollbooth to give Caesar his due before pulling onto the southbound lane of the newly repaired Mackinac Bridge. This would be his first trip across the span since it was reopened to traffic two weeks prior. The state of Michigan had commissioned a lot of work to the bombed structure over the past winter, and the governor had promised that the repaired portions were even safer and stronger than the original had been. He needed to reassure the public in every way possible, Colyer thought, because no matter what their elected officials said, there was a pretty large faction of the citizenry who refused to even come near the irradiated bridge.

Yet, the fact that the bridge had been the target of the first radioactive dirty bomb assault in the nation's history created a cult following. Apparently, there were enough strange people who thought it was cool to visit the site of a terrorist attack, in this case, one that might have been much worse than the World Trade Center disaster. Colyer shuddered to think what would've happened if both bombs had detonated at the height of the Bridge Walk. Michigan would have lost its governor, several congressmen, and probably several thousand of its voters in one fell swoop. A full two miles of the bridge's center would have collapsed into the Straits, and radiation levels would have been double what they were.

Even now, the incidence of respiratory ailments and lung cancer had increased a hundredfold among residents in the vicinities of Mackinaw City, Saint Ignace, and Mackinac Island. People were selling their homes at less than they owed, and new construction, once a booming business in this underpopulated part of the country, had fallen to none at all. Nobody was moving into the area, and nobody wanted to live within fifty miles of the Mackinac Bridge. The Department of the Interior and the Michigan Department of Natural Resources had exhausted their budgets to buy out landowners who wanted to move, adding their lands to public holdings, but there were thousands more who wanted to leave. As with every disaster, natural or man-made, the reach of governmental assistance fell far short of reaching everyone who needed it.

The second bomb had been found at the top of the Mackinac Point Lighthouse, and the Nuclear Emergency Search Team had been able to defuse and safely remove the device with no further mishap. Local cops had been quick to blame Rod Elliot as a key player in the terrorist attack, and the murders on the Betsy River. But it seemed apparent to Colyer that he'd, in fact, been instrumental in foiling both the timing of the attack, and the placement of the second bomb. It seemed clear that Elliot had been responsible for two of the killings, but both of those victims had been terrorists—he'd almost certainly had no part in the murders of his survival students. And he'd delivered McBraden to the authorities—that wasn't the act of a terrorist's ally. All in all, Elliot looked more like a hero than a villain, but a lot of locally sensitive questions were being answered just by dumping blame on a dead man. As always, local politicians were less interested in finding the truth than in absolving themselves of blame.

♦ ♦ ♦

Shannon Elliot knelt alone on the bank of the Betsy River. With both her hands, she held a simple urn with Rod's ashes inside. She bent her head and closed her eyes, causing a tear to be squeezed out to run down her cheek. She wasn't praying so much as reflecting on the good years she'd spent with a man who'd loved her more deeply than she knew how to describe, and who'd treated her like she was the most important thing in his life. And she wasn't mourning, except to acknowledge a sadness that there would be no more days with the man that she'd loved more than her own life. Rod had lived every day of his existence, and he wouldn't have wanted anyone to feel sorrow over his passing. He would have wanted his loved ones to sit around a fire, reminiscing and telling stories about his life.

Shannon dumped the ashen remains of her husband on the flowing water. She paused a moment in silence as the sluggish waters carried them toward mighty Lake Superior. Then she rose and wiped her palms against the thighs of her denim overalls. She had stories to tell.

ALSO AVAILABLE

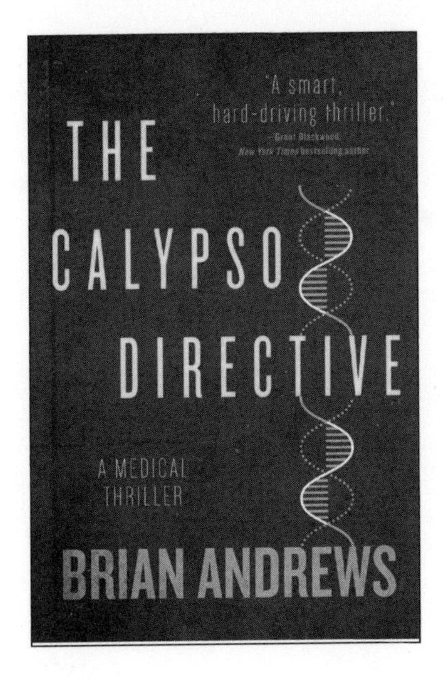

The Calypso Directive

A Medical Thriller

Brian Andrews

An unprecedented genetic mutation, an underground think tank, and an unscrupulous pharmaceutical company collide in this dazzling debut thriller.

For one hundred and fifty-five days, Will Foster has been locked in medical quarantine without his consent. The doctors claim he is infected with a deadly virus, but this is a lie. Encoded in his DNA is a mutation that provides immunity from disease for all who possess it, source code that Vyrogen Pharmaceuticals aims to commercialize as a multi-billion-dollar gene therapy.

Against all odds, Foster escapes his laboratory prison and steals a virulent strain of bubonic plague as insurance. To help him unravel the mystery inside him, Foster contacts the only person he can trust, a former lover and microbiologist living in Vienna, and the two become fugitives, hunted across the heart of Europe.

Under the guise of averting a plague pandemic, Vryogen hires an elite, underground group called the Think Tank to track down Foster. But the brilliant team discovers something unexpected—the ugly side of multinational pharmaceutical competition—and must choose between serving their client and saving Foster. Captivating, controversial, and courageous, Andrews's debut is sure to thrill and leave you wondering what secrets are locked in your DNA.

$15.99 Paperback • ISBN 978-1-62872-665-7

ALSO AVAILABLE

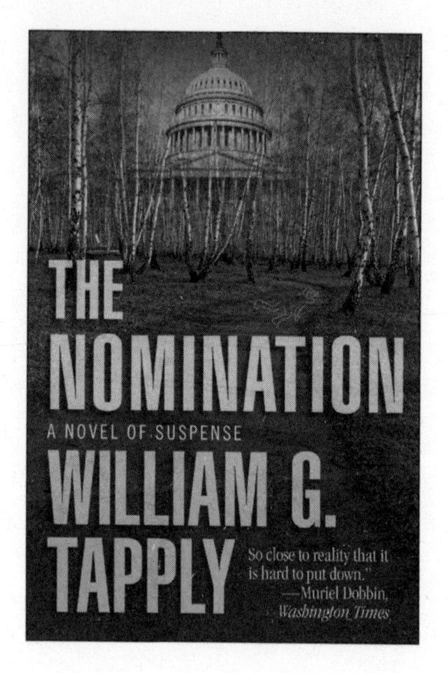

The Nomination

A Novel of Suspense
William G. Tapply

The Nomination is a fast-paced action and suspense thriller that brings events from the final days of the Vietnam War into direct conflict with contemporary American politics. Vietnam War hero and Massachusetts Judge Thomas Larrigan is hand-picked by his friend the president to fill the upcoming vacancy on the Supreme Court. Larrigan seems like the perfect candidate: a family man with an uncontroversial judicial record. The president's credibility needs a sure bet. Larrigan will do anything to win the nomination, but he has some old skeletons rattling around in his closet. He calls his old Marine buddy, now a hit man, to sweep the closet clean. But there are a few skeletons Larrigan doesn't know are still alive. *The Nomination* is the story of how lives can intersect in deception, desperation, revelation, death, and, ultimately, redemption.

$14.95 Paperback • ISBN 978-1-61608-555-1

ALSO AVAILABLE

Holding Lies

A Novel

John Larison

With *Holding Lies*, John Larison takes us deep into a thriving subculture of the Northwest, one born of ferns and firs, rain and hot springs, salmon and whitewater. He takes us even deeper into the troubles of Hank Hazelton, a fifty-nine-year-old river guide, as he struggles to reconnect with his daughter after a long estrangement. Before his daughter's arrival, Hank discovers a drift boat stranded below a rapid, its oarsman missing. Within days, the sheriff has opened a murder investigation, one that to Hank appears more about old grudges than objective evidence. When Hank himself becomes a suspect, he's forced to confront the violent past of his home valley . . . and his own culpability. In a novel about finding family in unlikely places, Larison breathes life into a community rich with history, sin, and hope, a place where bears still wander side streets and time is still marked by the seasons of the river. *Holding Lies* is a taut, big-hearted novel, steeped in the ecology of place and peopled with unforgettable characters.

$24.95 Hardcover • ISBN 978-1-61608-255-0

ALSO AVAILABLE

Process of Elimination

A Thriller

Arthur T. Bradley, PhD

A powerful international organization wants to tip the balance of global power by infiltrating the White House. At the direction of its mastermind, alias Pecos Bill, presidential candidates have become unwitting targets of a world-class sharpshooter.

A martial arts expert, a greedy corporate attorney, and a self-proclaimed conspiracy theorist form a shaky alliance initially intent on solving a missing persons case, only to get caught up in a bigger political plot in which they must uncover the assassin's identity before he can claim his next victim. Together, they race across the country, desperately trying to piece together an intricate puzzle of murder, deception, and betrayal through a mire of passion, behind-the-scenes deals, and false identities. Along the way, they encounter corrupt government agents, Secret Service cover-ups, and a high-speed car chase.

Only as bodies begin to pile up do the protagonists realize that the killer may be in their very midst, and that they must dig into each other's pasts to stop the deadly chain of events that has them in its crosshairs. In the tradition of Ludlum's Bourne series and James Patterson thrillers, Bradley's debut novel will leave you breathless and eager for more with every twist and turn.

$22.95 Hardcover • ISBN 978-1-62087-311-3

ALSO AVAILABLE

Removal

A Novel of Suspense

Peter Murphy

United States President Steve Wade believes his latest affair, with the beautiful Lucia Benoni, is a secret. When Lucia is murdered under mysterious circumstances, FBI agent Kelly Smith is called to investigate. As he dives deeper into the case, he uncovers links between Lucia, a hostile foreign power, a group of vicious white supremacists, and a shadowy high-placed Washington figure known only as "Fox."

As Wade continues to deny the affair, the press gets on the trail and latches onto the sensational breaking story with increasing tenacity. Because of the national security implications, there are demands in Congress for his impeachment. Vice President Ellen Trevathan should, by law, take power, but "Fox" and his associates have other plans. As time runs out, Kelly may hold the only key to preventing a coup d'etat and nothing short of civil war.

$24.95 Hardcover • ISBN 978-1-61145-762-9